Jasmine Blossoms

'Pleasure, Miss Parsons,' whispered the stranger as his lips caressed Joanna's earlobe. 'That's all we want from you, for you. To give and receive pleasure. You have nothing to fear. You won't be hurt.' He paused for a moment and pulled away before finishing his sentence. 'Unless that is what you desire.'

Joanna resisted the urge to tell him her name was Wilson, not Parsons, but what difference would it make? The stranger knew how to get to her, to turn her on: already she knew she wouldn't be able to resist much longer. She had nothing to lose and much to gain. Without a word she allowed the man to blindfold her and drive her to a mystery destination.

Jasmine Blossoms

SYLVIE OUELLETTE

Black Lace novels are sexual fantasies.
In real life, make sure you practise safe sex.

First published in 1997 by
Black Lace
20 Vauxhall Bridge Road
London
SW1V 2SA

Typeset by CentraCet Limited, Cambridge
Printed and bound in Great Britain by Clays Ltd, St Ives PLC

ISBN 9780753541012

The Random House Group Limited supports The Forest Stewardship
Council (FSC®), the leading international forest certification organisation.
Our books carrying the FSC label are printed on FSC® certified paper.
FSC is the only forest certification scheme endorsed by the leading
environmental organisations, including Greenpeace. Our
paper procurement policy can be found at
www.randomhouse.co.uk/environment

MIX
Paper from
responsible sources
FSC® C018072

Part One

Part One

Chapter One

The hands of the clerk behind the hotel counter were rugged, long and bony with unbending fingers, the hands of a man more at ease with heavy tasks than clerical work.

Mesmerised, Joanna watched as they fluttered over the computer keyboard. They hovered, punched a few keys, waited, then moved again. She couldn't stop staring at them, decidedly impressed by the sight of the round, wrinkled knuckles. For a brief moment, her imagination took over and she pictured those fingers hard and unyielding, caressing her naked body, knowing exactly where to pause, where to tease. Her nipples peaked and her heart beat fast. Now she could almost feel his fingers running up her bare thighs, gliding towards the inside, inexorably heading for a specific spot between her legs.

Impatient sighs from the people queuing behind her brought her back to reality. She took a deep breath and straightened up, quickly regaining her senses and coming to grips with her bleak situation: the hotel didn't have a booking in her name.

That was the last thing Joanna needed. She was jetlagged and fed up, and her back ached. Her clothes were becoming uncomfortable after the long flight to

Tokyo, and she desperately needed a bath. The elastic band of her cotton top cinched her ribcage right under her breasts and made her skin itch, as did the waistband of her leggings. The white shirt she wore over her outfit was now badly wrinkled and felt sticky. Her blond, wispy hair, which she had set in a neat braid before leaving home, was slowly coming loose, and her scalp itched. She felt like stamping in exasperation and her heel lifted slightly from the floor, but she managed to contain herself.

'Will this take much longer?' she asked in the best Japanese she could muster.

The clerk briefly looked at her, gave a dry smile, but didn't reply. None of this was his fault, but Joanna immediately disliked him just the same. He could apologise, or at least reply, she thought. He was, well, Japanese, and she knew how deferential these people usually were. She waited for him to say something, and grew even angrier when he didn't.

His face was thin and bony, just like his hands, his deep-set eyes almost completely hidden under heavy lids, his cheeks so hollow that under the glare of the ceiling lights they cast a shadow along his jaw line. Once again, Joanna looked at his hands. This time she thought they looked decidedly spooky. Everything from the man's lack of courtesy to his spiky gelled hair repelled her.

There was no booking in her name. She should have known this would happen, and she would have to brace herself for a repeat performance wherever she had to register over the next few days.

All this because of bloody Stacey! Why did the stupid woman have to resign three days before she was due to leave on the company's most important tour? Stacey had always been reliable in her job, one of the best buyers of exotic foods Joanna had ever worked with. She had a nose and a palate for the most exquisite – and often unusual – delicacies. Her resignation had been both unexpected and frustrating.

Personal reasons, she had said. What personal reasons? Joanna couldn't help wondering. The woman didn't even have a life! Her job was everything to her, or at least that was the impression she had always given everyone.

And why had she handed in her letter of resignation to Richard instead of Joanna? How had she managed to weasel her way out the Japan tour, not even working her notice?

Now Joanna had to take over. Although she had been promoted to marketing a couple of years ago and didn't have anything to do with buying any more, she was the only one who could fill in at short notice and trek to Tokyo for the conference and food fair. New products had priority; the publicity could wait. As could the files piling up on her desk, apparently.

Or, even worse, they could be passed on to dear Richard, who would like nothing better than to take Joanna's place and make his mark, albeit temporarily. Joanna knew he was itching to show everyone she wasn't irreplaceable and that he was the best one for her job. In fact, it was just like him to let Stacey skip the tour and resign without working her notice. He knew that would force Joanna to take over and be away for almost two months.

Oh, she had tried to find a way out. But in the end she had failed to come up with a better solution. It had all happened so fast. Now there was no way of knowing what stunts Richard would pull in her absence. It would be just like him not to hire anyone to replace Stacey, just to keep Joanna out of reach while he took her place. If only Stacey's departure hadn't been so sudden.

The clerk finally handed Joanna an electronic entry card for a room. Sharp pain shot through her shoulder as she picked up her bag and she almost dropped it. Her whole body ached, reminding her of the long tiring journey. She had left London such a long time ago already. Three planes and seventeen hours later, her mind was numb, but her body was acutely sore.

She made her way around the fountain in the middle of the foyer, a porter trailing behind with her luggage in tow. Blinking a couple of times, she looked up. Like a giant cage, the four walls of the foyer rose 30 storeys, as high as the building itself. At the very top, through the glass roof, the evening sky was but a blue patch. Inside, however, the powerful lighting was as strong as daylight.

The fountain was set off centre in a delightful rock garden. Dark, shiny pebbles were dotted along larger stones covered with thick, brilliant-green moss. Around the edges, coarse gravel had been expertly raked. The garden itself was spanned by a small, winding bridge made of warm, dark-red mahogany. The rich colours and exquisite display had been cleverly planned. Their soothing sight made Joanna feel better. She had made it this far. The rest would fall into place in due time.

She quickly glanced around, taking in every detail of the rest of the foyer. The tall palm trees looked too exotic, slightly out of place, and clashed with the more typically Japanese rock garden. Somewhere in the branches, birds were echoing each other's discourse, their songs at times drowned out by the cascading splashes of the fountain.

The whole thing was way overdone, Joanna decided. The contrast between the oriental and the exotic features was too pronounced. The sounds and sights were too strong, dizzying, and ruined the obvious attempt to make the foyer look like an affluent yet peaceful haven. It was tacky, in her opinion.

Despite her exhaustion, her mind had already switched into critical mode. After so many years working as a buyer, it had become a reflex. She would be spending the next eight weeks sampling a variety of food products to decide which ones her company would add to its line of imports. After a good night's sleep, her eyes, nose and taste buds would automatically shift into full gear.

The same thing with her language skills. A long time

ago, she had learnt Japanese well enough to be almost fluent, but she hadn't used it in a while. She hoped it would soon come back to her, otherwise it would be difficult to make herself understood once she started her tour of the provinces.

She was confident however. The tour was nothing new. She had done it all before, and although she didn't have Stacey's precious contacts all over Japan, she was one of the best at the job.

A young woman stood silently by the lift, dressed in a light blue kimono and wearing the traditional sandals with a wooden platform sole. She bowed to Joanna and pressed the call button.

'Bow to customer; press button,' Joanna muttered to herself. 'What a job.' The girl was obviously there for show.

The lift was a glass cage, overlooking the foyer as it went up. Joanna watched the tree tops shrink and noticed wires and loudspeakers cleverly concealed amidst the branches. She smiled to herself: there were no birds hiding in the trees. Even the chirping was make-believe. In the lift itself, there was cheap ambience music.

When she saw her room she winced. It was decorated in an anonymous, Western style, like all the major hotels in all the major cities of the world. Joanna had still hoped it would be different in Tokyo. She would have liked to immerse herself in a Japanese setting from the very first day, to be surrounded by colourful prints and rice paper screens, and sleep on a simple futon laid directly on the floor.

But instead the room was large and modern, impersonal. The bed was just an average spring mattress with a wooden headboard. The lamps were plain, European style. The only slightly exotic touch was an enormous basket of fruit on the small table by the window. Yellow star fruit and dark purple Japanese plums lay on a bed of pink lychees, welcoming her with a soothing mixture of light sweet aromas.

Joanna glanced at the attached card and immediately recognised its logo. It was from the organisers of the conference, wishing her a happy stay. Rather a commonplace gesture she thought but it pleased her.

The conference was due to begin the next afternoon. All the information for the delegates was in a thick glossy folder next to the fruit basket: colourful fliers from different companies; a map of the exhibits; a schedule of demonstrations and special events.

A name badge bore Stacey's name. Obviously, the organisers were still unaware that Miss Parsons had been replaced at the last minute as representative for International Emporium Plc by Joanna Wilson. This would have to be changed as soon as possible.

Joanna looked at her watch and worked out that she had fourteen hours to rest and get ready for the hard work awaiting her. Going anywhere tonight, however tempting the idea, was out of the question.

In the taxi on the way to the hotel, Tokyo had seemed different from what she remembered. The only familiar sight was the crowd on the street: hundreds of people dressed in simple dark clothes, fretfully moving in all directions in tiny hurried steps, seemingly in a constant panic.

The buildings looked ill matched, individually interesting from an architectural point of view, but put together in such a way as to make a weird ensemble: modern structures of glass and steel adorned by colourful billboards, sprouting in between smaller, more traditional, old buildings. Joanna felt the city was slowly losing its Oriental flavour. At first glance, many of the streets were more reminiscent of New York.

During her previous trips to Japan, several years ago, she had been too busy to do any sightseeing. Her memories were a thin collection of vague impressions. Maybe her schedule wouldn't be so hectic this time and she would be able to go out and play tourist.

She stared out of the window down to the street far below. In the early evening, the city still shone brightly.

The orange glow of the setting sun contrasted with the long purple shadows cast by each building. The neon signs flashed high above the street, illuminating everything in their path.

Up on the 24th floor, Joanna couldn't hear anything, but she remembered the sounds of the street seeping in through the half-open window of the taxi, carrying with them the aromas from the merchants' open-air grills. At the time, the strange mixture of cooked food and street pollution had made her nauseous. Now, the recollection made her mouth water.

But although she was childishly excited by the notion of exploring the city, at the moment she desperately needed to sleep. She turned from the window and realised the porter had silently left. A maid had walked in just as silently, a tiny, elderly woman wearing a pink smock. She had already started unpacking and most of Joanna's clothes were hanging in the closet, except for a few items which had been set aside.

The woman pointed out to Joanna these clothes needed to be ironed, gesturing profusely whilst pointing at the wrinkles and pretending to be ironing them right on the spot. Then she tilted her head and opened her eyes wide, as if to ask whether Joanna had understood.

'OK?' she finally asked, her voice melodious and fluid as a child's.

'OK,' said Joanna.

Leaving the maid to finish unpacking, Joanna walked into the bathroom. Large and well equipped, it looked like any other modern hotel bathroom. On the counter by the sink, a large basket had been set for the guests' convenience, filled with small black plastic bottles of shampoo and lotions, all bearing the hotel's crest. On top of a thick pile of folded towels lay a large white bottle of bath foam. Joanna picked it up, wondering why it looked so different from the other toiletries, and tried to read the characters on it.

All she could make out were the words printed in English: BATH FOAM SCENTED WITH JASMINE. The bottle was entirely white, adorned with a drawing of a thin sprig of jasmine bearing tiny pink flowers. There was no mention of a manufacturer or corporate address. It seemed to have been deliberately set apart from the rest of the products so carefully placed in the basket.

She started to run a bath and poured a large dollop into the powerful stream of water flowing from the tap. The water turned to thick foam and puffed up in a glistening pale-pink mass. The scent of jasmine rose and mixed with the steam from the bath water, enveloping her brain and mellowing yet reviving her tired mind. But the aroma was out of place: jasmine reminded Joanna of tea and rice, not bath foam.

She tossed the bottle back on top of the towels and quickly peeled off her clothes, letting them drop in a heap at her feet. She sighed as she stepped into the bath. Once sitting, her legs immediately felt lighter, their weight supported by the water which now reached her waist and tickled her belly button. The sudden warmth gave her goose bumps and she shivered.

The water rose further, slowly crawling up her ribcage. The suds brushed the underside of her breasts and fizzled. Her nipples stiffened in response, teased by the silky bubbles that seemed eager to reach them, and in reaction to the sudden assault of the hot water on her vulva.

Behind her, a plastic cushion had conveniently been placed against the edge of the bath. Everything in this bathroom was planned for comfort. She pulled out the elastic band holding her hair, quickly undid the braid by combing it with her fingers, leant back and closed her eyes. Her long hair floated and softly tickled her shoulders. Soon the water rose over her chest and she clumsily turned off the taps with her toes. Gradually, she felt her sore muscles unknotting.

But her mind was still focused on the task ahead. For the next five days, she would be dividing her time between lectures on food and demonstrations of cooking techniques from all over Asia. There would be talks on

10

spirits, sauces and traditional recipes adapted for the Western market. Joanna's job was to decide what would appeal to British consumers and to arrange for the importation of the different products.

That was the easy part. After that, she was scheduled to set off on a ten-day journey that would take her off the beaten track, visiting remote regions with a view to discovering what the organisers of the conference had overlooked. Once she was done in Japan, she would tackle Vietnam. After that, she would have to wait for directives from head office as to whether she should continue or whether someone else would come to take over the rest of the tour. If Richard had his way, the latter was unlikely.

Korea was on the list, along with Thailand, Malaysia and Indonesia – but the itinerary wasn't definite yet. Just a few days in each place, always on the go. Flights, hotels, meetings, tastings. If she spent all her energies working, Joanna wouldn't even have time to miss Harry.

Harry! She sat up suddenly, sending waves of water splashing over the edge of the tub. She had almost forgotten him! How could she? Her mind raced as she tried to figure out what time it was in London, where he would be at that moment.

By now he would have heard the hurried message she had left on his answering machine. An unexpected business trip. The lamest of excuses, only in her case it was true. Would he believe her? How would he react? More importantly, would he wait for her?

Joanna leant forward and bent her knees, encircling her legs with her arms and tilting her head on her right shoulder. Her breasts were pressed against her thighs, wet and slightly slippery with the moisturiser from the bath foam. Waves of water bobbed up and down her back, tickling and caressing her.

Her mind wandered as Harry's face slowly appeared behind her closed eyes. The memory of their last moments together came back vividly and she felt her nipples stiffening against her wet thighs. Even miles

11

away it seemed he still had a hold on her. She had worked so hard to get near him. Just as she thought she had him wrapped around her little finger, right where she wanted him, fate – and Stacey – had decided otherwise.

Her hands clenched violently around her ankles. Pain rose and she forced herself to let go. She had to think about something else. There was no way she could last through this trip if the memory of him kept haunting her. But it was too good to relinquish: the feel of his body pressed against hers, his tongue lightly brushing her earlobe, a lone finger tracing her hard nipples through the silk of her blouse; everything made her shiver.

She shouldn't have pushed him away that night. She had been bent on making him desire her even more, ready to tease him for as long as she could. It was a foolish game. He wanted her. But rather than abandon herself, she had toyed with him. He would simmer, she had decided.

Now she cursed herself. How stupid she had been! Would he still want her when she returned? Would she ever get a second chance? Perhaps she could ring him. From here. Then he would know she wasn't lying about the trip. After that, she would ring him regularly. At work. In the middle of the day. And talk so seductively he wouldn't be able to leave his desk for several minutes!

She leant back and let herself slide under the water to wet her hair. The suds filled her ears and their crackling melody drowned out her thoughts. A wicked smile slowly stretched her lips. She remembered how Harry had often playfully complained of the effect her voice had on him.

That's how it had all begun. As solicitor for her company, Harry had spoken to her on the telephone a few times, initially for business purposes. Gradually, their talk had turned to something more personal. Little by little, she had used words to entice him. When they had finally met, her gorgeous body had done the rest. Now that he had had a taste, would he wait another eight weeks to have her? Perhaps, she thought, her absence would only make him grow hotter.

Deciding that all was not lost, she sat up and washed her hair. She heard the door of the room closing and assumed it was the maid leaving. A few minutes later, however, she heard it opening again. Whoever it was left again almost immediately. Slightly puzzled, Joanna decided the maid had probably forgotten something and had come back to retrieve it. Who else would have a key?

She wrapped her hair in a towel and lazed in the bath for a few more minutes. Her fingertips toyed with the suds that now pearled on her skin, gliding down along the smooth curve of her breasts. Under the water, her hands continued down her abdomen, gently combing the fine hairs of her mound. Once she was back in London, if she had her way, it would be Harry's hands touching her. He would marvel at how soft and smooth her skin felt, just as she did right now. His lips would soon follow. By then, he would be so hungry for her that he wouldn't be able to control himself.

Instinctively, she moaned under her own touch. The sound of her voice shook her and she pulled her hand away. She couldn't let herself pine after Harry. It would make the whole trip unbearable. She would be cajoling and teasing whenever they talked, but the rest of the time she had to concentrate on her work. Starting now.

She got up and carefully stepped out of the bath. Water trickled down her back and legs. Now her body felt twice as heavy. The humid heat in the bathroom and the effort of getting up made her heart beat fast and a fine sweat pearled her forehead. Suddenly, she felt incredibly tired. No doubt the long flight and jetlag were catching up with her.

She patted herself dry then let the large towel drop on the floor. With a kick of her foot, she sent it to join her clothes in a loose pile. She didn't bother picking anything up. The maid would take care of that tomorrow.

Her moist skin was hot and silky smooth, smelling of jasmine. Now she was rather fond of this new fragrance. Grabbing the terry-cloth robe provided by the hotel, she ripped its plastic wrapping which she let fall to the floor, then threw the robe over her shoulders before going back into the bedroom.

Her eyes slowly got accustomed to the dimness. The only light in the room was faint and came from a small lamp on the bedside table. Glancing in that direction, she saw a corner of the bed cover and the blankets had been neatly turned down for her. Her handbag and briefcase lay on a table by the large window. All her clothes, her coat and her suitcase had been carefully stowed away. The service in this place was excellent, and Joanna decided she would make the most of it.

Lazily, she walked to the window, her bare feet leaving moist prints on the soft carpet. The robe slid off her shoulders as she crossed the room. She didn't make any effort to stop it. Her body was still warm from her bath; her skin needed to breathe.

On the table by the window she found a small calling card left on her briefcase, a card she hadn't noticed before. Its paleness contrasted sharply with the black leather and she wondered why she hadn't seen it earlier.

She picked it up absent-mindedly and glanced at the letters printed in pale lime green against a light pink background: WELCOME. WE WILL BE IN TOUCH WITH YOU SHORTLY.

There was no signature, nothing written on the reverse. Although anonymous, the card looked impressive and expensive. The cardboard was quite thick and pulpy, almost powdery; its rough texture caressed Joanna's fingers as she examined the letters printed on it.

This combination of pink and green was pleasing to the eye, as was the lettering. The Ws were stretched and elaborately flourished; the Ls slim and tall. It was impossible to tell whether the calligraphy was hand-

14

scripted or mechanically printed, but the card was indeed classy.

Joanna studied it for a while, vaguely puzzled, before tossing it in the wastepaper basket. It was pointless to try and figure out from where or whom it came. It could have been sent to the wrong room, Joanna concluded, and it didn't really seem important anyway.

Pulling the thick curtains open, she looked down towards the street. She didn't care that she was naked. In fact, she rather enjoyed the idea. The room was dim and no one could see her. Like a curious child she placed her hands on the glass pane. Her moist palms exuded a thin fog which settled on the glass, creating a vague outline.

On practically every building, large neon signs blinked in all directions, both above and below Joanna. The rays bathed her naked silhouette with glowing light, in alternating purple, orange and blue patterns. She stood immobile for a few minutes, enjoying the play of light on her pale ivory skin. This unusual caress, albeit a figment of her imagination, was nonetheless exciting, and she felt herself getting aroused.

Her mouth was dry and she slowly licked her lips. Shifting her weight, she rubbed her naked thighs together as she gradually leant forward to take a closer look at the street far below, stepping even more into the light. Her nipples unexpectedly touched the cold glass of the window and immediately grew hard, sending an icy bolt to her abdomen.

Joanna shuddered and stepped back in surprise, bringing her hands up to cover her breasts. Her palms, still moist but much cooler from their contact with the cold glass, felt like those of a stranger. Her breasts throbbed in her grasp, fluid and warm. All was silence, except for the sudden, loud pounding of her heart sounding in her ears. On the window the misty traces her hands had left were slowly disappearing. Beneath her knees the ventilation system went off with a click and sent up a cool breeze.

Joanna shuddered once again, finding the cold assault wickedly arousing, and swiftly drew the curtains before walking away from the window. Goose bumps rose and quickly subsided all over her body, but the effect on her loins lingered. Her body now craved contact. She needed to be touched, caressed. She yearned for warm flesh against her delicate skin.

Letting go of her breasts, she pulled off the towel wrapped around her head and let it drop to the floor. Roughly, she finger-combed her wet hair. So much for focusing on work, she thought. Perhaps that was easier said than done, considering how tired she was. It would get better tomorrow.

She was to spend the night alone, in a strange city, a strange bed. She would have to get accustomed to that, unable to indulge in this wantonness she wanted Harry to appease. There was no way she would let thoughts of what could have been drive her crazy.

Walking to the bed, she turned the light off and slipped between the cool sheets. Her head fell back on the pillow and she sighed. By now she was relaxed and sleepy, her mind going blank. Only her body remained awake, keenly so. Joanna knew she needed release. Only this once, she thought. She would start afresh tomorrow.

Slowly, lovingly, her hands ran over her body, which was still throbbing with desire. They covered every inch of her skin, lingering longer in those places where she was most sensitive. She rolled over a few times, stretching lasciviously and enjoying the feel of crisp cotton all over her skin.

Her hands wandered some more, her fingertips travelling in unison as they glided down her breasts and her abdomen before lightly flickering over her warm bush. Soon they grew lazy, as if drunk and unwilling to move, and Joanna fell into a deep slumber.

Chapter Two

A quick glance was enough for Joanna to see there were only a few women attending the food fair. She checked her watch: almost two o'clock. Although officially the food fair wasn't scheduled to start for another half an hour, the exhibition hall was already packed. Dozens of men in dark suits walked up and down the rows of stalls, laboriously making their way through the heavy crowd while examining the products on display with a critical eye. Most of them were Japanese. Every now and again Joanna would notice a few Westerners, Arabs and even Africans, but they seemed lost in a sea of Asian faces. Looking round, she remembered the first time she had come to Tokyo and how she had found the Japanese all looked the same.

Today, however, that wasn't the case. Young and old, tall and short, slim and fat all mingled as they consulted their schedules or exchanged business cards. Only three things remained constant: the dark suits, the solemn faces and the endless bowing.

Heads seemed constantly on the verge of colliding; the salt-and-pepper hair of the older men almost tangling with that of the younger delegates. No matter how they looked, they were all extremely polite and deferential, hardly ever smiling.

There were dozens of women in the large hall, but most of them were hostesses. Whether dressed in brightly coloured kimonos or in smart tailored suits, they all looked pretty and constantly smiled whilst showing off the products on display. The girls all acted incredibly demurely and practically never looked the men in the eye, preferring to cast their glances down and shyly raising their hands to their mouths to hide their smiles. Joanna knew this mousiness was somewhat faked, that they were striving to act the way Japanese men expected their women to be: docile and subservient. The men also took their role seriously, being polite but often abrupt with the girls, at times almost rude.

Joanna walked around the exhibition hall and observed the scene for a while. This type of behaviour was nothing new to her, but it was nonetheless surprising. Some of the men examined the girls the way they should have been examining the products on display.

The hostesses didn't seem to mind, however. In the Japanese world, a woman's role was to please and serve. That principle had been impressed on them at a very young age and they couldn't even imagine acting differently.

Joanna made a point of straightening up and walking tall. Some of the Japanese men were shorter than she. Joanna felt a smug satisfaction in looking down at them as they walked past and looked up. In a way, she was exacting revenge on behalf of all the hostesses, raised never to stray from the path set for them in childhood and never daring to address a man directly.

After a while Joanna could feel the men's eyes on her; discreet glances of admiration and curiosity. At that moment, there were no other Western women in sight. Joanna, tall, blond and more curvaceous than the tiny Japanese women, knew she stood out in the crowd. The feeling was delightful, almost exhilarating.

Initially she had hoped to blend in. The classic dark-blue suit she had chosen to wear over a thick, cream-coloured blouse made her look elegant, yet very professional. Her hair was carefully pinned in a slick bun at the base of her neck, her make-up subtle yet perfect.

But now she liked being the focus of attention and wished she had gone for a softer, more feminine look. She observed the men as they gathered around the displays. She was appalled by the way they constantly demanded explanations from the hostesses, snapping their fingers to attract their attention, practically grabbing the products from their hands. Joanna knew that if anyone tried to address her that way, she would tell them off in no uncertain words.

Not that she felt sorry for the women. Obviously, it was a role they knew they had to play. But Joanna just couldn't picture herself being that submissive. She was much too strong for that; she could never play some role just because it was what men expected from her. Just the opposite, in fact: she liked to call the shots, to be in charge.

She walked around for a while, making note of the stalls she wanted to go back to once the crowds thinned out. When she found a quiet corner, she stopped, fished out her schedule from her folder and quickly examined it. First on the list was a welcoming reception in the Tatami Room. That was in less than ten minutes. Joanna carefully studied her map, trying to figure out where she was and where she was supposed to go.

The room was at the opposite end of the exhibition hall. There was no time to waste. But as she hurriedly dodged her way through the crowd, her sense of smell kept slowing her down. So many enticing scents floated in the air and caught her attention.

Most of the participants were still preparing their stalls for the delegates, cutting up food and arranging it on plates for those who wanted a taste. Freshly cut fruit sent the strongest aroma, overpowering even the scent of grilled meats fragrant with the sauce in which they had been marinated before cooking. The fresh fish on display had a characteristic but not unpleasant odour. In some of the stalls, rice was cooking in large pots and its perfume competed with other scents. Together, they all mingled in an unusual, mouth-watering swirl.

Joanna's senses were now keen, and she suddenly felt hungry. She had eaten only a very light lunch because she knew there would be tasting sessions later in the afternoon. But before getting to that she had to attend the welcoming reception. She heard her stomach growling and smiled to herself: this would probably be a very interesting – and delicious – conference.

The Tatami Room was at the far end of the hall, down a short corridor. She found it right away. As soon as she entered, the thick wooden door closed behind her and the noises of the hall were suddenly shut out. In a fraction of a second, the atmosphere changed completely, from noisy and frantic to quiet and intimate.

The light was diffuse, coming from a large lone globe made of white rice paper and hanging from the ceiling. The four corners of the room were hidden behind dark, richly lacquered screens decorated with inlaid pieces of ivory and marquetry scenes depicting birds of paradise and flowing rivers. On the far wall, a large ancient-looking etching featured a scene from a banquet, with armies of samurai warriors dressed in traditional garb and women in lavish kimonos.

A young woman stepped forward, bent down in front of Joanna and helped her take off her shoes. Another woman took her briefcase and gestured for Joanna to make her way to the centre of the room.

The atmosphere was subdued, dim and quiet, slightly hypnotising. The only sound that could be heard was the wailing song of a lone *shamisen*, a string instrument with a long handle. The musician was an old man, his face wrinkled like a raisin, his eyes so deeply set they were almost impossible to see. But he was incredibly skilled; the fingers of one hand ran along the string, which the bow in his other hand sent vibrating. At least this time, Joanna thought, the sound was real, not the effect of a loudspeaker.

A group of about twenty people were kneeling around

a large low table. Only a few of them were Japanese; the others mostly Westerners. Several looked a bit uncomfortable, not knowing what to do or not used to kneeling.

There was only one empty spot left for Joanna, a thick silk cushion at the corner. As she quietly walked over and knelt, she noticed the table featured a big gap in the middle, where a geisha in a dark purple kimono was kneeling. Occasional whispers ran round the table, but no real conversation. The exotic music grew mesmerising, making words superfluous.

The man kneeling on Joanna's right turned to her and discreetly held out his hand a few inches above her knee.

'Hi! I'm Steve,' he whispered.

Joanna introduced herself, also whispering, and shook his hand. Her fingers fitted perfectly in his firm grasp and its warmth readily travelled up her arm.

She looked down, surprised to see his big hand entirely covering hers. His rolled-up sleeve revealed his forearm which looked strong. Joanna was shaken with a sudden realisation: he was the first man she had touched since leaving Harry, the first human contact. This notion was intriguing and exciting, and her blood raced. The man was incredibly handsome, with a thin nose and smooth cheeks. His warm smile made him the ideal candidate for a toothpaste advertisement: bright, white, perfectly set teeth and dark, luscious lips. He squinted slightly and his greeting seemed even more genuine.

Instinctively, Joanna's eyes narrowed in a sultry gaze and she gave him her most seductive smile. But it froze on her lips as he quickly let go of her hand and casually turned to his other neighbour. His welcome was meant as nothing more than a polite gesture. Incensed by his lack of interest but decidedly intrigued, Joanna continued to look at him, examining him out of the corner of her eye.

He didn't talk to his neighbour for very long either, yet he didn't turn back to Joanna. Instead, his eyes examined the room, sharply travelling from one object to the next. Even kneeling, he was much taller than Joanna. His accent sounded vaguely Texan. Something in the way he knelt straight yet relaxed revealed his self-assurance. The way he was dressed – worn jeans and a tan deerskin waistcoat – made her guess he wasn't the type who bothered with convention. The barely concealed smile still hanging at the corner of his mouth was both amused and cynical. His broad shoulders and strong hands gave him a healthy look, as did his tanned skin and his wavy blond, sun-bleached hair. All that was missing was the stetson hat, cowboy boots and mouthful of chewing tobacco, Joanna thought.

The geisha turned to Joanna and bowed. Her delicate ivory-white hand slowly poured sake in a small ceramic cup. Joanna couldn't help staring. It was impossible to tell the woman's age but she seemed quite young. Her face and neck were completely white, covered in several layers of *oshiroi*: a thick chalky white make-up uniformly spread from the roots of her hair down under the lining of her kimono. Her eyebrows and lashes were painted black. Her mouth, drawn in the shape of a pink rosebud, and faint rosy patches on her cheeks were the only sources of colour on her matt skin.

A delicate tassel of unhusked rice kernels dangled from her dark-brown wig, which was shaped into the traditional, thickly crowned bun. The wig looked heavy, yet the woman held her head high not betraying any strain, her poise perfect. A large black *obi* sash was fastened round her waist and chest, flattening her breasts and making the natural curves of her body indiscernible.

Her movements were slow and fluid, her fine wrists strong and steady. Her hands showed years of training. The large sleeves of her kimono didn't seem to bother her. She filled everyone's cup with sake, her precise movements elevating the task to something not unlike a religious ritual. After she finished pouring, she clasped her hands together and they disappeared as the large sleeves of the kimono glided down to cover them.

Joanna was hypnotised by the sight of her; how she looked and how she moved. She took the cup and slowly brought it to her lips, never taking her eyes off the woman. The sake was warm and its vapours drifted out on to her hand and wrist in a moist caress. She smelt the wine long before her mouth even touched the cup.

Her eyes watered and for an instant she held the cup level with her mouth without touching it. She closed her eyes. The porcelain was hot, and her fingertips quickly grew dry and sore. The vapours overwhelmed her and she was briefly tempted to put the cup back on the table.

However, her senses were already enticed, intrigued by the unusual warmth and perfume; she couldn't just put the wine down without tasting it. Her mouth finally came to rest on the hot cup.

She tilted it slightly, and at first her lips merely dipped into the warm liquid. Its sweet delicate taste seeped into her mouth and caressed her tongue. Her senses – taste, smell and touch – awoke and violently demanded more. She took a larger, thirsty sip.

The liquid turned into vapour in her mouth, warm and ethereal. She let it flow down her throat rather than really swallow it, feeling it gently coat the inside of her chest until it hit her stomach in a hot splash.

The sweet perfume lingered in her nostrils, gradually invading her head as well. She took another couple of sips, after which she felt curiously comfortable. Not quite drunk but pleasantly relaxed and uninhibited, reacting to the taste and smell rather than the alcohol. She turned to look at Steve once again.

His own cup was now empty and she saw that he was looking at the carafe on the table, where the geisha had left it. Joanna sensed he wanted a refill. She also knew that in Japan, propriety forbade people from pouring their own drinks; etiquette dictated that one had to fill another person's cup and hope the gesture would be reciprocated.

A smiled played on her lips as she noticed his eyes travelling from one cup to the next, looking for an empty one to fill, prompting its proprietor to return the favour. She was amused and impressed by his strategy. Too often she had been embarrassed by Westerners who weren't aware of this particular rule and boldly grabbed the carafe when they wanted more. Each time she had felt the shame and feared the Japanese would think her just as rude as her fellows.

Subtly yet boldly, she reached forward and took hold of the carafe. Steve's face lit up in a grateful smile as she poured the sake into his cup. She tried to make her movements as fluid and precise as the geisha's. Instead, she noticed her hand trembling and she bit her lip. Obviously, she lacked the training.

She set the carafe down, but not in the same spot. Rather, she set it in front of Steve; on purpose. Her arm extended and brushed against his in the process. Her instincts had taken over. She wanted to touch him just to see how he would react. She would gain his attention this time. As she felt her sleeve glide over his, she tilted her head and looked at him through half-shut eyes. Just having him next to her was curiously disturbing. She looked up at him, prepared to flash another inviting smile. His eyes were on his cup, however. He was paying absolutely no attention to her.

His lack of favourable response only fuelled Joanna's desire to flirt with him a little more overtly. His arm was only a few inches from hers and she decided to subtly lean in his direction until they touched, just to see whether he would pull away or respond. Gradually, she shifted her weight to the right, prepared to place her hand flat on the floor next to his knee to support herself. Her move had to be slow and appear casual.

Inch by inch, her shoulder neared Steve's arm. Soon she could smell the faint musky scent of the deerskin. She was enjoying herself tremendously. This was all a game to her; she aimed only to tease and was quite determined not to pursue this any further once she managed to get a reaction out of him.

But just as her shoulder met his, the music stopped. A Japanese man sitting across the table started to address the group. All the delegates straightened up, as did Steve, and Joanna realised it was now too late to do anything. He was out of her reach, in more ways than one. The conference had officially started and it was time to get down to business.

Joanna felt cross at being interrupted so abruptly, but at the same time she was reminded this wasn't the time or place to play stupid flirtatious games. She was here to work, after all.

Chapter Three

*L*ying on the man's back, Joanna let the tip of her tongue trace a wet path between his shoulder blades. Her hands hugged his ribcage on either side. Her thumbs dug into his muscular back; her fingertips were crushed between the bed and his nipples yet still able to toy with them wickedly.

Fire built between their bodies, the heat of her belly and his back reflecting off each other. She moaned with pleasure as she writhed. Her hips heaved against his buttocks, her loins growing warm and her moist flesh throbbing. In her throat sounds of pleasure rose with each breath, husky and sensuous.

The man didn't move. His skin gave under her touch, his body incredibly smooth. Soon he grew even hotter under her, warm and soft. Against her mouth his skin was curiously dry, almost powdery. Joanna felt it give under her tongue, wrinkling and slowing down her wet caresses. She pressed her face against him and continued moving lasciviously on top of him.

Her nipples also dug into his back, erect and extremely sensitive; her juices quickly pooled between her legs. Just caressing him was exciting enough to bring her almost to the point of orgasm. She moaned again, louder.

A moment later she woke up to the sound of her own voice. It took a moment to remember where she was. Against her naked skin the bedsheets were warm and damp from her sweat. She was alone, lying on top of the pillow she was hugging, the pillowcase drenched with her saliva.

Pushing herself up on to her elbows, she turned her head and glanced at the clock on the bedside table. It was still early. Her nipples were stiff and painfully erect. She let herself fall forward, her face landing deep in the thick pillow, and she stopped breathing for a few seconds, trying to calm the pounding of her heart. She felt hot and excited, once again yearning for the touch of a man's body. Never in her life had she awoken with such desire.

Then, in a flash, a face appeared in her mind: Steve. He was the man she had been caressing in her dream. He was the reason her flesh now craved its reward of pleasure. Even though he had only briefly and recently walked into her life, she realised she wanted him.

All he had done was introduce himself and shake her hand, but Joanna had been taken by his natural charm. After the welcoming reception, they had each gone their separate ways and she hadn't seen him since. The rest of her day had been spent dealing with distributors, tasting new delicacies, attending lectures and presentations. He had completely vanished from her sight and mind once the conference had started.

So why had he appeared in her dreams? And why was it so arousing? She turned on to her back and slowly lowered her hand to caress her throbbing flesh. It was soaking wet, its fragrance perceptible even through the bedsheets. Her dew had flowed down along her thighs and upwards to bathe the whole of her pelvis, merging with the sweat of her excitement to make the hairs of her mound slick and slightly sticky. She was so wet, wet with desire for the man.

Her fingertips came in contact with her vulva and readily melted into its wetness. Her clitoris was stiff and throbbing, its bud hard and aching. Her fingers easily glided inside her slick vagina, like a hot knife into soft butter, whilst her thumb teased her bud, caressing it and making it grow even longer and harder.

Once again the man appeared in her mind. She couldn't clearly remember his face but it was definitely Steve. She remembered better the feel of his arm brushing against hers and how she had wanted to touch him again. The memory of his hands was even clearer. She could still see his long fingers encircling the tiny cup of sake, still feel his warm touch from when he had shaken her hand.

Her thumb grew insistent on her tiny shaft, and somehow she wished it was his fingers she could feel on her flesh. Soon pleasure gathered within her, like a tornado forming and about to explode in devastation.

The muscles in her legs contracted violently, her toes pointing and her calves aching. She felt the familiar tingle deep inside her wet tunnel, playing against her fingers and guiding them to that place where her climax was soon to be born.

Her hips jerked a few times, at first shaking with mild spasms but soon echoing the strength of her orgasm powerfully. She heard herself call his name as she came and she smiled. Steve. She was saying it for the first time and she found the mix of letters incredibly erotic as they escaped her lips. She pronounced his name in a moan of joy that only served to heighten her pleasure.

She didn't care if she ever saw him again. The memory of him was sufficient to satisfy her. This way, she could use the man without him ever suspecting anything.

Her bras and underpants lay in a heap on the bed. Joanna couldn't decide which set to wear: the jade green lacy number, with push-up bra and minuscule thong, or the burgundy satin French knickers with matching camisole.

Knowing she would be kneeling for the best part of the evening, she opted for the latter. Comfort before sex-appeal. Besides, who would get to see them anyway? She grabbed the rest and threw them all back in the drawer.

Hurriedly, she slipped on her black velvet dress, a loose little item which neatly hugged her waist but flowed over her hips. Then she made her way down to the foyer. In the lift, she constantly glanced at her watch. The group was to gather at seven o'clock to depart half an hour later. She didn't want to be late, yet she hated being the first one to show up. Everyone should be there by now. This way, all heads would turn as she made her entrance.

Would Steve be there as well? Most probably. All day long, Joanna had caught herself keeping an eye out for him. Why had she dreamt about him that morning? He was a good-looking lad, of course, but definitely not her type.

Yet the sight of every blond head had startled her that day. It wasn't all that surprising. Most delegates were Asian and the few fair heads were a stark contrast to the jet black hair.

Would she see him tonight? A group of delegates from the West were on their way out of town, to some sort of country inn, for dinner and entertainment. Officially, it was meant as a night out to relax. But Joanna knew better. She had attended enough conferences to know she would secretly be evaluated. Nothing like a good meal and a few drinks to make people relax, and unwittingly reveal their true natures. Those who failed to behave themselves according to the Japanese rules of propriety would be noted, and as a result would probably have more trouble establishing the precious contacts necessary to get ahead in this type of business.

Joanna stepped out of the lift. Just as she expected, conversations stopped and heads turned as she came forward casually to join the group. Her blond hair flowed freely about her shoulders and bounced lightly as she walked. As if that weren't enough to attract everyone's attention, her unrestrained breasts bobbed under her dress, her nipples naughtily peaking against the silk of the camisole.

Not to worry, she knew she looked proper. Her black dress covered her knees, and not a single inch of cleavage was in view. Nevertheless, the smooth fabric gently brushed her curves with each sway of her hips and made her feel sexy. Her bare thighs softly rubbed together with each step and she could barely conceal her excitement.

She smiled at everyone she recognised and greeted them in turn, never giving anyone more than his share of attention before swiftly moving away. All eyes were on her and she basked in satisfaction for a moment. If only they could guess what a powerful arousing effect their stares had on her.

A couple of men came to her, smiling, and tried to engage her in conversation. She humoured them for a minute, yet let her eyes scan the crowd for more evidence that she was the only one everyone was looking at, be it blatantly or subtly. At the same time, she wanted to see whether Steve would be joining them.

Small groups had formed and everyone was mingling politely. Yet no one was immune to the sight of her. She could see heads turning her way often, if only briefly. She could also guess many of the men were in fact talking about her at that very moment.

That was exactly what she had planned. But just as she thought she had them all enthralled, the Valkyrie made her entrance and spoilt everything. In a fraction of a second, Joanna ceased to be the centre of attention, giving way to Greta, the New Yorker.

Another of the few women attending the conference, Greta was as loud as her clothes, which were anything but subtle. Her brightly coloured blouses, her incredibly short skirts and her impossibly high stilettos caught everyone's eye wherever she went, as did the cheap heavy jewellery dangling from her ears, her neck and her wrists.

Joanna had noticed her several times the previous

day. She remembered the nickname by which another delegate had referred to her and agreed it suited the woman perfectly. Although Greta wasn't very tall, her flamboyant golden frizzy hair gathered high on top of her head gave her extra inches and made her even more noticeable. Joanna could easily picture her perched on a shiny chariot, her hair sticking out from under a Viking's helmet, brandishing a sword and screaming at the top of her lungs as she charged towards the enemy.

In her early forties, the woman talked endlessly, to everybody, and was over-friendly to the point of being suffocating. She didn't shake hands with anyone more than once: being introduced gave her the green light to switch to impetuous hugs or powerful slaps across the back.

Wherever she went, she made her mark, interrupting speakers and babbling on loudly during demonstrations. Yet no one seemed offended. In fact, most of them were amused, for this behaviour was obviously natural to her. She didn't mean to be rude, she was just talkative and genuinely brash.

She walked among the gathered crowd, using her ample bosom to bump her way from one delegate to the next, and greeted everyone with little happy cries of surprise, plentiful hugs and way too many cries of 'Darling!'

Yet there was no doubt she was endearing. She knew how to take the floor and never relinquish it. Even the bright orange lipstick heavily smeared over her thick lips suited her. Overtly flirtatious, she gave everyone she addressed her undivided attention, albeit for a moment, and took a genuine interest in what they had to say.

Joanna would have liked her to go away, but couldn't help being impressed by the attention the woman attracted. Now, no one had any interest in Joanna. Greta had arrived and she was the star of the evening before it had even begun.

* * *

As Joanna stepped off the coach, the first thing to catch her eye was the large sign bearing the name of the inn, Jasmine Blossoms, painted in pale green on a pink background. In the early evening light, its paleness stood out, slightly fluorescent. There was something familiar about the lettering: the way the J was stretched; the slim tall L. She stared at it for a second, then shrugged off this vague impression of déjà vu and followed her colleagues inside.

The inn itself was a large building all on one level. Inside it was a maze, a series of rooms of various sizes, all separated by sliding panels of varying thickness.

The group was split up and dispersed into several rooms as soon as they arrived. Joanna knelt at the table and quickly examined her dinner companions. She was the only woman in a group of sixteen. Only a couple of faces were familiar. Thankfully, Greta was nowhere in sight.

Throughout the coach ride, the New Yorker's voice had drowned out the sound of the engines. Everyone had responded to her stupid jokes and the mood had been cheerful. But after a while the constant loud babbling had grown tiresome and Joanna was grateful to be rid of her childish laughter and squeals.

The hosts at her table were four Japanese men dressed in white, one sitting on each side of the table, addressing each guest in turn. Joanna was seated at a corner and barely took part in the conversation. She preferred to listen and observe, eager to see whether her suspicions were accurate.

Now and again, very precise questions were directed at a particular guest, and the four men exchanged brief glances after the reply. Each time, Joanna barely contained a smile of satisfaction. Just as she had thought, this was meant to find out more about the delegates, to see which ones were trustworthy.

Dinner itself was a colourful affair, starting with a delicate soup made with buckwheat noodles and several varieties of mushroom, followed by frugal servings of pickled vegetables. In all, the meal consisted of about fifteen dishes from different regions of Asia: steamed fish flavoured with oyster sauce and ginger, fried prawns rolled in seaweed, raw lobster with braised meats accompanied by fruit, all deliciously fragrant and presented with plentiful garnishes of carved raw vegetables.

Joanna sampled everything except for the dishes made with bean curd. Although in the past she had tasted practically everything deemed edible – even things that would never appear on a Western table – she had never got used to this particular ingredient. Be it fried, steamed or even barbecued, there was no way she could swallow the stuff.

Towards the end of the meal, the group was entertained by two geishas. One of them, Keiko, sang a bitter-sweet tale of dead lovers while her colleague Atsuko accompanied her on the *shamisen*. Everyone listened politely, the men at times leaning to whisper something in their neighbour's ear.

Joanna could easily guess what they were saying. Geishas held a fascination for Westerners, and she wasn't immune to them either. She couldn't tear her eyes away from the slim but straight bodies, their waists delicately wrapped in large *obi* sashes. The women looked like twins, two matching porcelain dolls, their faces a pure white, their hands and feet unusually small. One was dressed in mint green and the other in pale pink. After their song, they performed the ritual tea ceremony, then disappeared behind a sliding panel.

Shortly afterwards, one of the hosts turned to Joanna. Wanting to keep a clear head in preparation for the question she knew would soon be coming her way, she had made sure to stay away from the *sake*. Only briefly had she tasted it, more out of politeness, then put the cup back on the table. She knew that if she drank it, more would come. Instead, she nibbled on cucumbers to quench her thirst after saltier dishes. Now she was glad to have been so wise.

'What is the ultimate pleasure for you, Miss Parsons?' the host asked in a soft voice.

'Wilson,' Joanna muttered to herself. Although she had made the correction time and again, many still addressed her using Stacey's name, and by now she was fed up with constantly trying to set them straight.

She took a deep breath and waited before answering. The questions they had asked her companions had to do with business ethics or Western culture. Why were they getting so philosophical with her?

'Pleasure,' she replied cautiously, 'would be whatever I would find myself craving if I had to do without for a long time.' She kept her reply vague, on purpose, curious to see whether her hosts were trying to make small talk, or if they would press the issue.

'But surely this can mean many things,' countered another of the Japanese men. 'Can you be more specific?'

'For example,' she said slowly, 'there are certain types of food I would miss if I wasn't able to obtain them . . .'

'Yes, yes,' the man said impatiently. 'But what is the ultimate pleasure? The one thing you would rather die than be without?'

One of her colleagues leant forward, slightly drunk, and burped loudly. 'A good fuck,' he said. 'I would gladly pass on anything but that.'

The host seemed amused with that answer and immediately turned to Joanna. 'Indeed,' he said, his voice growing deep and slow. 'What about sexual pleasure? Do you value it more than fine food?'

Once again Joanna thought carefully before replying. 'Given the type of work I do,' she said, 'I have to value the pleasure I derive from food above all else.'

She sat back and took a sip of sake, satisfied that she had come up with the right answer. The first thing she had learnt about the Japanese was the value they gave their work. Their careers came ahead of their personal lives, even their own family. Considering that her hosts had made their careers in the food industry, Joanna knew she had to convince them food was also her priority.

Glances were exchanged between the hosts. A second later, they continued questioning the other guests. Joanna finished her drink. Knowing she had passed the test, she could now relax and enjoy the rest of the evening.

Soft laughter came from behind a translucent panel. Joanna stopped and listened for a while. The evening was getting boring, and she had excused herself to go in search of the bathroom. Coming back along a short corridor, she was in no hurry to go back to her table.

She held her breath as she listened to whispers and giggles. Soon she recognised the voices of Keiko and Atsuko, and she was amused to realise she was standing on the other side of the room where the geishas went when they weren't entertaining the guests. Now she remembered that earlier the girls had gone down this same corridor after their performance.

To her surprise, the panel suddenly slid open and an older woman beckoned her to come in. Immediately Joanna knew the woman was the *mama-san*, the one in charge of the geishas. She stepped in hesitantly, curious and excited.

Half a dozen cheerful young women welcomed her with broad smiles. Just as she had guessed, Joanna found herself in the middle of a large dressing room. One of the walls was lined with mirrors and fitted with a long dressing table. Towards the back, a rack supported dozens of colourful kimonos. On a counter top, dozens of jars lay waiting as did stands on which the large wigs had been placed. In every corner, jasmine shrubs grew from big pots on the floor, climbing towards the ceiling. Their tiny flowers, barely open, faintly exuded their characteristic aroma.

Keiko and Atsuko were sitting at the dressing table, removing their make-up. Now they each wore a simple cotton kimono, like a dressing gown. They had pulled them down off their shoulders to allow them to wipe off the make-up on the back of their necks. Underneath, they were naked and Joanna could see the reflection of their bare breasts in the mirror.

Without their wigs, they looked just like any other Japanese women. Keiko's hair was dark brown and styled in a short bob, making her look like a student. Atsuko had long thick sensuous hair falling freely on her bare shoulders, and so dark it shone with a vague bluish gleam.

Their breasts had now been released from the constraint of the thick *obi* sash and their nipples pointed proudly. Another girl walked around the room as she brushed her hair, completely naked, nonchalant and unashamed.

At first Joanna was taken aback. It was strange to realise that once the make-up, wig and kimono were removed, a geisha was an ordinary woman. Although the girl's stance and movements were unusually delicate and poised, there was no way of guessing the existence of her alter ego.

She turned to Atsuko and Keiko, who were still sitting in front of the mirror. The thick chalk-like *oshiroi* cream on their faces was only partially removed. Some of it had trickled down and pearled on their breasts. Once again, Joanna couldn't help staring at them. Only this time, she was aroused more than intrigued by the sight of their naked bodies.

The girls helped each other wipe off the white stains. Atsuko pulled her hair to one side and tilted her head so that Keiko could wipe her exposed neck. The sponge changed hands, and Atsuko pulled off Keiko's kimono completely to wash her upper back. Their movements were fluid and slow. Their hands travelled over each other's naked skin, and it looked to Joanna as if they were caressing one another.

But more striking was an enormous tattoo which adorned Keiko's back. A large dragon, a pale green and pink creature, surrounded by orange, yellow and red flames, had been permanently drawn on her skin as if it were a canvas. Aghast, Joanna glanced at Atsuko's back. There again she could see a tattoo, although her kimono still shielded most of it.

The *mama-san* caught Joanna's interested gaze and ushered her forward. She spoke a few words to the other geishas, who looked surprised for a minute, then broke into a fit of giggles. Two of them came to Joanna and started to undress her while the others rushed to the rack at the back and picked out a few kimonos.

Joanna was too surprised to react. Quickly, the girls pulled her dress over her head, then paused to examine her satin underwear. Glances were exchanged, followed by another collective fit of giggles. One of the girls came forward, lightly caressed the dark fabric, and encouraged the other to do the same. Together they finished undressing Joanna. By now, they were more interested in the underwear than the woman. Delicately holding up the pieces of clothing, they handled and examined the undies as if they were some precious trophy.

Once Joanna found herself standing naked in the middle of the room, she instinctively covered her breasts and her crotch with her hands. The girls didn't pay any attention to her. In front of the mirror, one held up the camisole to her chest as another quickly slipped on the knickers and pranced around while looking at her own reflection.

The *mama-san* laughed loudly and made Joanna sit down on a low stool. Two of the girls grabbed jars of white make-up and rapidly covered Joanna's face and neck. Behind her, the *mama-san* expertly gathered up Joanna's long blond hair and pinned it on top of her head. A few minutes later, a wig was placed on top.

Joanna turned to face the mirror. All she recognised was her naked body. Her face looked foreign, completely covered in white paste, her mouth painted like a rosebud and her eyes lined with black pencil. The *mama-san* stepped forward and dressed her with four different kimonos, one on top of the other. Finally, the large *obi* sash was placed across her chest and abdomen, then fastened at the back. The transformation was complete.

The *mama-san* walked to the back of the room, slid open another panel and gestured for Joanna to follow her. There was another dressing room, slightly smaller and empty, but with walls entirely covered in mirrors. Atsuko and Keiko, now completely naked and free from any trace of make-up, followed behind. The *mama-san* turned round and left, sliding the panel shut behind her.

Joanna stood in the middle and studied her reflection in the mirrors. She looked at herself from all angles, overwhelmed by the sight. The kimono on top was emerald green and richly embroidered with gold thread. The wig was heavy but easy to balance. Pulling back the sleeves, she was surprised to see how fine her wrists looked. Keiko brought her a pair of sandals and helped her put them on. Joanna pranced around, at first uneasy on such thick soles but soon gaining enough confidence to mimic the geishas' hurried tiny steps.

Her companions watched, covering their mouths with their hands as they giggled. After a while, they ushered Joanna back into the first room. She obeyed reluctantly, not yet having tired of admiring her new look.

Everyone else had gone. Docile and silent, she let her companions undress her. Her neck was a bit sore from the weight of the wig. Obviously it would take some training to get used to it. As the geishas removed it, Joanna felt her head spinning. And she knew it wasn't just from the wig: the sake she had drunk earlier probably played an important part as well. Everything around her served to make her mind numb: the amazing sight of the geishas' naked bodies, the large tattoos on their backs, the feel of the silk kimono against her bare skin, even the smell of the jasmine which now seemed even stronger and more intoxicating than previously.

Sitting on a low stool, she closed her eyes as the girls removed each layer of silk to once again reveal her naked body. Immediately, she looked around for her own clothes, or something else to cover herself with, but found nothing. She gave the two geishas a puzzled look. They were still naked and didn't seem at all bothered. Turning their back to her, they stood by the dressing table and filled a large bowl with warm water while gathering sponges and towels.

Joanna observed them secretively. Both women were incredibly slender and had a petite frame. Their minuscule waists made them look more like little girls, but their round and pert breasts were definitely those of a woman. But what most impressed Joanna was the sight of their backs, and she couldn't stop staring at them. Atsuko's tattoo was now in full view: a large, dark red bird, like a phoenix, painted against a pale green and pink flowery background. Together the geishas looked like works of art, a pair of painted naked statues for the visual enjoyment of the onlooker.

They turned around and smiled at Joanna as they came towards her. With wet sponges they started removing her make-up. Joanna shivered as drops of warm water dripped on to her lap. White streaks trailed down her chest and Atsuko wiped them away expertly. As she looked at herself in the mirror, Joanna gradually saw her face reappear. Soon her face and neck were clean, but the mix of water and white paste had trickled on to her lap and chest. By now, these were the only places the geishas were wiping.

Their sponges travelled skilfully over Joanna's bare breasts and her parted thighs, moving in a rather sensuous fashion. At first, Joanna thought nothing of her companions' daring gestures. But when they started to concentrate on her breasts, stroking her nipples which eagerly grew erect, she looked at each of them in turn, a little uneasy.

Suddenly, the sponges dropped to the floor and the two geishas continued rubbing Joanna's wet skin with their bare hands. She didn't react. Their gentle fingers brushed her stiff nipples in a manner that blatantly announced their lewd intentions.

Their touch filled Joanna with a rush of warmth. She

knew she couldn't refuse what they were offering her. Letting out a sigh, she closed her eyes. A woman's touch was nothing new to her, but in recent years she had only been with men and had practically forgotten how soft female skin felt.

Her own skin was wet and cool and reacted powerfully to the touch of their dainty hands, which were incredibly hot. Their expert fingers continued fondling Joanna's breasts until her nipples attained full erection. Little by little, the women had moved closer to Joanna and now their naked bodies rubbed against hers.

Joanna opened her eyes and immediately noticed the ecstatic looks on her lovers' faces. They weren't even looking at her. Eyes closed and smiling blissfully, each woman was concentrating on pleasuring Joanna. Their caresses were methodical and loving, like some sort of ritual devotion, as if they were worshipping her. They had the honour of serving and pleasing her.

They knelt by Joanna's side and soon their hands fluttered elsewhere on her bare skin, feeling her abdomen, her back and her thighs. Lips softly paused on her shoulders, warm and supple. Joanna let out a faint moan. Her senses were ablaze. The women moaned as well as they caressed and kissed her and their expression of delight aroused Joanna even further. She could feel their fingertips like hot embers travelling over her body, triggering a hot seething desire for more.

Instinctively, she opened her arms and the women huddled in her embrace. Their mouths fastened on her nipples and they suckled gently. She let her fingers comb through their thick hair, stroking their necks and gradually edging towards their adorned backs. Their skin was warm and soft, and Joanna let her hands wander at will. Finally she could reach down and touch the tattoos that had so mesmerised her. By now she was in such a state of arousal that she almost felt the colours under her fingertips.

The geishas took their time and proceeded slowly as they continued discovering Joanna's body. Now hot and impatient, Joanna guided their hands to her thighs which she parted readily. But the girls didn't want to be told what to do. Their tiny fingers slowly traced the inside of her legs, stroking them softly in large circles, gradually working their way towards the inside.

They slowly coaxed her into lying on the floor, amid the discarded kimonos. For a while Joanna remained still as they lay by her side and writhed against her, caressing her limbs and her abdomen with their own. All she could feel was the warmth of their soft skin pressed against hers, contrasting with the coolness of the silk kimonos underneath her.

Their wet mouths on her breasts were hungry and eager. Their hot breath brushed her wet skin and Joanna knew she could not stand it much longer. With a supreme effort, she resisted the urge to caress herself. Her dew had pooled between her legs and her aching clitoris was demanding immediate attention.

Thankfully, the geishas' lips soon followed their hands. Joanna shivered as they kissed her hot thighs. Her legs parted even wider, her knees bending as they began licking the inside of her legs. Now and again she heard them exchanging a few words, but she couldn't understand what they were saying. Keiko's mouth finally brushed her flesh and Joanna shivered with delight. Her arousal was unbearably intense by now. She needed the release and, since it was on offer, she wouldn't refuse it.

The geisha's tongue flickered over Joanna's clitoris and swirled endlessly. Atsuko rose to her feet and went rummaging in the drawers of the dressing table. At first Joanna paid little attention to her, but she gasped violently when she saw the enormous ivory phallus the girl had pulled out of a velvet case. Incredibly thick, with a rounded tip, it was intricately carved, with a pattern resembling bunches of small grapes.

Keiko's mouth pulled away, but her fingers never ceased tweaking Joanna's hard bud, bringing her closer to climax with each passing second. Coming back,

41

Atsuko knelt again and rubbed the ivory phallus against Joanna's wet folds, moving it with great dexterity up and down Joanna's slick labia to lubricate them thoroughly.

Joanna's hips jerked at the first tingle of her climax. Keiko didn't relent. Her fingers wriggled fast and hard, endlessly torturing their prey. The large dildo also added to the excitement, gliding over her wet and slick flesh, getting warmer and wetter. Joanna felt her vagina contract powerfully, clenching and relaxing as her first orgasm seized her. Her legs bucked then grew limp.

But just as the waves of pleasure began subsiding, Atsuko administered her coup de grace. Slowly but steadily, she inserted the ivory phallus inside the throbbing vagina. Joanna moaned as it stretched her, its girth filling her and rekindling her arousal. Atsuko twisted it around very slowly, mercilessly rubbing its knobbly surface against the inner walls.

Joanna could feel each bump on the phallus as it caressed her, triggering yet more pleasure. She reached another orgasm, more powerful than the previous one. Just when she thought this couldn't last much longer, Keiko bent down and took Joanna's stiff bud between her lips to suck it gently.

Joanna screamed with joy. This was too much for her to take. Pleasure rampaged through her again and again, and soon she grew oblivious to everything around her. She writhed on the floor, panting loudly, her mouth dry and her throat sore.

When she finally opened her eyes, she saw the girls hadn't left her side. And although their swollen breasts and erect nipples betrayed their own arousal, they hadn't caressed one another. The oddity of this situation wasn't lost on Joanna. They had done this solely for her benefit, not their own, taking more satisfaction in pleasuring her than themselves.

They helped her get back on her feet and brought her clothes out of a small chest. Joanna looked at herself in the mirror as she dressed. Her eyes shone brightly, and her hair was a bit tangled, but otherwise there was nothing to betray what she had just been through. Her legs still wobbly, she made her way back to the dining room.

The other guests had left their tables and gathered in small groups in a large reception area. Most of them were definitely tipsy, and no one seemed to notice that Joanna had returned. For once she was glad not to attract attention. With any luck, perhaps they hadn't noticed how long she had been gone either.

Above the conversations, Greta's voice rose loud and clear as she crudely announced she had to go in search of the ladies' room. Joanna was annoyed as the screeching voice brought her back to reality. Yet irritation quickly was replaced by dismay as she watched Greta go down the same corridor she herself had taken an hour earlier.

Joanna's heart started beating fast. Would Greta be tempted to stop at the geishas' dressing room? And if she did, would she be invited in and entitled to the same treat?

For a moment, Joanna was tempted to follow Greta round the corner and find a good place from which to eavesdrop. She resisted the urge however, standing idle and trying to keep track of time. That was the only way to know whether Greta had simply gone to the ladies or whether she had made an unexpected stop on her way back.

To her surprise, Greta came back only moments later. Joanna smiled to herself, beaming with smugness. Greta would never know what she had just missed.

Chapter Four

She couldn't bear to look at Steve. A couple of times he had tried to start a conversation, but Joanna had replied rather abruptly. What was she supposed to say to him? That only yesterday morning she had dreamt she was licking his back and pressing her wet pussy against his bare buttocks? That she had masturbated while thinking about him, then screamed his name as she climaxed? Indeed, that was all she could think about as she stood near him. Normally, she would have played on that. For her, seduction with words was easy. She had done it with Harry, and several men before him. Today, however, for the first time in years, her wits were failing her, her lascivious thoughts just couldn't translate into words. That's how powerful an effect Steve had on her.

He was standing just inches from her, silently watching a noodle-making demonstration. Joanna wasn't paying attention at all, although the crowd loudly expressed its admiration of the chef's skills.

More like an artist, the young cook expertly stretched the dough into long strands which he twirled through the air, folded in two, then stretched again. Joanna had seen it all before and couldn't concentrate.

Rather, she couldn't stop thinking about how excited

she was even now. After leaving the inn the previous night, her arousal hadn't completely subsided. For a second, she tried to imagine what Steve would say if she revealed what was on her mind at that moment. Confusion gave way to amusement and a wicked plan began forming in her mind.

All she had to do was stretch her neck and whisper in his ear. She could start by saying she had dreamt about him, the things they were doing together, then demurely pull away and pretend to be embarrassed. Soon after, she could tell him how excited she was just thinking about it now. She would glance at her own erect nipples and hope his eyes would follow.

Once she had his attention, she could go for the kill. First, tell him she was wet and getting hotter just being near him, then ask if he could sense it, perhaps even push it as far as asking him whether he could smell her feminine scent. That would surely drive him mad. What would she do afterwards? Probably leave it at that for the moment. Bask in the satisfaction of his attention.

She looked around, gauging her chances. It was risky. There was a lot of noise around them and whispering would be difficult. She would have to be loud enough for him to hear, but make sure no one else did. She couldn't chance having him misunderstand her or ask her to repeat. The effect would then be ruined.

Steve was wearing a thin cotton T-shirt and she a sleeveless blouse. Their bare arms were just inches from each other's: his muscular, tanned and slightly hairy; hers pale, slim and delicate. Now she longed just to brush against him, pretend to break innocently through the crowd to get a better view.

As she pondered the situation, she could feel her juices start to drench her knickers. Excitement grew and her flesh clenched faintly. The mere thought of making a move on him was wickedly stimulating. In front of them, the demonstration was proceeding. The other delegates watched intently. Joanna knew they wouldn't notice anything as she was standing at the back of the crowd. But there were still people walking past behind her, stopping for a little while to watch and then quickly going on their way.

She shuffled her feet slightly and stretched her neck, pretending she couldn't see very well. Taking a deep breath, she counted to ten and turned to Steve. But before the first word could even come out of her mouth, he turned and went. Joanna watched, dumbfounded, as the crowd closed around him, too surprised to go after him and not knowing whether to laugh or cry at her own foolishness. Why had she waited so long?

For a brief moment, she was tempted to follow him, wait until he stopped again and give it another try. But she knew he might then think she was chasing him. It would seem too obvious, and the surprise effect would be ruined.

The demonstration was over and the group was dispersing. Shaking with frustration, Joanna headed for the bar. She had to sit down, think and steady her nerves.

Southern Comfort with orange juice. The bartender gave her a puzzled look but Joanna couldn't care less. Delegates had been advised the bar would stock a wide variety of regional liqueurs and drinks for them to taste at leisure. Most of them had already enjoyed more than their share. But right now Joanna needed something western. She was in no mood to try something different.

Perched on a high leather-covered stool, she brushed her thighs together before crossing her legs. Her flesh was so wet she could feel the slickness; she could practically hear the wet sounds it usually made when she stroked it.

Her clitoris was so hard it ached. Thoughts just wouldn't go away and the arousal they generated didn't subside. She couldn't go on like this for much longer. She had put herself in this situation and she had to do something about it. As she subtly rocked on her seat, the thong of her knickers stretched and pressed against her folds, increasing the pressure on her swollen bud.

46

Tightly squeezing her legs, she contracted her buttocks then released them repeatedly. Each time, she couldn't help a faint sigh as her excitement grew. She needed release; she needed it now.

Hurriedly, she gulped down half her drink then glanced at her schedule and her watch. Exactly fifteen minutes before the next demonstration: pickled vegetables. That was one she didn't want to miss. It was precisely the kind of product her company would be interested in and she sensed it could become the new craze in snacks: colourful and loaded with flavours.

But instead, what she really wanted to do was go back to her room, lie on her bed, slip her hand inside her knickers and give herself the release she so desperately craved.

'You don't have time,' said the man next to her.

Startled, Joanna turned to look at him. She had vaguely noticed someone had come to sit on the stool on her right a moment ago but hadn't paid any attention to him. Obviously, the man had noticed her.

'Pardon me?' she replied.

He leant towards her slowly. He was just an average Japanese man, perhaps a bit taller than the norm, in his mid-thirties. His face was handsome, his features soft. Only his hair was bad, so coarse and untamed that it looked like a cheap wig. His eyes were quite big, perfectly almond shaped, and alight with childish amusement. The suit he wore was a shade of pale moss-green and his shirt pink. His tie – pure silk in a pink-and-green pattern – was a perfect match.

Joanna didn't stop to examine him further. Instead, she looked him straight in the eyes, trying to figure out what he could be thinking. Something about him made her suspect he was not a businessman. He didn't look as if he belonged at a food fair, for some reason. Perhaps the entertainment industry, she thought curiously. His eyes were black pearls that bore into hers as if he could read her mind. His cologne was quite strong but pleasant, a scent Joanna vaguely recognised but couldn't precisely identify. He smiled. She decided he was quite charming and returned his smile.

'You are wondering whether you have time to go back to your room and masturbate,' he said in a matter-of-fact tone.

Joanna's smile froze and she felt herself pale. At the same time, she noticed she was still rubbing her thighs together and immediately stopped. Her heart pounded fast. She was shocked by his blunt approach, yet she couldn't help being intrigued and wondered how he could have guessed.

He leant closer still.

'You are a very sensuous woman,' he said. His voice turned into a faint whisper. Despite his efforts, his accent was very pronounced, and at times Joanna wasn't quite sure that he was really saying what she thought she could hear.

'Don't try to deny it,' he continued. 'There is nothing you desire more right now than to have an orgasm. Your whole body aches for it. Your nipples are so stiff it is plain to anyone. I am sure your clitoris is even stiffer, probably aching.'

Joanna didn't reply. How could he know, she wondered. She looked straight ahead, feeling her cheeks grow red as she blushed. His hard breath on her temple did nothing to ease the heat spreading up from her chest.

He held up his right hand, reached towards her and lightly brushed her breasts through her blouse.

'You are hot, perhaps more hungry for sex than you have been in a long time,' he said in a low voice. 'Even after what happened last night you are not sated. You want more, always more. Right now, you have this incredible urge to masturbate. But there is no time for that. You must endure another few hours or risk missing something important at the food fair.'

Joanna was paralysed. The words spoken in such a thick accent, yet nonetheless unmistakable in meaning, made the situation surreal: both a nightmare and a dream come true. For the stranger knew exactly how she felt, but she didn't know how or why. And obviously he felt no embarrassment at saying it out loud.

His talk made her hotter still. He was right, and being told how obvious it was aroused her tremendously.

She looked round quickly. The barman had his back turned and was talking to customers at the far end of the bar. Other than that, there was no one else around. No one could see that her neighbour was now casually flicking her nipples with his fingertips.

His hand dropped on to her lap and his fingers glided under the hem of her loose cotton skirt. Joanna felt his fingers hot and soft, his touch light but intense. Looking down, she could see the bump his hand made under her skirt; his fingers barely discernible but his knuckles pointy and lifting gently as he caressed the top of her leg with his fingertips. Under the emerald green fabric, it looked like a thick snake recoiling before pouncing on an unwitting prey.

'Two minutes,' the man said. 'That's how long it will take me. And you will be grateful, I promise.'

For a moment, his caresses stopped. All Joanna could feel was the moist heat of his palm penetrating her skin and increasing her excitement. Instinctively, she uncrossed her legs and right away she cursed herself for it. Her body was acting independently of her mind. The soft fabric glided back over the man's hand and completely hid it from view, an accomplice to the stranger's licentious intentions, a traitor to Joanna's last hesitations.

Her flesh clenched violently, eager to be rewarded, and excited by the new turn of events. The pleasure so desperately craved was finally within reach. For a moment, Joanna wondered what on earth she was doing. Had she gone crazy? How could she let a complete stranger touch her like this?

Once again, she glanced round. Her lap was under the overhanging edge of the bar; no one would see anything. Still she hesitated. Taking a deep breath, she hoped to steady her pounding heart, but the scent of the man's cologne only served to arouse her even more. What was that fragrance? She knew she had smelt it before, but she couldn't remember exactly what it was.

'I can smell you,' he insisted as his lips brushed her earlobe. 'Let me. I won't ask for anything in return.'

Joanna gave in quickly, her aching flesh getting the better of her. Her need to be pleasured overtook any last shred of common sense. And the notion of having a stranger give her the release she craved, right here at the bar, was incredibly enticing. Slowly, she parted her legs. Already her breathing was shallow and fast. Her throat contracted and she wheezed a couple of times.

The stranger's hand immediately slipped between her thighs and his fingertips pushed aside the thong stretched over her flesh. She gasped as he touched her, and her reaction made him laugh softly.

'Brace yourself,' he said. 'You don't want your moans to attract attention, do you?'

Joanna shook her head. Closing her eyes, she tried to detach herself and imagine the scene from afar. His jacket was open, his left hand in his pocket holding the jacket to shield the view from behind them. Although his right hand was under her skirt and his knees practically touched her thigh, he sat tall and only his head was tilted towards her. It might have looked as if they were flirting, but nothing more.

With a trembling hand, she grabbed her folder and papers on the counter and tucked them between her elbow and her thigh on the other side, to shield her lap from that angle. No one would notice she hoped. And she knew she couldn't go back now. She didn't want to.

His fingertips paused on her wet flesh. She felt them warm and stiff as they covered the whole of her slit and lightly dug into her folds. Although he was of average build, his hand was big and covered the entire length of her vulva. He brushed his hand up and down slowly, moving it from the wrist.

Looking down again, she could see nothing but his

arm, half-hidden under her skirt. At times the fabric raised slightly and she had this vague image in her mind of a kitten playing under a carpet. The thought almost made her laugh but by now his caresses were so exhilarating that she quickly ceased to think. All she wanted was to enjoy what would happen next.

His index finger touched her aching bud and pressed on it slightly. Joanna bit her lip to muffle the moan rising in her throat. Closing her eyes, she tried to concentrate and slow down her breathing. There was no way she could abandon herself completely. Not here. Too bad.

She would have liked to turn around, recline against his chest, hike up her skirt, spread her legs wide and beg him to rub her hard and fast, to bring her to a peak as soon as possible.

'I can very easily picture you when you climax,' the man continued to whisper in her ear. 'I can see your naked body twitching, shaken with spasms as you come; your hips moving frantically to counter the motion of the hand rubbing you; your head shaking from side to side and your beautiful hair cast all around your face, falling into your mouth and sticking to your cheeks. I can also very well imagine your screams of pleasure, increasingly loud; your sobs as you beg for more.'

Dizzy with pleasure, Joanna reached out and grabbed her glass. Despite the storm rampaging through her flesh, she needed to keep her head cool. Her fingers clenched so tight she thought the glass would break.

She felt the muscles in her thighs contract as she climaxed, bit her lip to stifle her scream of joy, and desperately hoped no one could see her hips jerk slightly against the stranger's hand.

The man stopped the motion of his hand, but didn't pull away. He waited, looking at her intently, then resumed. Joanna climaxed again, almost immediately, and had to stop breathing completely to refrain from screaming.

'Enough,' she sobbed in a shaking voice. 'This is too much.'

She moved back on the barstool, jerking her hips sideways and closing her legs. The man pulled his hand away and immediately stood up.

'Enough?' he asked in an amused tone. 'But you're the one who asked for it.' He took something out of his breast pocket, which he slipped into the folder Joanna had put back on the bar.

She didn't really pay attention. Reeling from the pleasure that was still shaking her, all she could think about was the pounding of her heart. She couldn't even stand to look at the man, unsure of what she would see in his eyes.

'As you wish, Miss Parsons,' he said after a while. 'We'll be in touch shortly.'

Joanna was too shaken even to bother telling him she wasn't Stacey. Without looking behind her she could sense he had already left the bar. Her heart still beat fast. Common sense told her to get up and go and hide in her room, but Joanna knew she couldn't even walk. The last waves of pleasure were still causing her flesh to contract spasmodically from time to time; her thighs were weak.

With a precise but trembling hand, she grabbed her glass and emptied it in one gulp, then put it back on the counter with a bang. At the other end of the bar, the bartender briefly glanced in her direction but didn't say anything. He simply grabbed the bottle of Southern Comfort and headed back towards her.

'No orange juice this time,' Joanna said in a hoarse voice.

He poured the golden liquid over the shrunken ice cubes and walked away. In a panic, Joanna emptied it just as quickly as the previous one. This time the liquid was still warm, even fiery, as it fell straight to her stomach. She took a few deep breaths to steady herself. Now she really had to go back to the conference.

Thoughts raced through her mind but she had no time

for them. She had to get on with her work. Besides, she was too shaken to try making sense of what had just happen. She needed to cool down first.

But as she reached to grab her folder still on the countertop, her eye caught sight of something she had barely noticed before: the card the stranger had slipped in and which stuck out from between two pieces of paper. She started trembling again as she pulled it out, holding it only with her fingertips.

The card was almost exactly like the one she had found in her room the first night. It was the same thick and pulpy, almost powdery, cardboard; the same pale green lettering on a light pink background. Only the message was different: THIS IS ONLY A SAMPLE OF THINGS TO COME. WE ARE VERY PLEASED WITH YOU SO FAR. WE WILL BE IN TOUCH AGAIN SHORTLY.

Joanna's first impulse was to go back to her room and fetch the other card to compare them. Then she remembered that she had tossed it in the wastepaper basket and it was probably long gone by now. She cursed herself. She should have kept the card. Of course, at the time, there was no way of knowing how important it would become later on.

She stood idle for a moment, trying to make some sense out of this incredible situation. Who was sending the messages? And who was this man who had so casually approached her only a few minutes ago? He knew her, obviously. But why bother with silly cards if all he wanted was to bed her? Why the charade?

Somehow she sensed she was on the wrong track. He had approached her, given her pleasure, then walked away at her request. If he had wanted a quick bonk he would have insisted, or at least tried harder. And what on earth had he meant when he had said she was the one who had asked for it?

Perhaps his knowledge of English was limited and he had picked the wrong expression. She hadn't asked for anything! But although she felt his choice of words was probably inappropriate, his tone had implied that she had asked for it, literally.

An unexpected tingle deep inside her crotch made her shiver suddenly. Whoever the stranger was, and whatever he wanted, he definitely knew how to read her.

Joanna glanced at her watch, saw that she was almost late for the demonstration she wanted to attend, and grabbed her folder. There would always be time to make sense of all this later.

Chapter Five

The constant purr of the disk drive was slowly driving Joanna mad. For the past hour she had been trying to log on to the Internet, without any success. Although the hotel's business facilities were the finest she had seen in a long while, she just couldn't get it right.

Of course, it would have been easy simply to type her report and fax it back to London, but there was no way of knowing who would receive it at the other end. She couldn't chance sending it straight into Richard's greedy little hands, knowing he was capable of sabotaging her work. Electronic mail was the only solution.

If only she could get it to work. The previous evening, when she had overheard Steve saying he would also come to the business centre to do some work, Joanna had immediately concocted the perfect plan: she would come in ahead of him, pretend to be unable to find her way around the Internet, and conveniently wait for him to offer his help. Only now the tables had turned on her: she wouldn't have to pretend, she genuinely couldn't figure it out!

Of course, under normal circumstances, she would have deemed this type of game beneath her. But her state of mind was such that she needed to do something, anything, to regain control. Too many things had been happening since she had arrived, events beyond her, and she yearned to be in charge for a change. So she would seduce Steve. She would have him, on her terms. She would find a way to wrap him round her little finger, just like she had done with Harry and –

Harry! Once again she had completely forgotten about him. She was supposed to call him from time to time, to keep the fire of his desire burning from a distance so that he would be ripe when she returned. Pushing the chair away from her desk, she pondered for a moment. With everything she had been going through, Harry had been the last person on her mind. Between her hurried departure, all the work awaiting her here, her sudden lust for Steve, and the weird messages she couldn't comprehend, she hadn't had time to think about Harry. But eventually she would be back in London, back to normal life, and she needed to plan for her return.

Returning to the computer, she loaded the word processing program and dashed down a quick note. She complained about long nights on her own, how she missed the sound of his voice and the warmth it triggered inside her, and stated how eager she was to see him again. She didn't even have to think about it for very long. By now she knew Harry well enough to know exactly what made him tick.

Once the fax machine handed her back her copy, she put it through the shredder and went back to her desk. That would take care of Harry, at least for now. She would give him a ring later, plan it so that her call would reach him late in the evening, either live or on his answerphone. That way, the memory of her would stay with him through the night.

She sat and went through the Internet access programme again. She tried clicking here and there, typing a few words, turning off the system and rebooting, but to no avail. Grunting with irritation, she raised her fist and prepared to whack the keyboard. A hand caught hers in mid-air.

'Mind over matter,' said a voice behind her. 'You're more intelligent than the machine.'

Joanna recognised the voice and, without even turning around, she knew it was Steve. Perfect. She couldn't have timed it any better. Now that contact had been made, she had to think fast. She readily gave up on the idea of playing damsel in distress and childishly whining that the machine hated her. Since the bloody system didn't want to cooperate anyway, it was easier to act cool about it.

'I just can't work it out,' she said as she pushed her chair sideways to let him see the screen better. 'I am logged on, but the system refuses to deliver my message. No matter what I try, I can't send out my document.'

She casually leant back in her chair, leaving enough space for him to move closer. She knew she had reached her first goal when he stepped forward and grabbed hold of the computer mouse. She couldn't help the smile that stretched the corner of her mouth. He had fallen into her trap. And she didn't even have to pretend. Still, she had to proceed carefully. She remained silent as he clicked on a few icons, more or less repeating what she had done earlier.

For a moment, she felt as if he had almost forgotten about her, so she leant forward, nonchalantly brushing her shoulder against his thigh. He didn't move away. A couple of times, he glanced at her with a blank expression. Joanna simply looked at him, resisting the urge to flash him a seductive smile. She didn't want to be too obvious.

He shifted his weight from one leg to the other several times. He seemed uncomfortable having to lean over the desk. Joanna moved away slightly, and was delighted when he crouched down.

Now he was at her level. As he reached forward to check the connections on the computer, she could see his strong back, the fabric of his shirt stretched over it. She imagined it bare, picturing how she would run her

57

tongue along its length, let her fingernails lightly scratch his skin.

Just inches from his elbow, her short skirt had slid up slightly and left her bare thighs in plain view. He unwittingly brushed against her a few times. She pretended not to notice and didn't move away or come closer. She leant slightly forward, knowing that if he turned his head, even if only briefly, he would get a good view of her cleavage.

She started to count slowly in her head. Upon reaching ten, she would lean closer and let her breast touch his shoulder. Not too much, just enough for him to feel it.

She had barely reached seven when he stood up with a sigh and stepped back.

'Sorry,' he said. 'I guess you'll have to ask the clerk at the help desk. This stuff is beyond me.'

'I've already asked,' Joanna lied. 'They were supposed to send someone over, but I've been waiting for over 30 minutes already.'

'I see,' he said simply. 'I'm not too proficient with these things, and there's somebody else I've already promised to help . . .'

He didn't have time to finish his sentence. Behind them, a loud voice rose and Joanna knew there was nothing she could do to hold him back.

'There you are, darling!' Greta said. 'I'm sorry I'm late I had to get something in my room. Can we get started now?'

Steve gave Joanna a vague smile and walked away with Greta, in search of a free workstation. Baffled, Joanna watched them as they moved between the desks. She grew incensed when she saw Greta casually slip her hand under Steve's arm to pull him in one direction, then conveniently leave it there.

At that moment, Joanna knew the New Yorker was also after the Texan. And she was one long clear step ahead of the Brit.

* * *

Sitting on the unmade bed, Joanna couldn't help thinking that the past five days had been more exciting than a roller-coaster ride and had left her feeling just as disoriented.

Professionally, she had done well. Despite the initial problems with the computer, her reports had been filed and received with approval by her superiors.

As for the rest, well, it was a shambles. She wasn't any closer to Steve who, by the look of things, was probably in bed with Greta at that very moment. The New Yorker was brash and bold and she had got what she wanted. However Joanna couldn't care less at this point: she was off on her tour of the provinces and would never see him again.

As for the mysterious messages she had received, there had been no further developments. By now Joanna had concluded that the stranger from the bar had set his sights on some other victim and she wouldn't see him again either.

Which left her with Harry to work on. Only that morning she had given him a quick phone call. He was already asleep, for it was late night in London, but he had woken very quickly and his groggy 'hello' had transformed into genuine interest once he had realised who was calling.

Joanna felt happy with his enthusiastic reaction, yet she had also realised she was utterly bored with him. By now her interest in him had waned. He was too far away; she didn't want to wait until she was back in London to quell the desire that had been gently simmering within her ever since she had arrived in Tokyo. She needed something to sink her teeth into now. But, naturally, work was more important.

The knock on her door interrupted her train of thoughts. A moment later, the porter had hoisted her cases on to a trolley and was making his way to the lift. Joanna looked around one more time to make sure there wasn't anything she had left behind; perhaps a little card she hadn't noticed. But her effort was in vain. Other than the mess of discarded towels, empty crisp bags and wrinkled sweet wrappers strewn on the floor after a late-night binge the previous evening, nothing caught her eye.

Chapter Six

*A*lthough by now Joanna was used to being stared at, she couldn't help being amused by the blatant look of the young waiter. And she didn't miss any opportunity to return his smile.

The restaurant pretended to be a Texas café: Pete's Ranch and Roadside Diner. Joanna had chosen it by instinct. After a week spent tasting a wide array of fine unusual delicacies, she now craved junk food and knew she would be served something totally different here.

And then there was Steve. Although he was long gone by now, the word 'Texas' alone had been enough to bring him back into Joanna's mind. The restaurant was tasteless, the decoration over the top and probably as authentic as that of an English pub in the depths of Guatemala, but as she looked round she could very easily picture him in these surroundings. No doubt the place would make him laugh, but she didn't care about that.

She tucked into something that called itself a burrito: some kind of pancake filled with beans and peppers. Although it was the poorest imitation of the real thing she had ever come across, Joanna liked the taste of it. The dish was nicely spiced, the peppers crunchy, and the beans cooked to perfection. What she enjoyed most was the puddle of melted cheese which covered the plate and stretched endlessly into tiny strings as she childishly dug her fork into the mess and then pulled it away.

And using a fork was an additional blessing. Although Joanna had become an expert at the fine art of handling chopsticks, she needed something familiar, albeit innocuous, to lift her spirits at this moment. She engulfed chunk after large chunk, oblivious to the other patrons who probably thought the blond foreigner was either starving or totally lacking in table manners. But that didn't matter to her either. The only look she was aware of was that of the young waiter assigned to her table.

The mock cowboy outfit was by far the most ridiculous she had ever seen: the black denim jeans were fine, but the black shirt adorned with a shiny white fringe was decidedly naff. Even worse was the gold sheriff's badge pinned to his chest, made of cheap tarnished metal and bearing his name: Yukio.

But the young man in the ridiculous costume was nothing short of gorgeous. In his early twenties, he was taller than the norm and amazingly slender. His hair, although very dark, was incredibly wispy. It bobbed about his head as he walked, light and untamed.

All the staff were young and cheerful, but they all had problems walking in the Western boots. Perhaps someone should have told them it would be easier without the spurs, Joanna thought. But her new admirer seemed to have got the hang of it. His walk was terribly sexy as a result. His tight trousers revealed a slim waist and nicely shaped buttocks, so small and pert Joanna knew she could cover them entirely with her cupped hands.

When he came over to refill her water glass, she twisted her shoulders seductively, letting the opening of her blouse gape a little. She caught his glance as he quickly looked at her chest. She looked as well, pleased to see that her pink lacy bra was plainly visible and that the areola was barely covered by the half-cup.

Her eyes then caught his and he blushed. As he prepared to move away, Joanna put her hand over his, which was firmly clasped around the handle of the water jug. For a second, she couldn't help but think how his fingers reminded her of those of the hotel clerk, the one she had encountered when she had first arrived the previous week. They were just as long and bony. Only in this instance, she could feel them trembling under hers as they slowly released their hold on the water jug.

'Leave it,' she said in Japanese. 'This food is too hot for me.'

Yukio hesitated before leaving the jug on the table, and walked away as fast as he could. Joanna had to make a tremendous effort not to laugh out loud. This one would be easy. She didn't need to pretend, scheme, or play any game. She would go to him and be as blatant as she could.

She quietly finished her meal, complete with lime ice cream in a sweet tortilla, and paid her bill. She pretended to head for the door, but at the last minute headed down the dark corridor that led to the back of the building. She had noticed her prey going down there before, and she knew that's where he was at this moment.

All she found at the end of the corridor was a door, which she opened aggressively. She found herself in a small room filled with cases of tequila bottles, large tins of food piled all over the floor and a single low wooden stool. Yukio was sitting on the stool smoking a cigarette. When he saw Joanna come in, he sprang to his feet, threw his cigarette on the floor and quickly stepped on it to put it out. Uneasy, he mumbled a few words as if trying to explain what he was doing there.

Joanna knew he was surprised by her sudden arrival, but she wasn't about to start any sort of conversation. She crouched over the stool, dropped her handbag on the floor, grabbed the waiter by his belt and pulled him towards her, pleased to see his crotch was level with her face.

Swiftly, without a word, she undid his jeans and pulled them down. At first the man tried to stop her, but his protests were only perfunctory. As soon as his genitals were free, his hands fell to his sides and he remained idle.

Inches from Joanna's face, his young member hung in semi-hardness. Obviously, its owner was excited, but probably also surprised and perhaps even worried by her sudden attack. He smelt sexy, his pleasant male aroma mixing with that of tobacco to result in a strangely compelling perfume.

Joanna stared at his prick for a moment without touching it, admiring its proportions even at rest. Even though it wasn't very thick, its length was considerable. But what she liked best was that it was hers for the taking.

The thought excited her. It suddenly seemed like a long time since she had been with a man, let alone have one at her mercy like this. For now, all she wanted was to concentrate on pleasuring him. Later, he would come to her, ask for more. Then she would have him on her terms.

Softly, she caressed the smooth shaft with her fingertips. They fluttered along its length, lingering longer on the underside. Almost immediately, she felt it grow turgid, the vessels under the soft skin filling up with his arousal. The increase in blood flow brought it to a full erection, making the foreskin glide back over the darkening head as it gradually pointed to the ceiling.

Meanwhile, the young waiter hadn't budged. Joanna softly kissed his member, letting her dry lips follow her fingers for a while. When she felt Yukio tremble with delight, she switched to quick expert flicks of the tongue. By then he was incredibly stiff and Joanna licked her lips thoroughly before taking him in her mouth.

Even then, she felt him growing harder still. She placed her hands on his bare bum. Her palms and fingers fitted perfectly around the hard curves, her thumbs settling on the dimples on the side of his buttocks. A perfect fit, just as she had imagined. The realisation almost made her smile with satisfaction. Young flesh had always had that effect on her.

Pressing her hands on his behind, she pulled him closer as her wet lips glided further up along his shaft. In her mind, she could clearly see the image: her eager mouth engulfing him, her red lips clasped in a tight circle around his rod. The thought excited her and she felt her flesh drenched with her own desire, claiming its treat. But that would have to wait.

She heard him gasp as she took him completely and began sucking in earnest. After a moment she pulled away, but without releasing the suction. Against her chest she could feel the young man's legs trembling as her lips fastened harder around his glans and her tongue began circling the rounded tip.

His legs pushed against her breasts as he struggled to keep his balance. The waistband of his jeans, hard and unyielding, hung level with her chest. It grazed her stiff nipples through her clothes and she couldn't help moaning.

The stiff rod pulsed on her tongue as she increased the intensity of her caresses. She knew he was near his climax, so she released him completely, circled the base of his shaft tightly with her thumb and forefinger and held him fast.

For a moment, nothing happened. There was a pause during which they both stopped moaning and Joanna caught her breath. Gradually, the phallus she grasped returned to its resting state. Looking up, Joanna was amused by the perplexed expression on Yukio's face. Cupping her hands, she cradled both his limp prick and his balls for a moment, enjoying their warmth and youth.

Soon, however, she was hungry for him again. Holding on to his balls with her left hand, she wrapped her right hand around the flaccid shaft and quickly brought it back to arousal. Her lips glided over the head and she moved him in and out of her mouth rapidly, her wet lips sliding easily, her saliva mixing with the salty drops now seeping from the tiny slit.

She didn't stop to look up at him, but she could very well imagine that his bewilderment was now transformed into ecstasy. She knew she was good at pleasuring men. Handling him with both hands whilst her mouth never ceased torturing him, she felt him twitch in her mouth several times.

He bucked as he came, letting out a cry that sounded more like a whine of pain than one of joy. As soon as she received him, deep in her throat, Joanna pulled away. She didn't give him any time to recover. Grabbing her handbag, she sprang quickly to her feet. From the pocket of her jacket, she fished out the small card where she had written the name of her hotel and her room number and scribbled the time, 8 p.m.

That was to be their next encounter. Without a word, she slipped the card in his breast pocket. It didn't matter whether he was scheduled to work or already had plans. She knew he would find a way to be there.

As she was about to pull her hand away she hesitated and then grabbed the shiny star pinned to his chest, the tacky sheriff's badge. That would serve as a trophy.

She made her way out of the tiny room, as quickly and as silently as she had entered. Only once did she look back. The young waiter was standing idle, his trousers down around his ankles, his prick once again hanging limply, his expression as blank as when she had first come in. Soon enough, she knew, he would start wondering whether that had just happened. And he would have to come to her tonight, if only to make sure she wasn't a figment of his imagination.

Joanna hid in the shadows for a little while. From her hiding place, she had seen Yukio come into the hotel, and walk out again a few minutes later. She was late for their date. On purpose. He, on the other hand, had shown up fifteen minutes early. She knew he had been told she wasn't in her room, and that was probably driving him mad.

Now he was impatiently walking back and forth on the narrow pavement, glancing at his watch every minute or so. Joanna couldn't help noticing the loose trousers he was wearing this time, and guessed he was probably already hard and eager for her.

As he walked back towards the hotel, she strolled casually out of her hiding place. He saw her, stopped on the spot, then hurried towards her. She gave him a brief smile, gestured for him not to come near her and slowly made her way to her room.

Only a few seconds later, he knocked on her door. Joanna was pleased by his impatience, which tonight she would test to the limit. She counted to ten before sliding the panel open. For the first time since she had arrived in Japan she had a room decorated in traditional fashion. It was incredibly small, but the futon lying flat on the floor and the lavishly decorated panels on the walls were exactly what she had been hoping for. In these exotic surroundings, she felt more aroused than in some anonymous room. It suited her frame of mind perfectly and she prepared to let her passion erupt in the company of her young lover.

As he entered, he slammed the panel shut behind him and grabbed Joanna to pull her towards him. His kiss betrayed his passion, his youth and his impatience. Joanna was delighted by this transparency. His lips, soft and thin, were moist and cool like a child's. His tongue, obviously inexperienced, was eager; his embrace, strong and sensuous. His hands were impatient and quickly moved over her back and her hips.

Joanna pushed him away gently when he tried to slip his hands under her jacket. She couldn't let him take the lead. She ushered him to the low mattress, made him sit and stepped back. She offered a vision in black suede: a short skirt and matching jacket. Sheer black stockings covered her legs, their tops just reaching the hem of her mini-skirt. Slowly, she undid the front of her jacket to reveal a crimson silk blouse.

Never taking her eyes off him, she removed her jacket and nonchalantly let it fall to the floor before turning her back to him. With a measured flick of the wrist, she undid the zip of her skirt, then languidly swayed her hips to let it fall. Bending forward, she pushed her knickerless bottom towards his face as she picked her skirt off the floor.

She took her time before standing up again, wriggling her backside as she undid the tiny straps around her ankles and took off her sandals. She knew her fragrant slit was probably in plain view, within his reach, taunting him by displaying itself, wiggling slightly as Joanna removed her sandals. The straps of her suspender belt ran over her buttocks, gently grazing her bare skin and exciting her even more.

Getting back up, she turned round to face him again. His face was flushed, his lips red as he licked them. His eyes were now fixed on the triangle of golden hair just visible under the hem of her blouse. In his eyes she could read his desire and she sensed he was more than ready for her. But she would make him wait longer; much, much longer.

Casually, she walked to the mirror and took a good look at herself as she undid each button of her blouse. Indeed, that precious spot between her legs looked quite appealing. The thin fabric of the blouse barely hid her swollen sex, the moist folds now tingling with excitement.

Looking in the mirror, she could see her lover's reflection. Just one look told her he was dying to get up to come and help her take off her blouse. Yet she made no such invitation. Merciful, though, she didn't waste time undoing the buttons. For a moment she pretended to hurry up, build up his hope that she would soon offer herself to him. But all along she was only toying with him. She had no intention of giving in just yet.

The blouse glided down her shoulders and she let it

fall to the floor. She came near him, standing in her bra and suspender belt. Her nipples were hard and plainly visible through the stretched lace of her bra, and that was exactly what he was staring at as she stood motionless in front of him.

His trembling hand reached up to touch her but she pushed him away gently once again. Docile, he didn't insist. Yet she could see he was tremendously excited. His lips, swollen with blood, had grown redder still and a thin blue vein palpitated at his temple. His hands were slowly brushing the top of his thighs, pulling on the loose cotton of his trousers and drawing attention to the enormous bump throbbing between his legs.

Joanna paused for moment, contemplating her next move. One sign from her and he would pounce like a beast. But that would be too soon. Instead, she knelt in front of him and helped him take off his shirt. His chest, well developed and hairless, looked as smooth as leather. She lightly brushed it with her hands, gently flicking his hard nipples with her fingertips before moving on to undo his trousers.

With wickedly slow movements, she unbuckled his belt and pulled it out completely before tossing it on the side of the bed. Then she undid the buttons of his fly, one at a time, using only one hand whilst the other cupped one of his knees. He stood as she pulled down his trousers. His erect phallus sprang free, stiff and bigger than she remembered. He faintly thrust towards her mouth, as if by reflex, but Joanna ignored him. She continued undressing him until he stood completely naked, his clothes scattered all around her, then got back on her feet again.

She made him kneel on the futon, grabbed his hand and brought it to touch her moist sex. His novice fingers trembled as he caressed her hesitantly. Guiding him in a back and forth motion, she pushed his middle finger inside her. His hands were cool and their assault made her shiver. But soon enough the heat of her sex changed all that. She let out a loud sigh as he pushed in further, realising just how long it had been since the last time a man had penetrated her.

Slowly she let go of his hand, allowing him to discover her on his own. He hesitated still, clumsily rubbing her wet slit as she writhed against his palm to counter his movement. Her hips thrust instinctively, their motion a direct result of the excitement now burning within her. Again she imagined herself with Steve, and she fantasised having him at her mercy just as she did the young waiter. The memory of him made her moan. She wanted more; she wanted to come. Grabbing the young waiter's head, she pulled it towards her chest and guided his mouth towards her erect nipples.

He softly kissed them through the lace of her bra, letting his lips move around the erect peaks. She pushed his head from side to side, bidding him to reach under the fabric with his tongue to attack her nipples directly. She was almost annoyed at having to tell him what to do. But her irritation soon vanished as she heard him grunt and he rapidly grew more eager. They both breathed hard and loudly, moaning with delight as their bodies rubbed against each other. His free hand snaked around her waist and he pulled her closer still.

Against her thigh she could feel his hard dick pulsing and insisting. A fever seized her and suddenly she wanted him inside her. Freeing herself from his embrace, she knelt on the futon, right in front of him, and presented him with her naked bum.

He entered her without further ado. All at once he was in a trance, thrusting forcefully and digging his fingers into her hard buttocks. Joanna was elated. It seemed so long since she had been taken like this. To feel him inside her was sheer bliss. Yet despite her intense arousal, his inexperience did nothing to help her achieve the ultimate pleasure. He brought her to the edge and she remained there, close to the point of no return but without the extra stimulation she needed to climax.

Soon she could feel him on the verge of his own

orgasm. It was too early, she thought. She suddenly realised she had relinquished control, and she had to gain it back. Pushing him off, she turned around and moved to sit at the head of the bed. There, she parted her legs and offered her wet flesh for his contemplation.

Panting, he crawled on all fours towards the inviting pink folds. He was drunk with desire, his lips wet with his saliva, and almost drooling. Mesmerised by Joanna's flesh, he looked as though he feared the vision would disappear. Still hesitant, he lightly ran his fingertips along the glistening slit.

Joanna moaned with satisfaction. Teaching him would be sweet. Gently pushing his head down, she guided his mouth towards her swollen bud. He licked it briefly, as if only tasting it, then looked up at her. Joanna once again took his hand and pushed his fingers inside her before bidding him to taste her again.

This time he appeared more eager, and she leant back to enjoy the warm caress of his tongue coupled with that, a little rougher, of his fingers. Her pupil was docile and learnt quickly, yet he seemed to lack the enthusiasm and passion necessary to get her to climax. Again, the fire within her burnt fiercely, but not enough to trigger that devastating explosion she was craving. As she opened her eyes, she noticed his other hand wrapped around his shaft and realised most of his energy was spent for his own benefit.

She sat up, suddenly angry, and slapped his hand before grabbing it to bring it towards her flesh. Yukio looked at her, vaguely surprised and contrite, but obeyed her silent request. Joanna was doubly pleased. All she had to do was to remind him she was in charge tonight. Yet she knew she couldn't let her guard down. She couldn't completely abandon herself if she wanted to keep him at her mercy.

Dragging him off the mattress, she made him kneel on the floor as she stood in front of him with her legs apart. The young man followed, as if he knew he had no choice but to submit. This time she pulled him by the hair to make him kiss her flesh. He didn't resist and his tongue obediently resumed its caresses. His hands paused on Joanna's hips, softly stroking their smooth curves.

Joanna looked down towards him and was increasingly excited by his docility. He was the pupil and she the mistress, and the role pleased her tremendously. In the past, she had toyed with men in order to seduce them, but once they reached the bedroom they became equals. Now, this new-found satisfaction stemming from domination was exactly what she needed.

Every time he tried to stand or move, she forcefully pushed on his shoulders to instruct him to stay exactly where he was, pulling him by the hair when necessary. At times she had to fight the urge to laugh out loud. His tongue was merciless, and certainly untiring. It moved over her flesh with increased dexterity, and now Joanna knew that, given enough time, he would learn how to make her come. In the meantime, it was so good just to have him like this, like a puppet which she controlled completely.

Her student understood rapidly, and gave in to her desires. She made sure he kept his hands on her body at all times, not wanting him to pleasure himself. That could wait. Already his mouth had become voracious. His tongue foraged within her with increasing eagerness, bathing her with its soft warmth and triggering deep inside her a tingle which quickly transformed into arousal so intense she wondered if she could remain standing much longer.

Already her knees were trembling as she guided her lover's thumb towards her clitoris and showed him how to rub it, hard and fast. He did as instructed. Soon, her patience and her efforts paid off. She felt the wave of pleasure gathering within her folds, finally reaching its maximum, seizing her with all its might and piercing her so violently she couldn't help a loud cry.

At her feet, the young man still didn't stop teasing her. She came again and, pushing him away, collapsed on the bed as pleasure weakened her. He knelt between her parted legs and prepared to enter her. Suddenly regaining her senses, Joanna grabbed the thin leather belt that lay on the floor next to his trousers and lashed him on the back.

He whimpered, pulled away, and shook for a fraction of a second. Joanna looked at him defiantly. He finally understood that tonight he was there for her own benefit first. For a moment, they held each other's gaze. The young man's face now showed nothing but obedient passivity as he stood at the foot of the bed, his erection still at its maximum, but his body docile and immobile.

With a faint movement of the wrist, Joanna bade him come closer. She wanted more. Somehow, the wave of bliss that had just swept her hadn't been enough to satisfy her.

Kneeling on the bed, he set his mouth on her sex once again. This time, his tongue moved more lazily, insinuating itself along Joanna's sensitive slit, creeping up towards her bud inexorably but without the eagerness it had displayed earlier.

She shivered as it reached her bud, still stiff and aching from too much stimulation. Instinctively, she jerked her hips away and the young man didn't insist. He looked up at her, vaguely puzzled, and awaited her next order.

That was enough, she decided suddenly. Sitting up, she grabbed him by the hips and pulled him towards her. He entered her hesitantly, as if worried that she might change her mind or lash him again. Lying back on the pillow, she let him thrust at his own pace. She could tell he was inexperienced, and she knew he would come quickly. She let him have his way, feeling a faint tingle of pleasure as he filled her. She moaned softly, letting satisfaction sweep her, yet she was still hungry.

Yukio's eyes bulged, staring blankly at her, as he increased his rhythm. Now his passion was fully unleashed. His hips rammed into her thighs repeatedly, pushing her up against the head of the bed, but his enthusiasm did not translate into anything unusually enjoyable for her.

He cried out as he came, his mouth twisting in a grin of triumph and he collapsed on to her naked belly. She pushed him aside, rolled over and settled down to doze. Next time, she thought, she would have to hold out longer.

Chapter Seven

WE ARE GLAD YOU ENJOYED THE COMPANY OF OUR YOUNG FRIEND. HE INFORMS US YOU ARE AN EXCELLENT TEACHER.

Joanna stared blankly at the small card for a moment, only mildly puzzled by the message written on the now familiar combination of pink and green. More surprising was the present in the large box to which the card was affixed: a pink and green kimono.

With a powerful swing of her arms, she spread the garment on her mattress. It was large, with wide sleeves, and made entirely of pure silk, as was the thick *obi* sash neatly folded at the bottom of the box. And, just like the card, the kimono was the palest of pink, adorned with thin branches of green jasmine bearing tiny white blossoms.

This was something she could no longer ignore. There was definitely a pattern here, but what was the link? She knelt on the futon and absent-mindedly stroked the soft silk with the palm of her hand. The fabric was luxurious, absorbing the heat of her skin and reflecting it back. A shiver ran down Joanna's abdomen. It reminded her of her visit to the inn, the time she had tried on a similar kimono. In fact, it looked just like the one Keiko was wearing that evening. Or was it Atsuko?

She couldn't remember exactly. The feel of the soft silk on her bare skin was forever etched in her mind, and that was something she now longed to feel again.

A second later, she forced herself away from that train of thought. Reason took over and she made a supreme effort to remain focused. There could be no mistake now: the messages were indeed meant for her. But who was sending them? And why? Taking a deep breath, she forced herself to remember what she had initially so carelessly disregarded. The first card had been left in her room soon after her arrival. The second one was slipped into her folder by the man at the bar. This third one had been delivered with the kimono.

She shook herself as panic suddenly seized her. She didn't have time to dwell on this: she had to leave! She was late already! In a flash, she jumped to her feet, rolled the kimono into a big ball and tossed it back into its box. Sliding open the door to the closet, she pushed the box in with her foot. She couldn't afford to waste her time trying to guess what was going on; she had work to do.

As the train sped away from the station, Joanna slumped in her seat, still trying to catch her breath. The race through town had left her anxious, but thankfully the train was delayed leaving.

Her heart pounding and her throat dry, she closed her eyes and breathed deeply. Now she had time to focus on what lay ahead: in just over 30 minutes she would be in the village of Kiwashu. There, the weekly market supposedly had unusual dishes for sale, vegetables prepared according to regional recipes little known to outsiders, and prepared right there on the spot. At least, that was what Joanna remembered from one of Stacey's reports. This needed further investigating.

As she glanced out the window, she thought of how close she had come to missing out on this opportunity. She couldn't afford to let that happen. The mystery behind those strange messages had distracted her from her work, and that wasn't good. Just like the time when her encounter with the stranger at the bar had almost made her late for the demonstration she wanted to attend. Again this morning, the unexpected package had thrown her and she had almost missed her train.

For a moment, she began to suspect that perhaps this was the plan: maybe whoever was sending the messages simply wanted her to neglect her work, to be late, to miss important events. She closed her eyes again and tried to concentrate. It made sense, at least at first glance. But there remained one crucial question: who was behind all this? Who had an interest in making sure she botched the job?

A competitor? That was a possibility. Yet Joanna knew that in this business most companies wouldn't waste their time and money thinking up such childish plots. They fought their battles at the boardroom level.

No, it was a personal thing, she was sure of that. Someone wanted to discredit her. Joanna suddenly sat up and let out a small cry as the answer popped into her mind: Richard!

Of course! Having managed to get her to Japan, all he had to do was keep her distracted so that upon returning, she wouldn't have anything much to report on. The company directors wouldn't be pleased at that, to say the least. Richard could then use that against her. And since he knew quite a few people in Japan, this wasn't too difficult for him to arrange. He knew her itinerary, so it was be easy for him to hire someone to follow her.

She knew he was perfectly capable of pulling such a stunt. He had done worse. Only last year he had made her taste tainted ham, pretending it was a sample from a new company. When Joanna had mentioned the unusual taste, he had claimed it was because of the smoking process. The next morning, Joanna was unable to show up for work, stricken with severe food poisoning.

That day, they had a very important meeting with the company directors to discuss their marketing strategies.

Naturally, Richard had put his own ideas forward, in addition to taking credit for Joanna's hard work and meticulous market studies. To make matters worse, he had then started the rumour that Joanna's illness was fake, insisting that he had himself tried the ham and was perfectly all right.

It had taken Joanna months to regain her credibility. But she knew Richard would strike again. He just couldn't bear to see her get ahead of him. Ages ago, they had been close – very close – on a physical level. Close enough for Richard to know where Joanna's weaknesses lay, and how to use her lust to distract her from her work.

She sat back and let out a long sigh. She couldn't help smiling. Now that she was on to him, she wouldn't fall into his trap.

Part Two

Chapter Eight

*I*f Tokyo was modern and reminiscent of an American city, Kobe was in a class of its own. Little remained of the damage caused by the earthquake that had rocked the city a few years back. Most of the buildings had been rebuilt in a variety of styles, but with an elegance that gave most neighbourhoods a certain harmony.

Today Joanna was attending a seminar organised by the Japanese government's department of international trade. What she was most interested in was the part on exports. With the laws constantly changing, she needed to be updated before her company could add new products to its list.

As she made her way to the conference hall, a familiar sight caught her attention. Less than twenty yards away from her, a tall blond man stood out above the crowd. As he turned round and glanced vaguely in her direction, Joanna froze.

Steve! She stared intently, incredulous and unable to move. Yet she knew she wasn't dreaming. It was him. When she had left Tokyo, after the food fair ended, she had thought she would never see him again. Of course, it made sense for him to be here as well. After all, they were in the same line of business, and it was only natural that they should be interested in the same events.

Bumping into just about everyone standing in front of her, Joanna dashed towards him. She had to talk to him. This time, he would pay attention to her. Her mind raced to find something clever to say, but in the end her wits failed her and she decided to go for a cheerful and surprised 'hello'.

Just as she came within reach she stopped again. Out of nowhere appeared Greta, waving a wad of forms and colourful leaflets. Joanna stamped her foot. Not her again! Steve leant forward as the New Yorker handed him several of the papers before sliding her arm under his and leading him inside the conference hall. Obviously, they had come here together.

Once again, Joanna was cross. With her brash overtures and her blatant ways, Greta had succeeded in seducing the man Joanna had wanted to attack with subtlety and flair. The war was lost.

Now all Joanna could focus on was how much she despised the New Yorker. She was beyond annoyed or irritated, she just plain hated her. Of course, Greta had won for only one reason: her age had afforded her more experience. It was as simple as that.

But as she sat a few rows behind them, Joanna began to notice a few signs which led her to believe perhaps it wasn't all over for her. As Greta continued clinging to him, Steve appeared to show some annoyance. At one point, he even seized her hand, which was squeezing his thigh, and resolutely placed it on her own lap.

Joanna clearly saw Greta pouting as she leant towards him and whispered in his ear something that made him wince. Could the honeymoon be over already? Joanna smiled with satisfaction. If a blatant approach sometimes produced instant success, subtle seduction would perhaps ensure long-lasting enthralment. This, she knew, was worth aiming for.

Once the talk ended, Joanna was pleased to see that all the information given to the delegates was contained in the documents she had been handed. She had been too distracted by the sight of Steve and Greta to pay any attention to what was being said, too busy planning her next attack to bother taking notes.

She jumped to her feet as soon as the speaker finished his last sentence. She didn't want to waste any more time. Since there was only one door out of the hall, she knew that at some point the Americans would walk her way. All she had to do was stall by the door, wait for them to catch up and feign surprise as she noticed and greeted them. This time, she wouldn't let anything stop her.

To her amazement, it was Greta who noticed her first.

'Joanna! Darling!' she squealed as she lunged to embrace her. 'What a nice surprise! What are you doing here? Oh, how stupid of me! Of course, you're here for the seminar! Look, Steve! It's Joanna from London!'

For once, Joanna was relieved to let Greta do all the talking. Her verbiage seemed to annoy Steve, and that was exactly what she needed. The three of them made their way slowly to the foyer as Greta babbled endlessly, asking Joanna questions and answering them herself, never letting either Joanna or Steve utter a single word.

The New Yorker's high-pitched voice attracted everyone's attention, but as glances were directed towards the trio, it was Joanna they lingered on. For a second, she couldn't help but think how her situation was not all that different from when she was still in Tokyo. Once again she had to share the spotlight with the New Yorker, whose brash manners were effective but whose success was only short lived. But Joanna knew her class and her sense of style would let her have the last laugh. Both women would remain in the men's minds, but for different reasons: they would think of Greta with amusement, but Joanna would for them be an example of elegance and poise.

The delegates in attendance were mostly Westerners this time. Looking at Joanna was probably soothing if they had been away from home for a while. Apart from that, she knew she was, quite simply, a sight worth looking at. And that notion was incredibly empowering.

At the same time, she could feel Steve's eyes on her. She silently congratulated herself on her choice of clothing. If her loose, pale blue dress didn't look very professional in such surroundings, at least it was soft and feminine. Its pattern brought out the blue of her eyes. Her wispy blond hair, flowing freely on her shoulders and bare arms, looked seductive.

The feelings she had experienced whilst at the food fair resurfaced. She thrived on men's admiring glances. It was especially good when such fascination came from a man for whom she had lewd plans, like Steve. Once again he was just inches from her, his hard body right within her reach. And again she wanted him with all her being.

From the corner of her eye, she could see his hard biceps bulging under his white shirt sleeves and she could easily guess that his legs, back and chest were just as taut. She licked her lips nervously. The warmth of his body diffused in the space between them, and Joanna could feel it without even touching him. She longed to trace the sinews of his muscular body with her fingertips, to survey the roundness of his shoulders with the palm of her hand, to feel his animal heat radiate up her arms.

Her mouth watered expectantly as she recalled her dream, which played back vividly in her mind. Her imagination improved on it, defining a more elaborate scenario, which left her more aroused and wanton.

Most of all, she longed to feel his bare skin on hers, to rub her body all over his. Her nipples peaked as she imagined her chest pressed against his, writhing lasciviously. She remembered the part of her dream where she ran her tongue between his shoulder blades, and desperately wished to sell her soul to the devil if only she could do it in reality at that very moment.

The fact that she hadn't succeeded in seducing him only increased her desire. Steve had proved to be much more difficult than the young waiter from the diner. Or even Harry, for that matter. But she knew that the hardest-won battles were often the most satisfying. If it was to be true in this case as well, she shuddered to think how mind-blowing their encounter would be once she managed to win him over.

As they walked, Joanna sensed he was edging towards her. She didn't make any effort to move away. When his shoulder brushed hers, she contained herself and didn't show any of the heat now building up inside her. He was about to make a move, she could feel it. Her heart pounded and she felt her face flush. This was the opportunity she had been waiting for.

As Greta continued talking without even looking at them, Joanna turned her head towards Steve, ready to give her most inviting smile. But as she glanced coyly at him, she realised that the reason he was so close to her was simply because too many people were heading down the same corridor and he was actually moving away from them.

She tried to catch his eye, but to no avail. He kept staring straight in front of him, surveying the crowd and silently following Greta, who was bouncing along, opening the path for them.

'We're staying at the Sheraton,' she said to Joanna as they reached the door. 'Room 809. Why don't you give us a call this evening? Maybe we can get together for dinner? Are you coming, darling?'

Joanna nodded vaguely as she watched them walk away, wondering whether Greta had volunteered this information in a genuine effort to be friendly or if it was her way of telling Joanna that she and Steve were actually an item. Before she could work it out, Greta had grabbed Steve by the arm to lead him into a waiting taxi.

Dinner with Greta and Steve was now out of the question. Joanna cursed herself for reacting in such an immature way, but the arrival of yet another message had put her in such a bad mood that she knew she wouldn't be able to focus on gaining ground with Steve.

If she couldn't be at her best, she just didn't want to see him. In any case, she wouldn't even be good company.

She was much more annoyed now that the bloody messages were interfering with her personal life, in addition to her work. It had thrown her off to the extent that she was ready to give up on the Texan. She was willingly throwing away the last chance she had, for it was very unlikely she would bump into him ever again.

Sitting on the edge of the bed, she was so incensed she felt like crumpling the small card she held in her hand. This time the message consisted of an invitation for the next day. The time and address were flatly indicated, along with a simple PLEASE LET US NOW TAKE CARE OF YOU. COME AND VISIT US TOMORROW.

Just like the first message, this one had been left in her room, on the bedside table. That was going to be the end of the mystery, Joanna thought. Without hesitation, she determined to go, if only to find out finally who was behind all this. Then she remembered she had something planned around the same time. Rummaging through her briefcase, she fished out the now crumpled copy of her itinerary and quickly tried to calculate whether she could make both appointments.

She winced when she saw that she was scheduled to meet one of the directors of a desserts packaging company late that afternoon. Once again, the invitation interfered with her work, and a very important part of her trip. Desserts were popular, appealing to a large chunk of the population, and her company always strove to add new products to the ones they already offered. Indeed, this was a meeting she couldn't miss. But maybe she wouldn't have to.

First she would go to the address written on the card at 2 o'clock, as indicated. She wasn't quite sure where in the city the street was, but she had to take a chance. With any luck, she'd be out of there quickly enough to make the next appointment. She had to have faith in the taxi driver to get her there on time. It was risky, but she couldn't pass on this invitation. She had to know.

Chapter Nine

*F*rom what the porter of the hotel had told her, Joanna concluded that if she wanted to be in time for her second meeting, she had to get out of the first one very quickly. The location she was now headed for was in a totally different area of the city, miles away from where her business meeting was to take place. Making both meetings was still possible, according to Joanna's calculation. She had discounted using public transport. It seemed too complicated and wasn't reliable. Taking a taxi was the best solution, but even the fastest driver would take over an hour to get her to her next appointment.

This had to be worth the trouble, she said to herself, knowing she couldn't stay for more than 30 minutes. As a precaution, she had rung to say she would be probably be late for her second meeting. She had also inferred that she might be forced to reschedule altogether. The secretary on the other end of the line had not been very helpful. The woman was rather rude and had been unable to tell Joanna whether it was indeed possible for her to come the next day instead.

Joanna cursed herself for what she was about to do. Despite her best intentions, she was once again on the verge of neglecting her work for the benefit of a stranger, some coward who had to resort to mysterious messages to get her attention. But the mystery was compelling, and strangely addictive.

More than ever, she was convinced this was all Richard's idea. In fact, she half expected him to be there himself to greet her. Not in person, naturally. He was probably too busy scheming her downfall to waste precious time travelling to Japan just to get even with her. They would probably be linked by computer, via the Internet. Already Joanna was rehearsing in her mind the nasty reply she would eagerly type. No matter what he had to say, she was more than ready for him.

As she stepped out of the car, a weird sensation seized her. The building in front of her resembled a pagoda, some sort of temple. Built entirely of pale wood, it was topped by a roof of shiny red tiles. As she stood admiring its magnificence, Joanna still hesitated. Something was now troubling her. Not exactly a sense of doom, but the expectancy of a revelation. For a brief moment, she almost believed her suspicions about Richard were unfounded. Like a vague premonition, she had the feeling what was about to happen to her was bigger than that; it had nothing to do with him.

The main door was plain and painted black, without any window. As it opened, a little old lady dressed in a simple grey smock appeared and greeted Joanna, then moved aside to let her in. Joanna hesitated, unsure of what to expect, then shook herself and entered. This was silly; she had nothing to fear.

The little woman closed the door behind her and bent down to help Joanna take off her shoes. Curious, Joanna looked around and made an effort to take in every detail, hoping to discover some clue, albeit innocuous. The entrance hall was not as beautiful as the outside of the building, but simple and nonetheless welcoming. It reminded her of the inn at which she had dined near Tokyo. The walls were made of rice paper and she guessed they were all sliding panels. Behind one of them, she could hear the distant sound of laughter.

At first glance there was nothing here to give her any clue as to the identity of her correspondent. Not that she expected anyone just to show up straight away, but she was worried that perhaps it would take longer than expected for her to learn what she had been wanting to know. The thought made her extremely uneasy. If they kept her waiting too long, she would certainly be late for her next appointment. Faced with this possibility, she wondered if she would have the strength to leave should things start to drag.

Her critical mind was attuned to every aspect of the room as she desperately tried to establish where she was. There was no sign of any company name or logo. Yet Joanna was sure this was not a private dwelling. Mechanically, she followed the old lady who quickly led her from one room to the next, opening then closing successive sliding panels on the way. This strange procession was tedious. Each room was empty, except for an occasional print or etching on a wall, and there was nothing to tell Joanna what she wanted to know.

Finally, they reached a larger room, where piles of towels waited on racks. Joanna decided to ask what the mystery was all about, but before she could even speak the old lady slid open yet another panel. Joanna gasped, the words in her mouth now obsolete, as she understood what the mock pagoda actually was: a bath house.

Mesmerised, she slowly moved forward but didn't enter the room. This large room was the bath itself, a large, square space where three of the walls were practically hidden behind large vine-like plants. The ceiling was made of pale pink rice paper and diffused the light evenly. All round the large sunken tub was a platform of thin boards. On the edge of the tub, trays with cups and teapots had been left within the bathers' reach, as well as plates of fruit cut into small wedges.

The tub itself was not unlike a swimming pool, square and big enough to accommodate at least 30 people, and filled to the brim with steaming water. In the bath, about a dozen naked women soaked whilst chatting, most of them Japanese, but three of them Westerners. Their shoulders and heads were at times barely visible as the vapours rose from the water and enveloped them.

The scene was inviting. The warmth of the bath could be felt even from where Joanna was standing. The smell floating in the air was familiar and relaxing. Only then did Joanna realise that the massive vines growing all over the walls were jasmine, the same plant she had seen in the geishas' dressing room at the inn.

Joanna knew it would have been pointless to ask the little old lady anything; she was just an attendant and probably couldn't answer any of Joanna's questions. Already she was coming forward and gesturing for Joanna to disrobe, holding out a large wicker basket in which to leave her clothes.

Joanna obeyed mechanically. Although she didn't have much time, she knew this would do her good, and she saw no harm in joining the other women in the bath. She had come all the way here, and was too taken by the enthralling sight even to think otherwise at this point. The idea of being late for or missing her next meeting was still somewhere at the back of her mind, but by now her body was dictating her behaviour: all she wanted to do was accept the invitation.

She was keenly aware of her nakedness as she stood by the edge of the tub and found it exciting. She hoped all eyes would turn towards her, but the women in the tub didn't pay any attention to her.

Joanna however couldn't stop looking at them and furtively examined every woman in the bath. She couldn't help but remember the evening at the inn where she had spent such a delightful hour with the two young geishas so skilled in providing pleasure. There again, she had forgotten everything for the benefit of her own body. Suddenly, she knew it would be just the same today.

The attendant made her sit on a low stool and proceeded to give her a thorough scrub with a sponge and soapy water. Still reeling from surprise, Joanna said nothing. All she could think of was the time she had been given a similar treatment, in the geishas' dressing room. That evening, a simple sponge bath had turned into a powerful, exhilarating experience. This time, however, she doubted the old woman had such plans for her. Even when the attendant's hand lightly brushed the underside of Joanna's breast, there was nothing improper in her touch. Her job was to wash the customers, nothing more.

But for Joanna, the result was the same. Her skin broke out in goose bumps as the sponge glided over it and then left it exposed to the steamy air in the room. Her nipples contracted and Joanna fought the sigh that rose in her throat. Just when she thought it couldn't get any more arousing, the attendant made her part her legs and brought the sponge closer to her quivering flesh.

For a moment, Joanna wished the woman would drop the sponge and caress her just as the geishas had. But this time it just wouldn't happen. Once she was cleaned and rinsed, she was invited to step into the tub. One of the Westerners welcomed her with a brief nod, but no one else paid any attention to her. Another bather was pouring tea, her neighbour leaning against the wall of the bath with her head tilted back and her eyes closed; another pair was quietly chatting. Joanna remembered that, in Japan, bath houses were not unlike a local pub, where people congregate regularly to socialise.

For her, however, it was most unusual to share a bath with so many naked women. The details of the evening at the inn reappeared even more strongly in her mind and enhanced her excitement. The decor and set-up were so similar, down to every detail, as if both places had been designed by the same person.

The hot water crawled up her calf and her thigh as she entered the bath hesitantly and went down the submerged steps. She shivered as it reached her sex. She quickly looked around, embarrassed by the thought of someone noticing her reaction.

'First time, hey?' said the woman on her right.

Joanna paused and looked at her. The woman was much older than her, with a strong German accent that matched her square shoulders and short roughly cut blond hair. At first glance, she reminded Joanna of an over-trained Olympic swimmer: muscular and tough, a body trained like a machine, a soldier. Yet the smile the woman offered was genuine and welcoming.

'Do not be afraid,' the woman continued. 'It's very nice once you're in.'

And she was right, Joanna discovered as she reached the bottom. She crouched slightly and let the water rise slowly over her chest. Her nipples stiffened even more and her flesh contracted forcefully. Never would she have thought that a simple bath could be so sensuous. The temperature was just right and enveloped her comfortably; the water made her feel weightless. Her only desire was to let herself float and relax. She walked about for a little while, her feet barely pushing against the tiled bottom, using her arms to propel herself forward.

Once the initial thrill subsided, Joanna began to think more clearly. Since there was no way she could make it to her next meeting, she decided simply to enjoy herself. At the same time, she was cursing herself for giving in so easily. If Richard had indeed planned all this, he knew exactly what he was doing. But at least Joanna had the satisfaction of knowing she was now on to him. Soon enough she would find a way out of this dilemma, the dilemma of whether to indulge her body's lustful demands or whether to put her work first.

She stopped along the edge of the bath, reached out and picked up a chunk of fresh pineapple. The fruit was cold and firm, and its sweetness filled Joanna's mouth like an explosion. She waited before swallowing it, savouring its slightly acid tinge, then licked her fingers clean.

'I told you it would be nice, didn't I?' said the German.

Joanna simply smiled and nodded. She was expecting something to happen any minute. She knew that soon the mystery would come to an end, and she wanted to be prepared for it. In addition, the woman's friendliness was reminiscent of Greta's, and was slightly annoying. Joanna wanted to make the most of this relaxing state and also to keep her wits about her, should the revelation she was expecting suddenly manifest itself. She didn't want any distractions. She had to be ready for anything, at all times.

But as the woman kept on talking, Joanna began suspecting that perhaps this woman would be the one to give her the clues she had been looking for so eagerly. When the conversation turned to more intimate matters, Joanna straightened up and started paying attention.

'Japanese bath houses used to be for families, you know,' the woman whispered. 'Everyone in the same bath: men, women and children. It must have been quite embarrassing, no? I mean, all these naked bodies ... And beautiful bodies, aren't they? Just look at this woman on your left! Doesn't she have an attractive body?'

Joanna glanced sideways and nodded again. Next to her, a young Japanese woman was slowly rubbing her arms under the water, caressing her long limbs in a sensuous fashion. She was taller than the norm, and unusually curvaceous. Her breasts were large and shaped like pears. A fine wisp of dark hair had escaped from the bun on top of her head and casually floated over her right shoulder. Joanna's first impulse was to go to her and touch this lone silken strand of hair. But the woman didn't even look at her, and Joanna just couldn't bring herself to be so bold.

Her mind once again in a daze, Joanna wished the German would keep on talking. Just like when she had listened to the stranger at the bar, the words so daringly spoken in such a thick accent had a powerful arousing effect on her. The unusual surroundings were also contributing to her heightened state. But now the German remained quiet as she stared at a trio of Japanese women talking and giggling in a corner of the bath. All three were petite and young, and they also had gorgeous bodies, with small but perfectly round breasts, dark puckered nipples, and tiny waists begging to be embraced.

As she turned again to the foreigner, Joanna thought she saw a glimmer of lust quickly flash in the woman's dark eyes. Her heart pounded fast. This was a set-up, she just knew it. It was all too familiar by now, like a rerun of a film she had already seen. The German woman would keep on talking, the conversation getting more and more suggestive, and eventually Joanna would find herself being kissed and caressed by another group of lovely sensuous young Japanese women.

Only this time Joanna wouldn't remain idle. Indeed, she would endeavour to return the favour. In comparison, her evening with the young waiter would look like a teenager's first tryst. With these women, she would give her passion and her lust free reign. Today she wouldn't play any games, but would just be herself and get as much out of the encounter as she could, give as much as she would be allowed. But, most of all, she wouldn't stop until she was totally sated.

Slowly, she waded her way towards the German, wanting to test her suspicions. She half-expected the woman to reach out and touch her, but she wasn't sure when it would happen. To her surprise, the woman turned away and pranced about, her heavy body bobbing slightly and sending faint waves over the sides of the bath. Joanna stopped, moved back and rested her back against the flat wall of the pool. If this was her way of letting Joanna know she wasn't to make the first move, she had received the message loud and clear. Obviously, she would have to wait a little longer. Her assumptions were reinforced when she turned around and came back towards her.

'I feel so relaxed after I leave here, so free,' she announced. 'My body is liberated, and most of the time I don't even want to put my clothes on. I want to be naked, always naked. Maybe we should all be naked, all the time. This way, we could admire each others' bodies. You are very beautiful, you know. Do you have a lover?'

Joanna smiled at her. This was it, she thought.

'I have a lover,' she said slowly, 'but he's in London at the moment.'

'Ha! And do you miss him?'

Joanna didn't answer. Why had she said that? In essence, it wasn't exactly a lie: Harry was waiting for her, and it was only a matter of time before she would be with him again. As for the men she had met since she had arrived in Japan, she couldn't honestly say they were her lovers; just flings, really.

'Do you miss him?' the German repeated. 'Or do you miss the sex? Would you cheat on him while you're here?'

Once again, Joanna didn't say anything. Of course, she missed the sex. On any other terms, Harry wasn't all that important to her. Cheat on him? The thought had never even entered her mind. She hadn't made any commitment to him; she was free to go with anyone she pleased.

'You are not saying anything? Am I embarrassing you?'

The woman moved closer to Joanna as she spoke. For a moment, Joanna felt trapped. She already had her back against the wall, close to the corner of the pool. In a flash, she pictured the woman closing in on her, reaching out to caress her. The notion of being taken right then and there was strangely compelling, and Joanna shivered with both excitement and fright.

But the German stopped just inches from her, nodded slightly and started to whisper.

'Or are you aroused by what I've said?'

Joanna held her gaze but didn't reply. Of course, she was aroused. This was killing her. Her expectations had sent her blood racing ever since she had entered the bath house. If only the woman would look down at Joanna's chest, she would see her nipples proudly pointing, and would probably be able to guess how they throbbed. Joanna was so excited that she couldn't help brushing her thighs together; her flesh was swelling and her clitoris was so stiff that it ached. She wondered if it was obvious in her face, which she knew was flushed with anticipation.

Glancing down, she took another look at the woman's body. It was not unlike that of a man, really. Her chest was quite flat, her shoulders broad and square, her hips very narrow. Between her legs, the thatch of hair was the colour of toffee.

Joanna tried to imagine herself locked in a passionate embrace with such an androgynous body. The idea seemed awkward, but beguiling at the same time. Slowly, she reached out towards the compelling silhouette, but at the last moment something made her pull her arm back. She had to keep her cool. Although she was craving the contact, her mind had keenly refocused on the real reason why she was here: she had to find out exactly what was going on. That was paramount. Although she desperately wanted to abandoned herself, it would have to wait. She would show whoever was behind all this that it would take more than talk to make her lose control.

'I am sorry,' the woman said as she stepped back. 'I didn't mean to be so personal.'

'It's all right, really,' Joanna finally said. 'You didn't offend me.'

'Thank you.' The German gave her a broad smile. 'I won't disturb you any further. I have to leave now.'

Before Joanna could say anything, the woman went up the steps and dragged herself out of the tub, her muscular body now in plain view and glistening, with the water running down its length. Quickly she grabbed a towel and dried herself as she made her way out of the room. Just before sliding the panel shut behind her, she turned and waved briefly at Joanna.

That left Joanna more puzzled than ever. Had she missed something? Was that the invitation she had been expecting, yet had failed to accept? Or perhaps it was just a brief introduction, just to tease her? Surely there would be more to come.

At the other end of the bath, only two Japanese women remained. Joanna looked at them, but they paid no attention to her, nor to one another. She pondered whether she should go to them and try to engage them in conversation. Her Japanese had turned out to be much better than she had expected, and she was confident she could find something interesting to say.

One of the women then got out and was soon followed by the other one. That left Joanna all by herself in the large pool. Right, she thought. Now that she was on her own, anything could happen at any moment. Expectation combined with her state of arousal to make her situation practically unbearable. How much longer would this last? Would she be able to control herself when the time came?

Instinctively, she slipped her hand between her legs and gently caressed her swollen bud. She was so ripe, so eager to be pleasured. Her fingers easily found their way inside her tunnel and their intrusion made her moan with satisfaction. If she could make herself climax now, afterwards she would calm down and stay cool once her mysterious correspondent chose to reveal himself.

Even under the water she felt her warm dew escaping profusely. Her thumb naturally settled on her clitoris and quickly toyed with it, sending bolts of ecstasy coursing through her thighs. Her hand insisted and its movement made her whole arm sway. The water splashed lightly around Joanna's shoulders and chest, its noise reminiscent of the sound made by her own wet vulva when teased, the waves on the surface caressing her swollen breasts in a delightful tickle.

She came with a mere whimper, forcing herself not to scream her joy for fear that it would echo around the room and even be heard outside. Her orgasm was soon followed by another one, not as powerful but longer lasting, more satisfying that the previous one. As she pulled her hand away and breathed deeply to enjoy the explosion rampaging within her, she glanced round, suddenly worried. She held her breath for a second, listening intently for any sign that someone was within earshot.

A moment later, she was reassured that she was indeed all alone. She giggled nervously, feeling naughty for what she had just done, but happy to see that she had been right: now she felt calmer, her mind was focused and she was ready for what would come next.

It was a while before the sliding panel moved again. Joanna looked up expectantly, but was disappointed when she recognised the attendant. The old woman held up a large towel and, walking towards the top of the steps, motioned for Joanna to get out.

She obeyed readily, guessing nothing would happen while she stayed in the bath. Once she was dry, she followed the attendant silently into the next room. Her heart jumped as she passed the threshold. By now she was almost afraid of what she was going to find.

On a low stool, her clothes awaited her; her shoes, handbag and briefcase were right next to them. She dressed quickly as the woman watched, then followed her again. Although the details of her arrival were somewhat blurred by now, she knew she was being taken back through the same rooms as before, only in reverse.

A sneaky suspicion started to form in her mind, only to become solid fact when the attendant opened the last door. To her amazement, Joanna found herself back on the pavement. A taxi pulled over, the old lady opened the door, and mechanically Joanna got in.

The driver looked at her in his rear-view mirror, waiting for her to tell him where she wanted to go. It took Joanna a few seconds to come to her senses. By now it was dark. She gave him the name and address of her hotel. Sitting back, she started to laugh softly at her own stupidity, only now beginning to realise that what she had expected just wouldn't materialise.

Chapter Ten

*F*or the seventh time, Joanna reread the card: LET US NOW TAKE CARE OF YOU. Indeed, her afternoon at the bath house had been very relaxing. How silly of her to think it was meant as a rendezvous with the person sending the messages! It was just something to throw her off; tempting enough to make her skip her meeting, but in no way meant to enlighten her.

It was a trap, and she had fallen into it head first. Once again, she had put her work aside in order to satisfy her instincts. She had let her lust lead the way. Even as she had soaked in the bath, her imagination had got the better of her. Was the German woman planted there to reinforce her expectations, to encourage her to stay put? That was likely. It was just another trick, another way of awakening her desire only to use it against her.

More than ever, Joanna was certain Richard was behind all this. The timing was perfect; he knew exactly what to do to make her forget where her priorities lay. This would be the last time she would fall for it, however. From now on, she would fight temptation, she would do whatever she could to make sure her job came first.

The knock on the door interrupted her train of

thoughts. Still holding the card in her hand, Joanna absent-mindedly went to see who it was. Mechanically, she took the fax the clerk handed her and didn't even respond to the boy's curt bow. Closing the door behind him, she walked slowly back to the bed, slightly disappointed to recognise her company's letterhead on the top page.

Yet at the same time, it was a soothing sight; a link with the real world, something tangible and familiar, without any mystery behind it. She scanned the three pages, not unduly surprised to see there was a change in her itinerary. The train tickets would be ready and waiting for her at the front desk the next morning.

She sighed and let the papers drop to the floor. That was nothing unusual, but the message itself was a strong reminder that she had been less than professional and, to a certain extent, that she had been neglecting her work for her own benefit. But it wasn't too late. By coming up with some brilliant discoveries she could still get her act together and undo the damage. As she pondered what she could do to redeem herself, she was only slightly aware of the piece of paper being slid under her door.

At first she thought nothing of it, guessing it was perhaps an additional page of the fax. But then she wondered why the bearer hadn't knocked. Curious, she jumped to her feet and went back to the door. On the carpet, the piece of paper awaited her.

It was a sheet from a notepad, folded in two. As she picked it up, Joanna saw that it was in the familiar pale pink colour and she paused before opening it. Just as she suspected, the left-hand side of the sheet was adorned by a thin sprig of jasmine. It was another message from her mysterious correspondent. Only this time it wasn't on a card but on stationery.

WE HOPE YOU ENJOYED YOUR AFTERNOON AT THE BATH HOUSE. WE ARE AWARE THERE HAVE BEEN CHANGES TO YOUR SCHEDULE AND WE WILL TRY TO REVIEW OUR PLANS ACCORDINGLY. WE WILL BE IN TOUCH SHORTLY.

Joanna crumpled the paper into a ball and threw it angrily across the room. This time, Richard was going too far. She knew the messages had to be from him, or at least from someone working for him. How else could anyone here know that her office had advised her of changes? And the fact that both messages had reached her around the same time only served to confirm her suspicions.

She looked at her watch, quickly worked out what time it was in London and grabbed the telephone. She would settle this once and for all. There were several beeps on the line before she heard the familiar double purr of the phone at the other end. Joanna braced herself, ready to give Richard an earful as soon as he picked up the receiver.

But, to her surprise, a female voice answered instead, a voice Joanna didn't recognise.

'Could I speak to Richard Damon, please?'

The woman at the other end hesitated for a second. 'I'll transfer you to Mr Reynolds. Won't be a moment.'

Before Joanna could protest, she heard a click and knew she was already on hold. Why on earth was this silly woman putting her through to Mike Reynolds? He was Richard's and her superior, but she had clearly asked to speak to Richard.

'Mike? This is Joanna. I'm calling from Japan. Can I speak to Richard? It's quite urgent.'

'Richard? Well . . .' Mike hesitated as well. What was going on over there? Joanna wondered.

'Joanna,' Mike finally said. 'I'm sorry you have to hear it like this, but I'm afraid Richard is no longer with us.'

Joanna wanted to scream. He was gone! Of course, he was most likely working for some competitor now. They probably had their own representative out here in Japan, with the same mission, and Richard wanted her out of the picture.

'Do you have a number for him? I must speak to him today.'

'No, no. You don't understand. I meant ... Joanna, I'm afraid Richard has died.'

For a moment, Joanna wasn't sure she had heard correctly. She swallowed hard, trying to make some sense out of what was going on.

'There was a big accident on the motorway,' Mike continued. 'The police said he had died instantly. It's been very difficult here since then. I'm afraid we haven't had time to find somebody to take over for you in Japan and –'

'When did he die?' Joanna interrupted.

'The day after you left. We thought of contacting you, but we didn't want you to worry about anything other than your work. Besides, there wasn't anything you could have done from where you were, right? Also –'

'What about the changes I received today?' Joanna interrupted again. 'Was he aware of that?'

'The changes? Oh no, that only came up a couple of days ago. Why?'

'No reason,' Joanna replied. 'Listen, it's late now and I need to get some sleep. I'll send you a full report by e-mail as soon as I get to the next hotel, all right?'

She hung up without waiting for his reply. For a while she remained there, her hand curled round the receiver. Richard had died. Fine, good riddance, she thought. But then she realised she wasn't any closer to solving the mystery.

Of course, there was always the possibility that he had left instructions in advance, planned the whole thing before she had left, and now his orders were still being carried out.

Ironically, she couldn't help thinking that the joke was now on him. He had carefully planned her downfall, but he wouldn't be there to see it happen. Provided she let it happen in the first place. Good riddance, indeed.

Juggling her bag, her sunglasses, her hat and her note-pad, Joanna cursed herself for not having better planned her outing that day. She had dropped everything in turn, and it was a miracle she hadn't lost anything.

The market she was touring was large but totally disorganised. Stalls were not arranged in neat rows, but set up wherever the owners had fancied. With practically every step, Joanna bumped into people, stalls, large containers. She twirled about like a mad weathervane, completely disoriented and unsure where she was going next.

Some stalls had meat hanging at eye level. This had knocked off her hat so often she had finally decided she would risk getting a sunburn rather than put her hat back on every few seconds.

Then there were her sunglasses, another nuisance. A couple of times she had got lost and had found herself in a part of the market where merchants sold fabric and household items. It had taken her a while to find her way round. Some of the stalls had awnings so big they shielded the sun completely, making the place dark and gloomy. So the sunglasses had to be taken off as well. As if that weren't annoying enough, she was also constantly tripping over live chickens running all over the place.

Still, she had made some interesting discoveries so all this aggravation was not in vain. Once she had surveyed the produce on offer, she moved on to the next phase of her tour, a trick she had learnt many years ago: customer-watching. In such a market, where most of the customers were either local housewives or restaurant owners, Joanna knew that their expertise would be useful to her. They knew what they wanted, and where to look for it. In turn, Joanna would learn from them what was most popular. She could also ask for recipes or special ways to prepare what they were buying.

She scanned the crowd for a moment, looking for a place to start. Her attention was diverted when she noticed a man who looked familiar. She thought she recognised him from the conference in Tokyo. Moving closer, she donned her hat and sunglasses. Naturally, she knew they weren't much of a disguise. As the only foreigner in the market, she was too obvious to hope to remain unnoticed. But at least the glasses would allow her to study him secretly.

The more she looked at him, the more she was sure it was the same man she had chatted with a couple of times at the conference in Tokyo. He was Japanese but he worked for a company based in Manchester, a competitor of Joanna's firm.

At first she found it odd that they should be in the same place at the same time. Japan was a big country, and there were thousands of markets. On second thought, she realised her itinerary had been devised to take her from the food fair to the exports seminar, then on to another conference in Kyoto. It wasn't impossible that someone else in the same line of business would have followed the same logic and chosen to stop at some of the same places. Besides, part of the trip had been arranged by the Japanese government's department of trade and tourism, so it did make sense.

On the other hand, it was just as possible that he knew her itinerary, and that his presence at the market wasn't a mere coincidence. Could he be the one behind all those mysterious messages? She soon forgot about work and took to following the man's every move. She wanted to know where he was headed next. So the prey would become the hunter, she thought with satisfaction. The game lasted for the better part of an hour. She heard people complain as she stood idle in the middle of an aisle, blocking their path, but she didn't care. It was much more important to find out whatever she could about the man, whose name she was trying very hard to remember.

She was disappointed when he gathered his purchases, made his way out of the market and hopped into a waiting taxi. Perhaps he didn't even know she was there and had been to the market for his own reasons. Joanna cursed herself once again. Now she was getting paranoid! She had no proof that the man was there to spy on her, but she had let her suspicions take away her sense of priorities. The whole thing was definitely getting out of hand. How hard would she have to kick herself to stop it from happening again?

Chapter Eleven

*J*ust as Joanna had suspected, many of the delegates from the Tokyo food fair were now attending the conference in Kyoto. She nodded a greeting to those she recognised, now realising that most of these men had probably not been far from her since she had left Tokyo, travelling in the same direction, and she hadn't even had a clue.

That realisation reinforced the idea that any of them could have been behind those mysterious messages. They were all potential competitors, on different levels. And since she was now beginning to think that Richard didn't have anything to do with them, it was the only other possible explanation.

As everyone gathered in the hospitality suite, Joanna tried to see whether anyone in particular was paying her more attention than the rest. Surely, her Nemesis would be keeping an eye on her at every moment. Lost in thought, she was startled when a pointy finger probed her shoulder in a none too gentle manner. She turned around and practically jumped with surprise when she recognised Greta.

'We meet again!' the New Yorker exploded in a loud cheerful voice.

Joanna didn't know how to welcome the news. At

first, annoyance grabbed her in the pit of her stomach. She didn't need the flamboyant Valkyrie distracting her at that point but she resisted the urge to tell her to get lost. Another thought rose in her mind, and she decided she was almost pleased to see her: if Greta was here, Steve couldn't be very far behind.

In a fraction of a second, her mood changed radically. Just knowing that she'd see Steve again empowered her. All was not lost on that front. It gave her something to look forward to, something to focus on so that she could put all this business of silly messages behind her.

'It's soooo nice to see you again,' Greta purred as she embraced Joanna in a tight hug. 'How have you been? What a shame you couldn't join us for dinner in Kobe. We had a marvellous time. Of course, I always have a marvellous time when I'm with Steve.'

She winked as she spoke his name. Joanna seized the occasion and didn't give Greta any time to continue babbling.

'How is Steve?' she asked in all innocence. 'Will he be attending the conference?'

'He's here,' Greta replied as she looked around the room. 'Although I must admit I haven't seen much of him since we arrived. He's got a lot of work to take care of, you know. He insisted we take separate rooms because he works late into the night and he doesn't want to disturb me, and sometimes he locks himself in there for hours on end . . .'

She kept talking but Joanna wasn't paying attention any more. From what Greta had just said, it appeared to her that Steve's work had more to do with getting rid of the New Yorker than keeping up with directives from head office. That was a good sign. Since they would all be at the conference for the next three days, Joanna could now rehash her plan to get Steve for herself.

With all the mystery surrounding the messages she had been receiving, she felt she no longer had any control over her life. At least, with Steve, she would be calling the shots.

'Ah!' Greta squeaked in an excited little voice. 'There he is!'

Joanna turned round and saw Steve talking with a woman at the far end of the room. Like a cheetah, Greta leapt and barged her way through the crowd, not even stopping to apologise when her intrusion caused a couple of delegates to spill their drinks.

Joanna was tempted to follow behind, albeit in a more leisurely fashion. It was the perfect opportunity to say hello, engage in conversation and see for herself what the situation was between those two.

But as she read Steve's annoyed glance towards Greta when she forcefully grabbed his arm, Joanna was glad she hadn't moved. She had to see him one to one, with nothing to take his attention away from her, especially not Greta.

When she saw Steve heading her way across the bar, Joanna knew the lucky break she had been hoping for had just happened. She had been waiting for this all day, ever since Greta had dragged him away. Now, thankfully, the Valkyrie was nowhere in sight. She waved at him but didn't make any effort to go to him. Instead, he was the one who came towards her.

'Hi!' he said in a friendly tone as he stopped and smiled at her. 'What are you doing here so late?'

'I couldn't sleep,' Joanna lied. 'I thought a small drink would help me relax.'

She waited for him to make the next move, desperately wishing he'd ask her if she wanted company. Of course, she couldn't confess she had been spending most of her free time in the bar just in case he happened to pass by.

He gestured towards the empty armchair next to hers.

'Mind if I join you?' he asked.

Joanna pretended to hesitate for a moment.

'Please do,' she said in a husky voice. 'But I'm afraid I'm not very good company.'

She examined him furtively as he slumped in the

chair. He reached over, grabbed a handful of spicy almonds from the bowl on the table between them, and nonchalantly popped them in his mouth, one by one.

In the dim light, he looked even more handsome than Joanna remembered. Despite the hotel's impeccable air-conditioning system, it seemed that Steve was too hot to bother putting on proper clothes. All he had on was a pair of running shorts and a sleeveless top. His hair was still damp and the soapy aroma lingering around him told her he had just stepped out of the shower. His trainers were worn out and the laces undone. It was obvious he wasn't planning to go out, and straight away Joanna suspected that he was just looking for an escape from Greta's overbearing presence.

For Joanna, it was like an early Christmas present, something beguiling waiting to be unwrapped. His legs, long, muscular and oh-so gorgeous, were in plain view as he settled in his seat. His shorts were made of a thin, shiny fabric and although the fit was meant to be loose, Joanna couldn't help notice how the bump between his legs showed up.

Her wild imagination could easily picture the creature hiding underneath the fabric. At the moment it was at rest, but Joanna knew waking it up would be a delightful challenge. She was confident that, given a chance, she could get it out of its torpor. Her grip tightened automatically round her glass and her fingers moved up and down as if caressing him instead. The hard, smooth surface of the glass only led her to focus on his dick, on how it would feel in her hand.

As her mood shifted and she found herself aroused, she could almost taste it in her mouth. Now she was hungry not only for the man but for his manhood. She imagined it, stiff and throbbing, getting even harder on her tongue as she sucked it earnestly, wanting to push him to his peak as soon as possible. He would buck under the strain, forcing her to take him even further in the hot furnace of her mouth and –

'Don't you think?' Steve repeated.

Joanna was startled out of her reverie.

'Pardon me? I'm afraid I didn't quite understand what you meant?'

Steve gave her a puzzled look. 'I said: I think it's quite unusual to enjoy such warm weather at this time of year in Japan, don't you think?' As he spoke, he took another almond from the bowl and lightly tossed it from one hand to the next before eating it.

Joanna shook herself and desperately tried to find something clever to say.

'I don't know,' she admitted sheepishly. 'I don't pay much attention to these things. I pack a few things on spec and no matter where I go I know I can always buy more practical clothes.'

'So you travel without much luggage, then?'

Suddenly finding her wits, Joanna seized the occasion to steer the conversation to her advantage.

'I pack tons of underwear,' she replied in a whisper. 'I'm very choosy when it comes to that. There are quite a few items I just can't do without.'

As she spoke, she innocently leant towards him, over the table, letting her blouse gape and offering him a clear view of the sheer black bra she had on underneath. She bit her lip to contain a giggle of excitement when she noticed his glance swerving exactly where she wanted it to go. Now that the foundation was laid, there was no better time to build.

'You see,' she continued in the same tone, 'women are very particular when it comes to what touches their skin.'

She stopped talking for a moment, waiting to see if he would pick up on her line, and also to show him she wasn't a mindless talking machine like Greta. He gave her a brief smile before replying.

'It's the same thing with men, you know. That's why there's so much advertising for men's underwear in recent years. There's big money in that.'

Joanna almost cringed. This wasn't what she wanted to hear; he wasn't picking up at all!

'Yes, but men's underwear is all the same, cotton,' she ventured. 'I like lace, satin, silk. Sometimes, depending on what I'm wearing, a silk dress for instance, I prefer to go without any underwear at all.'

She paused for effect. As she waited for him to say something, she writhed slightly in her chair, rubbing her bare thighs together at the same time. She saw he didn't miss that, but still he didn't show any sign of picking up on her meaning.

'That would be handy on a day like today,' he said finally. 'It's so hot out I can barely stand it. And, believe me, I've seen hot weather before!'

Despite his effort to pursue a banal conversation, Joanna detected a tremble in his voice which gave her hope that he was not unmoved. She was getting to him. Finally. That was good, but she didn't want to come on too strong or be too obvious. Later, after another couple of drinks, she'd try again.

Then, just as she was about to ask him if he wanted another drink, he put his glass on the table and stood up.

'That's enough for tonight,' he announced. He yawned, not even bothering to put his hand in front of his mouth, and stretched briefly. 'I have a lot of work to tackle tomorrow,' he said. 'I'd better go to sleep now. Good night.'

Before Joanna could say anything, he had turned around and made his way out of the bar. Left alone, she couldn't decide what to make of it. All she could think of was the last sight she caught of him: his pert round bottom under the shiny fabric of his shorts. Too bad she couldn't see the front! She cursed herself for not having looked for that certain sign that their conversation was starting to get too personal for him.

Had he left because he really had work to do? Because he was tired? Or was it just an excuse to get away from her, like he was doing to Greta? Or, on the other hand, did he have to get away because it was getting too much for him?

Joanna smiled and emptied her glass, deciding she preferred the latter explanation. She had definitely gained some ground tonight. But still it wasn't enough. If anything, it was all the more frustrating. She wanted to take charge for a while. Her ego was in serious need of a boost. If only she could toy with Steve as she had with Harry.

As the lift brought her to her floor, she felt she needed confirmation that she hadn't lost her touch. She decided to ring Harry. He would be at work at this hour, and that was the best time for her, the perfect way to toy with him, to tease him. After all, he had often confessed that her seductive talk had more effect on him when he sat at his desk. It added an extra naughty flavour to their conversation, he had said.

She dialled slowly, rehearsing in her head what she was going to say to him. At the other end, his 'hello' sounded cold and impersonal, but as soon as Joanna purred his name, the tone of his voice changed drastically.

'I miss you,' she said in her most seductive voice.

'I miss you too, darling,' he replied. 'I can't wait to see you. When are you coming back?'

'I don't know,' she whined. She grabbed a satsuma from the bowl on her bedside table and peeled it slowly. Its fragrance dispersed as the skin broke, its juice spraying her hands, and its scent unexpectedly excited her. 'Everything is so boring here, so routine,' she said. 'It's all work and no play; I barely have a minute to myself.'

'Good,' Harry said. 'At least I know you won't be looking at other men while you're there!'

'Other men?' Joanna feigned surprise. 'Darling, there's nobody here even worth looking at. They're either fat or old, or totally uninteresting. Besides, I can only think of you since I left. I can't wait to see you again . . .'

She let her voice trail on purpose, as a bait for him to ask the question she knew always came next.

'And then what?'

She took a moment before replying. She popped a

112

segment of satsuma in her mouth, bit into it slowly and let its tangy juice slide down the back of her throat. 'I can't wait to run my hands all over that gorgeous body of yours,' she finally whispered after swallowing.

'And?'

'And pick up where we left off last time. I'm kicking myself for not having let you have your way with me. I was foolish. I thought it was only proper not to give in so soon, but now all I can think about is your tongue on my neck. You know, you made such an impression on me that night. Just thinking about it makes me shiver.'

'Really?'

'I am so hot for you baby,' she lied. It was all a game. She didn't want to let her guard down. There was no point in getting aroused now if there was no man to satisfy her. But already she could hear Harry breathing faster, and she knew she had to give him her best line ever. She grabbed another segment and sucked it loudly before speaking again.

'If only you could see me right now,' she continued in a husky voice.

'But I can't,' he said breathlessly. 'What would I see? And what are you eating?'

'Well, for one, I am lying completely naked on my bed. I'm eating a satsuma. I squeezed it between my fingers and let the juice dribble all over my bare breasts.'

'Are you sure you want to get into this?' Harry asked cautiously. 'You never know who may be listening on this line. And this is an overseas call, you know.'

'I couldn't care less about that. I'm all wet just thinking about you. My nipples are incredibly hard, aching to feel your tongue circling round them.' She let out a faint moan, just to reinforce her point. In reality, she was trying very hard not to laugh out loud. He would never know that she was still fully clothed and had yet to spill a single drop of juice.

Harry didn't reply. 'Are you hard, darling?' she asked in a whisper. 'I can't wait to hold that beautiful prick of yours in my hands, you know.'

'And?'

'And caress it slowly along its length, up and down, with my fingertips.'

She paused, still trying not to laugh, as she heard him swallow hard. He was so easy to manipulate. Not at all like Steve. As her thoughts shifted towards the Texan, she began imagining she was talking to him instead. Instantly, she felt her flesh lubricate and she knew she was playing a dangerous game. But so what, she thought? It could only help her get in the right frame of mind for the next time she saw him.

'Then,' she continued, 'I would take you in my mouth. You have no idea how hungry I am for you.'

'I know, baby,' he interrupted. 'I want you, too.'

As he spoke, Joanna quickly tossed aside what was left of her satsuma and reclined against the pillow. Slipping one hand under her dress, she pulled down her knickers and briefly caressed herself. Just as she had felt, her flesh was hot and moist with want, although the man fuelling her arousal wasn't the one she was talking to on the phone. When she didn't reply, Harry suddenly got worried.

'Hello? Are you still there?'

'I am,' Joanna sighed.

'What's going on? Are you doing what I think you're doing?'

'I am.'

This time she wasn't lying. So many times she had pretended to masturbate while on the phone to Harry; for once she wouldn't have to fake it.

Writhing on the bed, she repeatedly plunged her fingers inside her clenching vagina, caressing her inner wall whilst her thumb flickered over her clitoris.

'Can anybody see you?' she asked.

'No,' Harry replied. 'I'm in my office and the door is closed.'

'Then do it,' Joanna ordered. 'Do it with me. Now!'

He didn't reply. What would it take to make him obey, Joanna wondered? She moaned loudly, bringing her wet fingers to her mouth and tasting her own juices before resuming her caresses on her slick flesh.

'Do it, Harry!' she implored. 'Undo your trousers and slip your hand inside. Do it for me.'

She heard the faint noise of a zip and smiled to herself. 'Keep going,' she said as she panted. 'Take it in your hand. Is it as hard and big as I imagine it is?'

'Yes,' he confessed breathlessly.

'Hold it tight. Stroke it up and down.'

'I don't know,' Harry protested faintly. 'What if somebody walks in?'

'What if they don't?' Joanna countered. 'Remember how you said you'd like us to come at the same time? Well, here's your chance. Stroke it, Harry, hard and fast.'

As she spoke, she increased the motion of her hand on her own sex. Now she knew he was obeying. His breath was fast, and already strangled cries were reaching her over the line.

'This is so good, darling. So good,' she moaned. 'If only you were here for real. I wish I could pleasure you myself. My pussy is so hungry for you. I want you inside me, now. I want you so bad.'

'So do I, darling,' he replied between moans. 'I can't wait to feel your soft skin under my fingers. I want to taste your pussy, slip my tongue inside and make you squeal until you beg for mercy.'

Joanna bit her lip. As pleasure swept her, the only name she wanted to scream was Steve's. But she held back. Despite the wave of bliss shaking her, she knew she couldn't completely abandon herself. She couldn't betray herself.

She heard Harry grunt and she knew he had come as well. They remained silent for a moment, catching their breath.

'Was that good, sweetheart?' he asked. His voice was not unlike that of a little boy, wanting to know if he had done well.

'Very good,' she lied. For although she could still feel

115

her flesh quiver, sending faint bolts of pleasure through her pelvis, Joanna wasn't entirely satisfied. She needed more than this. She needed Steve.

'I've got to go now,' she said. 'Don't forget me too soon.'

'I won't,' he promised. 'If anything, I am more impatient to have you back than ever. The things I will do to you when you come back – '

'Yes, I know,' Joanna interrupted. 'I'll ring you again in a few days.' She hung up before he had time to say anything. He had played right into her hands. Once again she was in control. Yet satisfaction still eluded her.

Chapter Twelve

*I*t had to be Richard, Joanna reasoned. Since the morning when she had received a fax from her office and simultaneously a message from her 'secret admirer' it had all been quiet. No other messages, no other sign that someone was watching her. The last communication dated from three days ago.

Obviously Richard's accomplices hadn't been able to keep track of her. This could only be explained by his sudden passing. He had probably left instructions with his people in Japan just before Joanna had left, but he hadn't made provision for an unexpected change in schedule. As a result, Joanna had been able to concentrate on her work, and now the anonymous messages were slowly vanishing from her mind.

The same was true of Steve. She had hardly seen him at the conference. And it seemed Greta had also lost her hold on him. The ebullient New Yorker was still following him about like an enthusiastic puppy, but she had cooled down a bit. Still, it hadn't done anything to help Joanna advance on that front.

From a few brief conversations, she had managed to gather that they were likely to meet again. But since there had been changes to her itinerary, she couldn't be so sure any more. If she were to bump into them again, so much the better. Otherwise, well, she would have to make do with what-could-have-beens.

The cryptic messages she had received before were the furthest thing from her mind as she opened the envelope. At first, she thought it was simply further directives from her office. But when she recognised the pale green sprig of jasmine adorning the pink card stapled to the first page, she felt her heart skip a beat. Just when she least expected it, another message.

This time, it left no room for speculation. IT IS TIME FOR US TO MEET. The page to which the card was stapled was in fact a road map. Joanna was instructed to make her way to a rendezvous point the next day, late in the afternoon.

Her first reaction was to reach for her briefcase and check her schedule for that day. To her surprise, making the rendezvous wouldn't interfere with any meetings. She didn't have anything planned for the following morning either. Was that a ploy to ensure she would show up?

The meeting point was outside the city, but at first glance easy to get to. Suddenly, it seemed almost too easy. I'm not going, Joanna thought. She'd had enough of these childish games. For all she knew, it could be just another wild goose chase, like the time she had gone to the bath house expecting answers to her questions, only to come back feeling even more puzzled.

If they really wanted to see her, they would have to come to her, she decided. She didn't have any time to waste on this.

She checked her watch for the fourth time, cursing herself. Why had she come? Once again, temptation and curiosity had been stronger than plain common sense, and now Joanna found herself alone on an empty road, with no means of getting back to the city. If only she had asked the taxi to wait!

The person she was supposed to meet was now more

than fifteen minutes late. She should have stuck to her first resolution and stayed at the hotel. She had nothing planned that evening and she probably would have ended up being bored to tears, but at least she would have been safe.

She took a first step along the road, hoping she wouldn't have to go very far before meeting someone from whom she could hitch a ride. The thought of bumping into some lunatic, even a mass murderer, entered her mind. But she couldn't let that worry her. She was in enough trouble already.

She waved frantically as a car appeared from around the bend in the road. It stopped right in front of her and the back door opened. It was a big car, much bigger than the average Japanese one; more like a limousine. The dark tinted windows wouldn't allow her to see much of what was inside, but she could see there was at least one passenger in the back seat, a man.

'Do you speak English?' she asked as she bent forward to speak to him.

'Yes, Miss Parsons,' said the man. 'I humbly apologise for being late. Please do get in.'

Joanna was stunned. She had given up on anyone appearing, but now it seemed she hadn't been stood up after all. She hesitated. Accepting the invitation would perhaps bring her one step closer to solving the mystery, but could she really get in a car with a stranger, a man whose face she couldn't even see?

The passenger gave an order to the driver, who turned off the engine. Slowly, the man got out and walked towards Joanna.

Her heart jumped when she saw his suit: a pale shade of green, just like the one worn by the man from the bar. But it wasn't him. Yet there was no mistake to be made: even the pink shirt was identical, not to mention the tie. The face had changed, but this man was just as handsome as the stranger from the bar, albeit a few years older. And his eyes were smaller, more mysterious.

Another thing both men had in common was unusually thick hair, coarse and unruly, like a wig.

He walked towards Joanna with tremendous self-assurance and class. He was as tall as she was, although his broad shoulders made him look taller, more impressive. As he approached, the cool air blew in her direction and carried his fragrance which she recognised: jasmine.

The scent stirred her memories and the effect on her was overwhelming. Suddenly, she was there again: sitting at the bar, with the stranger next to her casually slipping his hand between her legs to pleasure her.

'I can see you are still not convinced we are really those you have asked to meet,' the man said. 'Let me assure you, there is no reason for you to hesitate.'

Joanna didn't reply. What on earth was he talking about? She couldn't even surmise he was talking to the wrong person. Although he had addressed her by Stacey's name, she knew he was indeed the man she had come here to meet.

'Who are you?' she said loudly in a defiant tone. 'What do you want from me?'

The man laughed softly. 'You may call me Torima. Of course, it is not my real name. And, really, you should know better than to pretend you don't know what this is all about. Come. What you've been waiting for is within your reach.'

Joanna didn't budge as he turned and started to walk back towards the car. She couldn't think of anything to say, but she knew there was no way she was going to follow him. When he saw she hadn't followed him, the stranger came back towards her.

'I can understand you are angry about all these delays,' the man said softly. 'But there's no need for this attitude. You know what we can offer you has no price, and is well worth waiting for.'

Joanna listened carefully to every word, hoping to catch something, some kind of clue that would reveal what this was all about.

'You know you will not regret this,' he continued. He

edged towards her, coming closer than before. As his hand reached up, Joanna knew he was going to touch her but she didn't move. Her instincts were telling her to let him have his way, just like the man at the bar.

And, as she had guessed, his fingertips slowly brushed her breasts. Her nipples stiffened readily. His other hand followed the curve of her waist and lightly fondled her buttocks. As he pulled her towards him, Joanna gasped. Under his clothes, she could feel his body, hard and trim. Her hips instinctively pushed against his. Immediately, Joanna realised she wanted him. She wanted to be taken by a real man, something that hadn't happened for a long time.

The stranger obviously knew how to get to her: already she knew that she wouldn't resist much longer. The links were forming in her mind, reminding her of the pleasure that had swept her when the stranger from the bar had persuaded her to let him touch her. It would be just the same with this man; she knew that much.

'Pleasure, Miss Parsons,' he whispered as his lips caressed her earlobe. 'That's all we want from you, for you. To give and receive pleasure. You have nothing to fear. You won't be hurt.' He paused for a moment and pulled away before finishing his sentence. 'Unless that is what you desire.'

She resisted the urge to tell him her name wasn't Parsons but Wilson. What difference would it make, anyway? The mistake had been made so often she had stopped correcting and couldn't be bothered to do so now.

The man stood so close to her she could still feel the heat of his body. She gave up trying to rationalise. No matter how disconcerted she was by this mystery, her instincts were telling her that the man wasn't lying: she had nothing to lose, and much to gain – pleasure. Without a word, she got in the car. The man got in after her and closed the door behind him.

'We hope you understand the need for this,' he said as he pulled out a piece of black fabric.

Joanna remained idle as he blindfolded her. She wasn't afraid any more. Having accepting that fighting her instincts was pointless, she was filled with trust. And, more than anything, she was incredibly aroused.

They drove for quite a long time. Not a single word was exchanged. Joanna felt hot but calm. Eventually, they stopped and she was helped out of the car, still blindfolded. Both the stranger and his driver helped her along what seemed like a narrow path made of cobblestones. She could hear music and occasionally her nose caught whiffs of cooking, but there was nothing else to tell her where they had taken her. There were practically no noises, except for a lone cricket and the very distant rumble of traffic. The cool air was slightly humid and gave her the impression that they were in the country, but those were the only clues.

Once inside, the blindfold was removed. Joanna was overwhelmed by the light assaulting her eyes. The room in which she found herself was enclosed by rice paper panels, and was not unlike several places she had been before: the bath house, the inn near Tokyo, one of the hotels where she had stayed.

She wasn't even surprised when a panel slid open. Torima left and two geishas came in. The scene was so familiar that Joanna's heart began pounding in anticipation. Now, for the first time, she knew what was coming next. They undressed her and she felt herself melt. An exact re-enactment!

This was confirmed when she saw the kimono one of the geishas held out for her: pale pink and adorned by wispy green springs of jasmine. It was exactly like the one she had received as a present a few days earlier. Finally, the puzzle in her head was coming together. Now there could be no mistake: whoever these people were, they had made jasmine blossoms their emblem.

That would explain the bottle of bath foam left in her bathroom, the letterhead and the cards, even the ties of those men. There had been jasmine everywhere: in the geishas' dressing room, the bath house. Every detail had carefully been taken into consideration.

The only thing leaving her confused was that the geishas were now helping her put on the kimono, whereas Joanna had been expecting something else. Her logic was telling her that before long she would find herself naked again, with the geishas, and partaking in a passionate quest for never-ending pleasure.

But, to her surprise, another panel slid open, this time on her right. Joanna turned sideways and watched, hypnotised, as it opened on to another room. It was a large banqueting hall, almost completely empty, and with a very high ceiling. Alongside the wall on the left-hand side, about a dozen people were kneeling in a single row behind a low table arranged in a crescent.

It was as if they were expecting something to happen in front of them, in the middle of all this empty space. In front of them, at the other end of the banqueting hall, an enormous door was closed. It was massive, made of dark lacquered wood and adorned by big metal studs.

As Joanna peered in, the people behind the table looked towards her and bowed in unison. Mechanically, she bowed back.

Behind her, Torima reappeared. He too had changed into a kimono, entirely black and embroidered with gold threads in the jasmine sprigs pattern that was now so familiar. He looked like a samurai, something out of an old film. Only then did Joanna realise she had been right when she had guessed he was wearing a wig. Now that it had been removed, she could see his real hair, which was long and tied into a bun on top of his head.

He placed his hand on the small of her back and gently ushered her into the room. Everyone smiled at her and bowed again. The men in attendance were all Japanese and were dressed in the same fashion as Torima. Joanna recognised one of them as the stranger from the bar. He, too, had removed his wig and his own hair was skilfully arranged. He smiled and bowed at her.

The women, however, were Westerners. Although they all wore kimonos like Joanna's, they weren't made up to look like geishas for they didn't wear any white make-up or black wigs. As her eyes travelled from one woman to the next, Joanna filled in another piece of the puzzle.

The kimonos were reversible, and some women wore theirs inside out, revealing the pink sprigs on a green background. For Joanna, it conveyed a strong image that took her one step closer to solving the mystery: Keiko and Atsuko, when they were entertaining the dinner guests at the inn, had been wearing exactly the same kimonos. She hadn't realised it at the time, but all the clues were there from the beginning. And all this time she had thought it was just one of Richard's cheap ploys. This was more elaborate than even he could ever have planned.

Not a single sound was made as she entered the room. The table was lavishly set with elaborate dishes which hadn't been touched. They had been waiting for her. She was invited to sit at the centre of the table. She was the only one who didn't have to kneel. Rather, she was provided with some sort of legless chair, made entirely of cushions, and slightly reclining. As she sat, Torima encouraged her to stretch out her legs. This way, she couldn't reach the table, but she didn't really mind. Food was the last thing she was thinking of at that moment. Everyone was still staring at her, but not a word was exchanged. Joanna's mind raced with dozens of questions, but she sensed now wasn't the right time.

Torima knelt next to her. He clapped his hands, and suddenly the party began. The music started, coming out of nowhere, and all the guests helped themselves to the food on the table. Two young men appeared on either side of Joanna. One after the other, they picked up the dishes on the table and brought them within Joanna's reach.

She ate without really thinking about what she was putting in her mouth. Several of the dishes were served in the traditional Japanese fashion, brought to her in a square shallow lacquered box. There was a lot of raw fish, small servings of oddly shaped mushrooms, and the usual noodle soup which everyone slurped loudly. The flavours and textures mixed in Joanna's mouth as she savoured each bite, every morsel awakening her senses.

The two attendants never left her side. They brought the dishes for her to sample with pointy chopsticks, but at times they even fed her themselves and joyfully Joanna let them. To drink she had a choice of tea, sake, plum wine and liqueur. All she had to do was point and the cup was brought to her lips.

She let herself relax, intoxicated by such an overwhelming display of delicacies. On either side of her, the other guests were also gorging themselves, using both chopsticks and bare fingers to pick up their food, sometimes directly from the serving trays.

Although the guests casually chatted amongst themselves, no one talked to Joanna. Even Torima, who now and again turned to smile at her, never uttered a word. She observed the scene for a while, soon noticing one constant: the guests kept glancing towards the empty space in front of them. Only then did Joanna notice the lights along the ceiling were aimed directly for that spot. Obviously, everyone was expecting a floor show at some point. By then, her surroundings seemed so familiar to Joanna that she even expected Keiko and Atsuko to show up at any moment, to entertain them with songs and dances.

Chapter Thirteen

*T*he aromas from the dishes floated and mixed in the air. They filled Joanna's nostrils and amplified the taste of the food as she put it in her mouth. Soft music contributed to a comfortable ambience, but although Joanna knew it wasn't a recording she couldn't tell exactly where the musicians were. It was easy to assume they were probably behind one of the panels, but it didn't really matter.

The atmosphere had changed drastically from when she had entered the room: from rather cold and formal to totally uninhibited. Now it was exactly like any other dinner party: mostly cheerful and at times even rowdy. The food was plentiful, varied and exquisite. The amount of sake Joanna had drunk was also a contributing factor to the state of blissful relaxation in which she now found herself.

Although she had been here for well over an hour, no one had said anything to her. Torima was very attentive and constantly smiling, but beyond informing Joanna about the dishes presented to her, he didn't try to engage her in conversation. Yet it was obvious that Joanna was the focus of silent attention, being made to feel like a queen and waited on by two lovely young men.

She could sense she was the topic of conversation, yet

she felt no maliciousness. Rather, everyone seemed pleased by her presence among them, as if she were a guest of honour, a trophy on a shelf to be admired. And, for once, she didn't even have to work at it.

At some point the music stopped. The lights above them were dimmed, making the empty space in front of them only more obvious. The guests stopped eating and straightened up.

Two young Japanese women appeared through the side door and came towards Joanna. The other guests moved away slightly to allow them more space. The women were both dressed in white and carried towels and small bottles. At first glance, they looked like beauticians, and Joanna guessed she would be entitled to yet another treat.

One of them knelt next to Joanna's legs and proceeded to massage her feet. The other young woman delicately opened Joanna's kimono and pulled away the sides to expose her naked body.

Joanna felt the hair on the back on her neck rise on end. At first, she was horrified to be exposed in such an unceremonious way. As her skin was uncovered, the cool air in the room made her shiver. But she didn't dare stop the women. She looked around, rather worried, but a moment later she was pleased by the other guests' reaction. Ohs and ahs of admiration reached her as they all stared at her, stretching their necks to see her better.

Such a display of appreciation was indeed flattering, and the alcohol flowing in her veins had left her hot and uninhibited. When tiny hands began spreading jasmine-scented lotion on her thighs, her stomach and her breasts, she simply took a deep breath, let out a long sigh, and decided to relax and enjoy it. The massages were sensuous but not so daring as to be unduly arousing. Above all else, they were mostly pleasant and soothing.

Joanna was beginning to think she might fall asleep when suddenly, from outside the room, a gong resonated loudly. She was startled, stirred, and in a fraction of a second found herself wide awake. The other guests also became more attentive, intently staring at the large door in front of them. Only a moment later, it opened.

A man stepped in hesitantly, escorted by the two young men who had waited on Joanna earlier. He stared at everyone in turn and appeared uneasy, even somewhat feverish. Joanna couldn't help but think of how he looked like he didn't belong in such a place. He was dressed in a dark smart suit, with his tie properly done and his hair neatly combed. Immediately, Joanna understood he was a *salary-man*, just an average Japanese bloke working in an anonymous office, in an anonymous building.

One of the women stood up and went to him, bidding him stand right in the middle of the empty space. Next to him, she also looked out of place. Joanna hadn't paid much attention to her before, but now she couldn't help but notice how strikingly beautiful she was. Her skin was the colour of coffee, and her vaguely Hispanic features made her look South American, perhaps Brazilian. The pink kimono definitely didn't suit her; she would have looked better in a pareo or sarong, in bold colours.

The man looked at her, then glanced towards the people still at the table. His eyes paused on Joanna and he gasped. His eyes opened wide and he licked his lips nervously. Joanna writhed with satisfaction. It was extremely gratifying to be reminded once again of how beautiful she was. In the semi-darkness, her skin glowed softly and looked even more velvet-like. Her nipples had grown stiff and dark and pointed insolently toward the man. If he wanted to look, she would let him. Obviously, what he saw pleased him.

Torima pushed away the bottles and the dishes in front of Joanna, clearing the space to afford the beholder a better view. Everyone around the table smiled, but no one said anything. In the man's eyes, Joanna could read both fear and excitement. She guessed the fear was motivated by the unknown, for he looked like he didn't quite know what to expect. But his excitement was obvious in the bulge stretching the front of his trousers.

Joanna wasn't surprised by the latter, but she was amused by the expression on his face. By now she had grown accustomed to solemn glares and polite smiles, and his bewilderment was a welcome change.

The gong resonated once again, and it was Joanna's turn to gasp when the woman standing next to the man suddenly dropped her kimono. Underneath, she was half-naked and simply wore a sheer corset made entirely of fine white lace. Joanna immediately recognised the garment as French and admired its quality. It was beautifully crafted, just strong enough to emphasise nicely the slender figure of the woman by cinching the waist and lifting her bare breasts without cupping them. Yet it seemed delicate enough to make it a delight to wear, and made her skin look even darker. Although the woman was probably in her early 40s, she was impressive to behold; rather short and stout, but neatly sculpted and amazingly firm.

Joanna's eyes wandered all over her body, along with those of the man, and stopped at the same place as his: the junction of the legs. Under the frilly lace, an enormous luxuriant thatch of thick black hair was plainly visible. Along its edge, on the right-hand side, a thin sprig of jasmine had been tattooed, the vine clinging to her bush and following its contour to curve at the top.

Joanna saw the man lick his lips at the sight of such abundance. She remembered how she had once heard that in Japan pubic hair was considered the ultimate taboo. Even in the most risqué pornographic magazines, the hair was hidden or mechanically erased from the photos. As a result, Japanese men often developed a fetish, a fixation that could only be appeased by the sight of an unusually well-furnished mound.

The woman's other assets were her gorgeous breasts, adorned by large black nipples so stiff and erect they were practically begging to be suckled. As she admired them, Joanna also noticed two abundant forests tucked under the woman's armpits. They added something primitive to her, a raunchy and feline aura. Silently, she walked around the man, moving about as lithely and graciously as a dancer. The man followed her every move by turning his head, never letting her out of his sight, but obviously unaware of what he was supposed to do.

Joanna shifted in her seat, trying to fight the surge of arousal now invading her. She was eagerly anticipating what would happen next. The woman waved her hand towards one of the attendants still flanking the *salaryman*. Without uttering a single word, he obediently brought her a riding crop which he passed to her with a deep bow. Joanna was impressed. Obviously, he knew the drill.

The Spaniard only said a few words, and although her Japanese was atrocious, their meaning was unequivocal: undress and kneel. The *salary-man* didn't need to be told twice. He obeyed promptly and shed his clothes at record speed. Soon he knelt, completely naked, in front of the woman who exercised such a fascination over him. His body was average, not very tall but nicely shaped. His organ, already erect, was just as unremarkable.

But Joanna wasn't too disappointed: the man himself wasn't the focus of her interest at that moment. She was much more curious about what her dinner companion would do with him.

The woman walked around the prostrate figure a few times without so much as brushing him; either to examine him or to test his patience, Joanna thought. Nonchalantly, she then let the flexible tip of the riding crop run up along the ridge of his spine. The man twitched faintly, but didn't try to move away or reach out to her.

She stopped in front of him and, standing precariously on one leg, offered him the other, putting her pointed toes on his lap and pressing her knee towards his mouth.

Without wasting any time, the man eagerly kissed and licked the whole length of her calf and shin. His eagerness was only matched by the speed of execution. His tongue moved swiftly and didn't miss a single spot.

His mistress seemed pleased, but when his hands came to grab her leg to pull it closer to his wet lips, she directed the riding crop in a precise blow on his forearm. The man squealed in pain.

'Don't touch,' she ordered.

Sitting back on his heels, he looked at her defiantly for a moment. But as soon as his eyes resumed their journey over her appealing body, he once again bowed his head in submission. Hesitantly, he kissed her leg again, curbing his enthusiasm for a while but soon letting his passion resurface.

Yet although he seemed to enjoy his humiliating position, now and again it became obvious that he couldn't restrain himself. Often his hands came forward in an attempt to touch the woman, but pulled away just in time to avoid another strike. When his mouth strayed above the mistress's knee, she pushed his head down forcefully and intimated that he should wait for her instructions.

As she watched from the other side of the table, Joanna felt more and more excited. She was impressed by the way the woman toyed with her slave, allowing him to touch her only as she pleased, never hesitating to strike with the crop when he strayed.

The other guests also watched silently, mesmerised by this performance, never flinching or betraying the way they felt. Only Joanna showed signs of agitation. Voyeurism was something she had never experienced before, and she found it tremendously arousing. Her blood coursed through her veins to converge in her breasts and her pelvis, making her hot and wanton. Every time the *salary-man* dared to do something forbidden, Joanna shifted in her seat in anticipation of the forthcoming strike, which made her feel even more wicked.

The woman set her foot back on the floor and stood in front of her slave, legs parted. The man remained still, as if hypnotised by the enormous mound of hair now just inches from his face. She grabbed him by his hair and pulled his head towards her waiting flesh. His eyes closed in fervour as he stuck out his tongue readily. Without further ado, he frantically rubbed his face over her silken mound, grunting loudly as he let his tongue trail all over it. He bent down even further, setting his hands on the floor for balance as he lapped endlessly.

At first, the woman didn't react, but soon her slave's eager caresses began to affect her visibly. Her pelvis slowly swayed and ground against his face. Her face betrayed the pleasure that swelled within her as he grew more enthusiastic with each passing second. When his hands finally came up to grab her thighs and pull her even closer to his mouth, she didn't try to stop him.

Yet that was all she would let him do. When his hand strayed and he grabbed his own stiff phallus, the woman noticed immediately and mercilessly lashed him until he let go. He remained docile for a while, but she once again had to stop him a little later when he tried to reach up and touch her generous breasts.

Although the woman seemed keenly aware of the possibility that her slave might try to stray again, that didn't stop her from enjoying herself. Her breath soon grew shallow and she whined repeatedly. Her hips swayed majestically, her round buttocks contracting as she thrust towards her slave's mouth, her thighs trembling under the strength of the pleasure gathering within her.

Joanna's throat was dry but she was unable to take her eyes away from them, too enthralled even to think about taking a sip of sake. In just a few seconds, she knew the woman would climax right in front of them, and she couldn't wait for that moment.

The woman's head jerked back and forth a few times, forcing her hair to come undone and fall all over her shoulders and breasts. At the same time, she began hitting her slave's bottom with the riding crop, each blow making him grunt both in pleasure and in pain. Even as her orgasm came, she didn't stop the thrashing. Down on all fours, his dick straight and engorged, the *salary-man* climaxed under the blows. He didn't have much time to recover, however.

The woman stepped back unexpectedly. The two attendants rushed forward to help the man on to his feet and lead him hurriedly out of the room. Staggering, the man needed considerable coaxing. As he walked away reluctantly, he kept his head turned, looking behind him as if unwilling to leave just yet, perhaps even hoping for more. But already the Spaniard had donned her kimono and returned to sit at the table. As she took her place and the door of the room closed shut behind the *salary-man*, everyone round the table broke into a round of applause. She blushed and bowed modestly.

Joanna was flabbergasted. Thousands of thoughts flashed through her head, and she was dying to ask what that was all about. Was it real or just a cleverly constructed play? She didn't have time to ask, however. The gong resonated again and another man, looking just as scared but excited as the first, appeared in the doorway. This time another woman, tall, blond and vaguely Swedish looking, stood up and went to him. This one was younger, probably in her late twenties, but she exuded a calm and a coolness that led Joanna to believe that she had just as much experience in the field of domination as the Spaniard did.

Somehow, Joanna expected a repeat performance of what she had just witnessed, but when the kimono fell around the woman's ankles, she knew she was wrong. Underneath, the girl was dressed in leather from head to toe. Her body was just as slender as it was tall. The *salary-man*, shorter than the previous one, barely reached her armpits.

As he stared, his eyes bulging and unblinking, the girl pulled on two zippers circling her breasts. To Joanna's amazement, the leather cups fell to the floor and revealed small but perfectly rounded breasts, each adorned by a pale, erect and pierced nipple. The girl wriggled her shoulders, making her breasts wobble and the rings dangle insolently in front of the man's face.

Only then did Joanna notice his hands were tied behind his back. Obediently, he stuck out his tongue. He knew what to do and not a word was exchanged. The woman continued twisting her shoulders and guided the tip of her breasts over his mouth. She swayed in a slow, lascivious motion, using his lips and tongue to caress herself.

Unwittingly, Joanna echoed the motion, moving her shoulders in tempo with the girl's, as if she also had a man's mouth to abuse. She realised what she was doing and suddenly stopped. A bit embarrassed, she looked at Torima. He was looking at her and had plainly seen what she was doing, but he didn't say anything. He smiled, nodded, then turned his head to enjoy the show once again.

By now the girl had undone the *salary-man*'s trousers and pulled them down round his ankles. Under the hem of his white shirt his dick sprang out proudly, brushing against the tip of his tie.

An attendant brought a long slim chain. The woman wound it round her slave's prick, then slowly pulled on it so that it enveloped its length and rolled around it. The man shivered but didn't make any effort to pull away. The mistress and the slave held each other's gaze as she cruelly pulled on the chain. It unrolled from around his shaft at considerable speed, gliding along his skin seemingly without any friction.

Next, the girl passed the chain between the man's legs and tugged on it to make it glide back and forth. The man trembled at the knees and his erection seemed only the more prominent. Still standing in front of him, the girl undid a long zip between her legs and swiftly displayed all her flesh. Her mound was bare, closely shaven, and Joanna felt her mouth go dry at the sight of it. It also bore a tattoo of jasmine blossoms, but this one was a full bush instead of a lone sprig.

With wickedly slow movements of her hands and hips, the girl inserted the chain inside her tunnel, link by link. Joanna shuddered at the thought, as if she could feel it herself. Once the chain was almost completely in, the girl twirled the few links that were still protruding and writhed as the chain inside her moved in reply.

She moaned as she slowly pulled it out again. The metal links reappeared, glistening and covered with her dew. The girl let the chain bunch up in her hand and used it to rub her slit, panting incessantly as she pleasured herself.

The *salary-man* was sweating profusely, licking his lips constantly as he watched. The girl's back arched as she climaxed with a loud cry that echoed round the room. Grabbing the chain, still slick with her juices, she rubbed it against the man's mouth, smiling naughtily as she watched the expression of bliss which instantly appeared on his face.

As she was taller, she had to look down at him. The expression on her face was one of sheer contempt. Without a word, she let the chain drop to the floor, grabbed his buttocks in both hands and brought his hips toward hers.

Throwing her leg around his waist, she impaled herself upon his dick and encouraged him to thrust. Holding on to him for support, she cried again and again as pleasure swept her. She held him firmly, never allowing him to stop thrusting. The man was exhausted. At times he nearly lost his balance as he had to support the woman, who was standing on one leg. But obviously he had no desire to stop. At one point, however, the girl decided she had had enough. She pulled away, quickly donned her kimono and returned to the table. Just as before, two attendants appeared who pulled up the *salary-man*'s trousers and ushered him out of the room. And, just as before, the man kept looking behind him in

135

silent protest, unwilling to leave having received so little satisfaction.

This man's exit was also followed by a round of applause. The session had been shorter than the previous one but just as intense. Joanna's palms were moist, and she could feel sweat trickling down her back. Her senses were ablaze, her heart pounding with excitement and her head spinning. Both scenes had been surreal, like a dream, yet there was no mistaking the effect they had on her.

After the applause died down, the lights were switched back on and more food was brought in. Conversations resumed as if nothing had happened. Still, no one deemed it necessary to talk to Joanna about what they had just witnessed.

As she settled back in her seat and tried to calm down, it took Joanna some time to realise that the new dishes were all phallic representations. There were mushrooms which had unmistakably been chosen for their shape, as well as long fat asparagus, whole cucumbers artistically carved and carrots whose rounded tips made them resemble a man's erect penis. The vegetables were arranged to stand upright, each accompanied by a couple of hard boiled eggs at the base, and laid on a bed of parsley to mimic pubic hair.

Even the sake cups had been taken away and replaced by another set. These cups were shaped like a phallic mushroom with a hole pierced in the glans, allowing the liquid to be sucked. Joanna remembered having seen these in a souvenir shop, but she thought they were meant as a joke and never would have believed anyone actually used them. But as she glanced round the table, she realised they were in fact *de rigueur* with her dining companions who thought nothing of sipping their drink in such a lewd fashion.

As they were brought in, the dishes were first presented to Joanna, who didn't quite know what was expected of her. The vast array of vegetables didn't look like a dish to eat, but rather an implement for her to put to other use. Looking round, she saw that the other guests were not paying much attention to her so she refrained from taking anything. She wasn't hungry any more. Her stomach was comfortably full and the new dishes being brought in weren't all that appetising so she didn't wish to sample them.

Her dinner companions, who had initially been so enthralled by the sight of her, wouldn't even glance in her direction any more, let alone talk to her. But Joanna no longer cared. In fact, she was quickly getting bored. After the excitement of the show, she was now in a lull, her heart having returned to its regular pace and her body numb after such a rush.

The only thing she was conscious of was the skilful massage still being administered by the two geishas. By now Joanna's body glowed with a faint sheen from the lotion applied everywhere. The girls' touch had turned into a more daring caress, their fingertips gently rubbing the inside of her legs and expertly flickering over her nipples to keep them erect. Joanna was aroused as a result. But rather than a violent hungry eagerness, what she felt was a mellow gently simmering heat.

Just as she settled back to continue relaxing, the lights went out and the gong resonated a third time. The door opened again and a large contraption was rolled in. Simultaneously, all eyes turned to look at Joanna.

She gasped in amazement as she watched a man being pushed forward on a mobile platform. Hanging by his wrists from some sort of rack, he was completely naked from the neck down. The only thing he wore was a leather mask which entirely covered his head save for his nose. There were zippers over his eyes and mouth. Those over his eyes were fastened, whereas the one over his mouth had been pulled open. There, an enormous rubber ball, held in place by a chain fastened behind his head, gagged him.

Despite his precarious position, the man was already erect. Joanna didn't need to see his face to know he was yet another *salary-man*, brought into this temple of lust

137

to serve as a willing slave. There was no way of knowing how he must have felt. Only his heaving chest betrayed his fear. For there was no way for him to know what would be coming next, but it was indeed very easy for Joanna to guess.

Torima turned to Joanna. 'Come,' he said as he held out his hand towards her. 'The time has come for you to show us what you are capable of.'

Joanna stood obediently and silently let him lead her to the middle of the room. Her heart pounded. Now she understood why everyone was staring at her: it was her turn to supply the entertainment. The thought both excited and horrified her at the same time. She would never know what to do. Yet the prospect was so enticing that she was willing to go along with anything they would ask of her.

Torima took her kimono and went back to the table. Now Joanna stood naked in front of her audience. Curiously, she didn't feel shame but pride, and she was wickedly pleased by the notion of providing the entertainment. Between her legs, her juices had collected and were now bathing the inside of her thighs. Her blood rushed to her abdomen and rekindled the heat of her arousal. She held the power.

Again she stared at the man, only now noticing his ankles were in shackles. At his feet, a whole panoply of torture devices had been left for her: nipple clamps, a whip, a riding crop, a large leather dildo, a vibrator, a chain and even a few contraptions she had never seen before. Instruments of pain and pleasure. The pleasure would be hers, naturally, and the pain for this faceless slave obediently waiting for her to have her way with him.

What was she to do? Anything she fancied, obviously. Judging from what the two other women had done earlier, Joanna guessed she had to torture her slave, leave him wanting more, never give him satisfaction. In the process, she was allowed – even expected – to take

138

as much pleasure as she could. The thought was overwhelmingly alluring.

Stepping on to the platform, she came closer to the man but didn't touch him. All the hair on his body had been removed, from his neck to his ankles. He was very muscular, trim and fit, and covered with jasmine-scented oil. Under his skin she could see his muscles play as he pulled in vain on his restraints. She set her hands flat on his chest and slowly let them glide down towards his abdomen. Surprised, the man fidgeted but didn't try to move away. Not that he could even if he wanted to.

Joanna felt elated. Not only could he not see what was happening, but she realised he probably couldn't hear anything either. Several of his senses had been numbed. He couldn't see, hear, touch or taste her. All he had left was the possibility of feeling what she was going to do to him, but there would be no way for him to see it coming. Every caress, no matter how rough or gentle, would be a surprise.

He was all hers, to tease, to torture, to toy with. This was better than anything she'd ever experienced. There would be no need for naughty conversation or elaborate seduction schemes. This one was already hers. He was at her mercy.

She felt his skin, amazingly soft, break into goose bumps under her fingertips as they approached his hairless pubis. At that moment she would have liked to see his eyes, know that he wanted her, read the fear and desire on his face. Yet she knew that her treatment would be more efficient, both frightening and arousing, if he couldn't see her.

Her hand ran upwards again and settled on his chest. Underneath, she could feel his heart pounding prodigiously hard and fast. In contrast, Joanna was now strangely calm, even amused. Swiftly, she reached down and picked up the two small metal clamps. Using only her tongue, she worried his nipples until they stood stiff and swollen. The man moaned under her caresses but a second later he cried out in pain as Joanna fastened the clamps in place. She stood back, silently watching him reel from the surprise.

His dick throbbed in the air, the shaft shaken by small spasms and the purplish head shedding tiny tears of excitement. Joanna was disappointed by its smallness, but she quickly dismissed it. Tonight her pleasure would come mostly out of domination.

Picking up a rod made of thick braided straw, she briskly slapped his thighs, concentrating mostly on the inside and gradually moving dangerously close to his sac which hung limp. Soon the man's skin rose in welts and Joanna had mercy on him. There would be time for more later.

Slowly, she crept up behind him, treading carefully so he wouldn't know she was there. His legs were parted wide, causing his buttocks to spread, making the puckered ring of his anus plainly visible. As quietly as she could, Joanna grabbed the whip and gauged the girth of its handle. As her fingers closed round it, a naughty thought rose in her mind and she couldn't resist it. Parting her legs wide, she pushed the handle deep inside her vagina, letting it stretch her mercilessly, wetting it with her own juices.

Although at first she had only meant to lubricate it, its rough caress was so pleasant that for a moment she almost forgot the task at hand. She pushed it in and out a few times, attempting to quell the hunger of her flesh. She sighed loudly, but soon grew weary. Besides, she didn't want to keep her slave waiting any longer.

Without any warning, she inserted the handle deep inside the man's arsehole. He bucked under the attack, letting out a strangled yelp, and thrust forward in a vain attempt to escape. The restraints held him back.

Joanna pushed the handle as deep as possible, then waited a moment to let her prey recover from the shock. Never letting go of the whip, she twirled it to tease the man's inside. She watched, mesmerised by the sight of his thighs tensing as she continued assaulting him.

Before long the man stopped reacting. No matter what Joanna did, his moans grew feeble and his body lethargic. Joanna was disappointed. She figured he probably needed constant, renewed and varied stimulation. Slowly, she pulled the handle out and let the whip fall to the floor. She stared at it as it lay limply, now no more threatening than the other implements, no longer of any use to her.

Her eyes paused on something unusual, a contraption made of several leather straps. As she picked it up, she realised it was a dildo with a harness, something for her to wear so she could pretend to be male, albeit from her slave's point of view.

She managed to put it on in a flash, amazed by how quickly she had worked out the proper way to wear it. Two large leather straps were worn over the shoulders, like braces, pressing against her swollen breasts and gently tickling her nipples. There was another strap, fastening round the waist and holding the large leather dildo right on top of her pubis. Finally, the last strap had to be slipped between her legs and fastened at the back. This was the part Joanna found by far the best feature of this weird contraption. Her flesh, now wet, swollen and unbelievably sensitive, was unceremoniously attacked by this last strap, providing her with exquisite torture every time she moved.

Her slave couldn't see what she was doing but, judging by the amount of sweat pearling on his back, he knew she would soon continue what she had started.

She positioned herself behind him, legs apart and solidly planted on the ground. Parting his arse-cheeks with her thumbs, she penetrated him with a swift movement of the hips, just as roughly as she had inserted the handle of the whip.

And, just as before, the man bucked under the attack. His reaction only served to fuel Joanna's excitement. She began thrusting immediately, powerfully, taking him like a man, her hands forcefully holding on to his hips.

Soon, she forgot her surroundings. The strap between

her legs rubbed sharply with every jab she gave and brought her closer to orgasm. The treatment she was inflicting on her willing slave, be it humiliating, painful, frightening or even pleasurable, brought her an immense high. She increased her momentum until she came, no longer willing to wait. She was the mistress, she was owed pleasure and she wanted it now.

Her belly was slick with the sweat trickling down the man's back. In her grasp, he was now as limp as a rag doll, having ceased to resist and simply given in to her desire. Yet now and again she could feel him twitch as she withdrew, pulling out until the tip of dildo almost fell out of its target. But every time she pushed in again there was a certain point at which her slave's arousal seemed to be enhanced. Despite the cavalier treatment he had endured at her hands, he was still fully erect, perhaps even more excited than before.

But as her orgasm swept her and subsided, Joanna was exhausted. Her position was not comfortable; her knees had grown weak and wobbly. She pulled out completely, got rid of the cumbersome gear and knelt on the platform.

Her flesh clenched faintly and, although her climax had been quite powerful, Joanna knew this would not be enough for her. She wanted more, as soon as possible. But she wouldn't allow the man any satisfaction.

Down on all fours, she slowly made her way around the platform until she came to kneel in front of him. Inches from her face, his stiff prick was offered to her contemplation. Although fully erect, it hadn't grown much bigger than its resting state. His balls had hardened and his sac was tighter. It wouldn't take much to make him come.

Just as she pondered what to do next, one of the attendants came up to her and handed her a velvet pouch. Joanna opened it and fished out something that was perhaps the most appropriate answer.

It was a penile sheath carved out of ivory: a latticed, hollow tube topped with a glans. Joanna immediately recognised its potential and couldn't wait to try it. Her exhaustion quickly vanished as she found herself fretfully excited.

She picked up one of the rings that lay amongst the panoply of torture devices and slipped it round the man's stiff rod. This way, she could be sure he would maintain his erection. The hollow tube fitted perfectly over the man's shaft, tight enough to stay in place but loose enough not to afford him any unwanted stimulation. She stared at it for a moment, admiring the contrast between the ivory lattice and the dark, purplish skin visible through the small, carved-out holes.

She rose to her feet and, just like the tall girl before her, threw her leg around her slave's waist. Her fingers quickly guided his covered phallus towards her eager flesh and she impaled herself upon it. Its intricate pattern tickled delightfully and she moaned loudly as it filled her.

The man didn't move. His face was just an inch from her chest, for she was much taller than him. However, blindfolded and gagged, there was nothing he could do to her. Holding on to his shoulders for balance, Joanna bounced on one leg, letting out a small cry each time the ivory-covered member penetrated and stretched her tunnel. She held on for as long as she could, feeling the muscles in her legs burn as a result of exhaustion and extreme arousal. For it was there, deep inside her thighs, that pleasure was born before it rose to her pelvis.

Her arousal peaked and she came again. This time there was no reaction from her slave. Pleasure was hers, and hers alone. It pierced her like a bolt, sending shock waves through her abdomen, rampaging through her entire body, making her toes curl and her hands clench violently around the man's shoulders.

Even more exhilarating was the notion that the man took absolutely no satisfaction. He was a faceless stranger and would remain so, a body offered for her sole benefit. She kept on going for a while, wanting more, much more. When she grew tired, she pulled away, changed legs, repositioned herself and resumed her bouncing. Pleasure rose and subsided, then gathered again in an endless series of orgasms. For the first time in many months, if not years, Joanna Wilson finally felt entirely satisfied.

She was hot, sore, out of breath, but filled with such contentment that she couldn't even believe it herself. Now the man held absolutely no interest for her. She had taken what she wanted; she had no need for him. She moved away, turned her back on him, and slowly walked back towards the table. She knew the attendants would take care of him. Her dinner companions broke into a loud round of applause. Just like the women who had performed before her, Joanna couldn't help blushing modestly.

Its roar brought her back to reality. She didn't need to look behind her to know the man was being wheeled out of the room; she didn't need to see his face to guess he was probably completely bewildered by her sudden lack of interest. Was he happy about what had just happened? Frustrated? Angry? It didn't matter, at least not to Joanna.

'You did very well,' Torima finally said as he threw the kimono over her shoulders.

Joanna knelt at the table, next to him. To her surprise, most of the guests stood up and left the room. Dinner was over, and Joanna found herself alone with her host and two other Japanese men, one of whom was the stranger from the bar.

'We are very pleased with you,' Torima continued. Whereas up till now he had hardly said anything to her, now he seemed unwilling to remain silent. 'The men who come to us are looking for a very special woman, very domineering, very cruel. It's not always easy for us to recruit candidates who will so perfectly fulfil their fantasies of submission.'

So, this is what the place is all about, Joanna realised. Not that it was much of a surprise. The men who had been brought into the room tonight were looking for a kick. She knew that the average *salary-man* was used to his woman – be it girlfriend or wife – being docile and submissive. For them, the ultimate thrill lay in the exchange of roles.

'I never thought I had it in me,' she confessed in an exhausted voice. Now that her host seemed much more talkative, Joanna felt relief that she could finally pour her heart out. 'I have to admit I enjoyed this tremendously. Most of the men I know need much more convincing, more coercing, and I never feel they are entirely at my mercy.'

She stopped to catch her breath and swallowed a large gulp of sake. The men were still looking at her, their eyes and their smiles encouraging her to keep talking.

'Recently,' she said as the alcohol started coursing through her veins and put her in a confident mood, 'there was this man at the conference, some bloke from Texas. I wanted so much to seduce him, but he didn't seem at all interested. It's been very annoying. I needed what happened tonight to relieve this frustration.'

The men didn't reply but looked at one another in such a way that Joanna suspected they were exchanging some silent message. Before she could ask what that look meant, Torima spoke again.

'We are very pleased with you,' he repeated. 'When you first contacted us, we were very sceptical about your abilities. On your previous trips to Japan, we were told by our observers that you were more the quiet quaint type. You seemed to be so shy and withdrawn, we doubted you were capable of domination. I suppose, as they say, that still waters really do run deep.'

'Me? Shy and withdrawn?' Joanna laughed incredulously. 'That's something I've never heard before! And what on earth are you talking about? My last trips to Japan date back many years, and I was never here for very long. And I most certainly never contacted you!'

'You most certainly did, Miss Parsons,' Torima countered. 'We still have the letter and – '

'I am not Stacey Parsons!' Joanna interrupted

145

impatiently. She realised she had raised her voice and took a deep breath to calm herself down. 'Ever since I arrived here I've been mistaken for her and, quite frankly, I'm getting fed up with it!'

The men looked at one another with puzzled expressions. Somehow, Joanna felt them stiffen, as if instinctively distancing themselves from her.

'But aren't you the representative for International Emporium plc, based in south-west London?' Torima asked cautiously.

'Yes,' Joanna answered with a tinge of condescension. 'But Stacey resigned three days before she was due to leave, and I filled in at such short notice.'

Once again, the men all looked at one another.

'There's been a mistake,' Torima finally said. 'We had agreed with Miss Parsons that we would keep track of her via the name of your company. We weren't aware there had been a change.'

Suddenly, everything became clear to Joanna. All this time, they had thought she was Stacey. All the mysterious messages weren't meant for her at all. Somehow, a while back, Stacey had started something she obviously couldn't pursue. Were these people the reason why she had resigned? Had she chickened out at the last minute, unsure of whether she could take on the role that would be expected of her? Yet she must have known that her replacement would be sent straight into some kind of trap.

Stacey had explained that personal reasons had motivated her resignation. At the time, Joanna had assumed there was something holding her back in London. But in the light of what she had just heard, it might very well have been that those 'personal reasons' were right here in this room, and resigning was the only way she could avoid them.

The men started talking among themselves in Japanese. Lost in her thoughts Joanna didn't pay attention to what they were saying. All she noticed was that they

146

were talking very fast and often not loud enough for her to understand.

Finally, after what sounded like an argument, the stranger from the bar said something which obviously pleased the others tremendously. One of the men jumped to his feet and promptly left the room. Torima turned to Joanna.

'We do not normally invite someone to join our group this way,' he said. 'Traditionally, it is a much longer process. However, having seen what an outstanding asset you could be to us, we have decided to waive the preliminary tests and waiting period, both of which Miss Parsons had fulfilled.'

Joanna looked at them blankly. Was that his way of telling her everything was fine?

'You must, however, submit to at least one other entry requirement. Usually, this comes before the final test, which you passed superbly this evening, but we will make an exception in your case.'

Joanna nodded faintly. After what she had been through tonight, she was more than willing to go along with anything they asked of her. If it meant never having to work at seducing anyone, to derive pleasure out of cruelly torturing willing victims, she was ready for anything. Already the man who had left the room was returning and bringing back with him several sheets of paper.

'Here is what we want from you,' Torima said. 'If you pass this final test you will be allowed to become part of our group. Otherwise, you will never hear from us again. Do you understand?'

Joanna nodded again. Her heart pounded. What was he going to ask of her? Was there any chance of failure?

'Earlier, you mentioned there was a man attending the conference, an American from Texas, I believe.'

Joanna kept nodding, puzzled as to why he would mention Steve.

'We want you to seduce him,' Torima said bluntly. 'From what you have said, it has so far proved to be a rather difficult task, if not impossible. We want to see how good you can be once you set your mind to it. Get the man to make love to you, without using any deceptive tricks, drugs or anything of that sort, and we will deem you to have succeeded.'

Joanna didn't reply at first. What a wicked plan it was. But what a waste of time and effort for her. After what she had just been through, she didn't want Steve any more. Trying to seduce him would be a step backwards. Now that she knew what it was like to have someone submit to be tortured, toyed with, dominated by her, Steve held no interest for Joanna. He would be too much work. But could she get out of the challenge her host had set up for her? How cruel of them to let her see what a joy total, unconditional domination could be, only to be kept from the opportunity of further enjoyment because of some traditional rules and stupid tests.

On the other hand, what Joanna had experienced tonight was beyond belief, and she was ready to do anything for a chance to become part of their group. Unless she found a way to make them change their mind, or at least give her a less daunting task. First of all, she had no idea where Steve and Greta would be by now, and her previous attempts had been so futile she doubted she could, even out of desperation, be more successful this time round. Besides, how long would it take just to track him down? But even as the thought rose in her mind, she saw it was in fact her way out.

'What you are asking me is impossible,' she said, trying to sound calm and collected. 'I have no idea where the man is by now. For all I know, he could very well be on his way back to America.'

Torima smiled, grabbed the papers out of his companion's hands and gave them to Joanna.

'We know where he is,' he said smugly. 'Here is his itinerary. Your paths will cross again next Thursday when you arrive in Osaka. The two of you will be staying at the same hotel for 48 hours. That should give you plenty of time to seduce him. If you fail, you will never hear from us again. But if you are successful, you will be officially invited to join us if you please.'

A young man came in, carrying a large green bottle on a tray which he left in front of her host. Joanna barely paid any attention, however. These men knew she was due to bump into Steve again. Whatever this organisation was, it was obviously one step ahead of her.

'How will you know whether I have succeeded?' she asked suspiciously.

'We will, do not worry,' Torima replied as he poured a beige liquid into a crystal goblet. 'Have some plum liqueur, it will help you relax.'

Joanna shook her head. The last thing she needed at this moment was more alcohol. She had three days to come up with some way to seduce Steve. Every minute counted, and she couldn't let anything cloud her judgement.

'If you don't mind, I'd like to go now,' she said simply.

'Very well,' Torima said as he slowly rose to his feet. 'You will understand, however, that we will need to blindfold you for the journey back. We cannot reveal to you the location of this building just yet.'

Joanna followed him silently. Her clothes were given back to her, and she was left to dress in private. At this point, however, it didn't make much of a difference.

Part Three

Chapter Fourteen

*J*oanna was surprised to wake up so late the next morning. The combination of constant extreme excitement and the amount of alcohol she had drunk had taken its toll on her. As her mind mulled over the events of the previous night, for a moment she wondered if it had all been a dream. She couldn't even explain it to herself. But when her eyes fell upon the papers she had left on the table by the window, she knew it had all been real.

Dragging herself out of bed, she went to fetch the thin pile and quickly glanced at Steve's itinerary. It wasn't all that different from hers, and she quickly recognised the places and times when they had met. Their paths had in fact crossed on another occasion, and she hadn't even known it. Way back in Tokyo, after the conference, he had been invited to the same cooking demonstration as she had, although at a different time.

As she mechanically turned a page, she noticed something that suddenly jogged her memory: the evening foreign delegates had been taken to an inn outside the city. She had the same entry on her papers, only here the name of the place was actually indicated: Jasmine Blossoms.

The image in her head took a clearer form. No wonder

the sign looked familiar back then: the lettering was the same as on the cards she had been receiving, and it was the same pale green on pink background. Of course, it must be Torima's place! The more she thought about it, the more convinced she became that it was indeed the same building where she had been taken the previous night.

And, judging by how long it had taken to get there, it was probably located somewhere between here and Tokyo. It was a pity she hadn't paid attention to where they were going that night. Of course, as far as Joanna was concerned, it was all Greta's fault. The New Yorker's high-pitched voice had annoyed and distracted Joanna, and she had often closed her eyes in an attempt to tune out.

And last night, Torima had blindfolded her. But Joanna now knew where to find them, by simple deduction. It was all a bit too easy, in a way. Did they really think she was that stupid? She was a step ahead of them, and she felt confident she would soon devise a plan to turn this to her advantage.

She quickly slipped on the dress that lay in a heap at the foot of her bed, not even taking the time to put on her knickers first. That was the least of her concerns. Storming out of her room, papers in hand, she decided the lift would be too slow and practically ran down the flight of stairs to the front desk.

In the foyer, a group of tourists had just arrived and were dragging their luggage towards the counter. Joanna rushed forward and managed to get there first, congratulating herself for having avoided the queue.

'Can you help me?' she asked, still out of breath, as she shoved the papers in the clerk's face. 'I need to find the address for this place.'

The woman stepped back, smiled and took a second to see exactly what Joanna was pointing to.

'Jasmine Blossoms?' she asked with only a faint trace of an accent. 'What is it?'

'Some sort of banqueting place, an inn,' Joanna

replied. She couldn't exactly tell what the place was, if indeed it had any other purpose than the rituals to which she had been initiated the previous night. 'I think it's about halfway between here and Tokyo.'

The woman shook her head. 'I have never heard of it,' she said as she turned to another clerk, an older man who had just come to join her behind the counter. Showing him the paper, she addressed him in Japanese. She spoke fast but Joanna managed to understand a few words like 'rural', 'unknown' and 'private'. After shaking their heads at each other, both clerks came back to her.

'We don't know any such place,' the male clerk said. 'Are you sure about the name? It's very unusual to find inns or restaurants with English names outside of the major cities. I'm sure I would remember.'

'It was right there, in big letters, on a panel,' Joanna stated. 'I saw it with my own eyes.'

'It could have been a private home,' the woman replied. 'In that case we wouldn't be able to help you.'

'It was a large building,' Joanna explained. 'All on one floor, but with a lot of rooms, banqueting halls, all connecting and separated with sliding panels made of rice paper.'

Both clerks laughed softly and looked at her rather condescendingly. 'That could be just about anywhere,' the man said.

'We were entertained by geishas singing,' Joanna continued. 'There was jasmine everywhere, in every room. The building itself was in the country, in the woods and . . .'

The man interrupted her. 'We have no idea where this could be,' he said. This time his voice betrayed his impatience and for a moment Joanna felt as though he might have been able to help her out but simply didn't want to. Already both clerks had turned to the people waiting in line behind Joanna, no longer paying attention to her.

She took her papers and sheepishly made her way

back to her room, now realising her chances of finding the place on her own were very slim. Besides, there was always the possibility that the sign had been put up that night for her benefit. Naturally, if she had been Stacey, she would have picked up the clue, which perhaps was what they had been aiming at.

A moment ago, she was ready to go out and find them. Now she was on the verge of giving up. At first glance, it had seemed like a good idea, but she wasn't so sure any more. The same was true about their plan to have her seduce Steve. The more she pondered it, the more daunting it seemed.

In the lift, she leant against the wall and bowed her head in disappointment. The papers were now crumpled in her hands and she stared at them absent-mindedly. If she chose to give it a try, she knew the challenge would be great. Her work would most likely suffer because of it. She was on the last leg of her tour of Japan and she would have to e-mail her last report in just a few days. She wouldn't have much to say if she let herself be side-tracked by such a crazy venture.

But as she once again read the entry of their visit to Jasmine Blossoms, she remembered how the two geishas had caressed and teased her and how good she had felt. Now she was sure it was the same place she had been the previous night. The inn probably filled two purposes: to provide Japanese men with the excitement they craved, and the perfect place to invite foreign women and put them through some sort of screening process.

Her thighs rubbed lightly as she walked along the corridor to her room. Common sense told her to drop the whole idea. Yet at the same time, the tingle now growing amidst the folds of her sex was unmistakable. If she managed to seduce Steve, she would win on two counts. First, she would gain the personal satisfaction of having him. After that, she would be invited back to the Jasmine Blossoms inn, wherever and whatever it was, and from then on she knew her life would change forever.

She closed the door of her bedroom behind her and leant against it. Just thinking about Steve had made her wet again, and her heart pounded at the thought of him arriving to stay at the same hotel in just a couple of days.

What would she do with him? Would he be submissive, like those *salary-men* she had seen the previous night? Or would she be in for a night of passion, where each of them would demand to be pleasured, and then oblige in submitting to the other?

The thought of being in control was terribly arousing. And she knew she would be if she succeeded. But at the moment, 'they' were the ones in control. And she didn't like it at all.

Chapter Fifteen

*B*eing aware of Steve's arrival before he even set foot in the hotel was a nice change for Joanna. Knowing his whereabouts gave her the edge she needed to put her plan into action. This time, she just wouldn't give up. She would act surprised to see him, naturally, and at the same time find a way to get rid of Greta. Once the Valkyrie was out of the picture, Joanna would go for the kill.

Unfortunately, she hadn't worked out the fine details of that part. She would have to trust her instincts. For one thing, she already knew talking about her underwear was futile. It hadn't worked the last time and on second thought it was rather childish, to say the least. She would need something either much more subtle so that the poor man wouldn't know what hit him, or something much more direct so there would be no mistaking her intentions.

Somehow she doubted the latter was the best approach. There was always the possibility that Steve would refuse her invitation, no matter how blatantly she issued it. There was always the chance that whatever was going on between him and Greta had developed, and if he were the faithful type that would leave Joanna out in the cold.

Her heart jumped when she saw him walking casually round the stalls. This food fair was in no way comparable with the one they had attended in Tokyo, and for that Joanna was grateful. Sushi and ramen noodles were already popular in the UK and she had no interest in them. The rest of the stuff on display was boring, and there was absolutely nothing new for her to sink her teeth into.

That would allow her to concentrate all her energies on Steve. She pretended not to see him as he walked in her direction, but she couldn't help noticing that he was alone. Where had he left Greta? Could she be just a few feet behind, or had he left her in another city? Even better: could she be on her way back to New York?

Joanna now realised that if the people from Jasmine Blossoms were informed of her whereabouts and Steve's, they probably also knew about Greta's. She should have asked them, she realised. But of course it was too late now. She cursed herself for not having thought of it, but a moment later she also realised she would know soon enough anyway.

As Steve stopped by the stall where Joanna was standing, she made a point of engaging the hostess in a loud and complicated conversation about different types of seaweed.

That morning, she had carefully thought out all the details. She had chosen to wear something simple but revealing: a pair of flared hipster gabardine trousers in a funky shade of electric blue that revealed her taut stomach and tiny belly button. Her white satin top was tied in a loose knot between her breasts. Underneath, her bare breasts bobbed slightly as she walked. Her erect nipples were only faintly visible from a distance, but much more so if the onlooker came closer. And if the onlooker was Steve, the man responsible for her near-permanent state of arousal, the effect on them could only be greatly enhanced.

She knew she had scored points when his voice resounded in her ears.

'Joanna! What a lovely surprise!'

She briefly smiled at him but finished her conversation with the hostess before turning to him.

'Hello Steve. How have you been? And how is Greta? Is she around?'

'Oh, she's around, somewhere,' he answered vaguely.

'Are you staying until tomorrow evening?'

'Saturday morning, actually. After that I'm off to the Philippines.'

'I see. Well, it was nice seeing you again. I'll be seeing you around, I'm sure.'

Before he had time to reply, she flashed him another brief smile, turned round and walked away.

Good, she thought as she made her way to the foyer. At least he had seen her, and he was the one who had come to her. It was much better than having been ignored, as she had been before, and she saw it as a good omen.

Tonight would be the night, Joanna had decided. Not that she had much choice in the matter: tomorrow would be the last time she saw Steve, if indeed he stayed until the end of the conference.

As she walked round the bar, she demurely returned all the smiles cast her way. She had a suspicion that one of these men was there to spy on her and, not knowing exactly who it was, she had to treat everyone with superlative cordiality.

As soon as she spotted Steve, she slumped casually in a soft leather-covered armchair, making sure she was within his field of vision. Just like the other night, the table by her side was loaded with bowls containing an assortment of nuts, crispy chick peas, sesame sticks and salted watermelon seeds. Joanna saw this as a good sign, knowing food was one of Steve's weaknesses.

He looked towards her and waved. Joanna feigned surprise, returned his greeting, but didn't make any move to betray how badly she wanted to go to him. She settled in her seat, crossed her slender legs and held them tightly closed. She had decided not to wear anything underneath her slinky, shiny red dress. She knew he would notice. Men always noticed the absence of panty lines. It kept them guessing whether the lady had anything under her clothes or if it simply didn't show. In that respect, if Steve was just like any other man, he too would surely wonder.

And, for Joanna, it felt tremendously naughty. The tight fabric hugged her figure perfectly and lightly rubbed against her bare buttocks as she moved. The notion of being so exposed excited her, and she knew this heightened state of arousal was just what she needed to embolden her seduction scheme. She knew there was nothing more irresistible to a man than a woman who was hot for him and wasn't afraid to let it show.

Steve was standing near the bar, surrounded by three women. Joanna couldn't help but think how handsome he looked tonight, as usual. His white cotton shirt was slightly wrinkled, the top button undone and his tie loosened. Again tonight, his rolled up sleeves gave her a good view of his arms, the arms she couldn't wait to find herself in.

Greta was still nowhere in sight. The three women, all Westerners, were vying for his attention, endlessly smiling at him, occasionally touching his arm as they addressed him, even echoing his gestures by mimicking his stance whilst subtly closing in on him.

Joanna observed the scene from afar. She couldn't believe how blatant these women were, at times even elbowing one another in some nasty competition to get near him. If only they paid attention to the expression on his face, they would back off right away. For Steve didn't seem at all flattered by this excess of attention. He stood tall and aloof, his arms tightly crossed over his chest in a silent defensive stance. It was clear that he was barely listening to them. All three women talked at the same time, trying to keep him interested but not taking any cues from his vague replies and lack of eye contact.

In fact, his eyes were everywhere but on the women around him. At some point, he even turned his back to them to address the waiter. Now and again, he also looked at Joanna, and for a moment she felt perhaps he wanted to come over and talk to her instead.

As the waiter handed him a drink, he broke free of his female admirers and walked towards Joanna. This was exactly what she had hoped for and she had to bite her lip to stop her smile of satisfaction from becoming too obvious. She watched and sank back into her seat as he approached. Now she had seen that a direct attack didn't have much of an effect on him and she knew she had to remain detached and let him do the chasing.

Yet her victory was short lived. Just as she thought Steve was about to fall into her web she watched, incredulous, as he suddenly noticed a group of men a little further away and headed straight over to join them.

It was only natural, Joanna reasoned. Having spent the past few days in Greta's company, and the last half-hour surrounded by overbearing females, he probably needed some breathing space. But something was telling her he would come back to her eventually. Just as his lack of interest had fuelled her desire to be with him, she knew that the reverse was also true. He would come over and talk to her, if only because she hadn't manifested any interest. In the meantime, she couldn't let him see her disappointment. Rather, she nodded at him as he passed her and pretended to continue her nonchalant observation of the crowd around the bar.

Several people tried to engage her in conversation, but although she made a supreme effort to remain polite, she didn't invite anyone to join her. She had to be alone for when Steve came to talk to her. She knew he would; it was only a matter of time. Also, since she was within earshot of the group with which he was now standing, she suspected that some serious eavesdropping couldn't hurt. Maybe he would say something useful to help her devise a plan. Now that she knew how subtle she had to be, she needed more ammunition if she was to make him fall for her tonight.

From the moment she started paying attention, the answer came to her.

'It was indeed delicious,' one of the men said with a heavy Italian accent. 'I never thought the Japanese had so many different ways of preparing squid.'

'I don't care much for squid myself,' said another one. 'But I really appreciated the whole package.'

The conversation veered towards marketing strategies, but Steve managed to get it back to the topic of food. What they were discussing was the freebie, a box full of seafood and other delicacies that several delegates had received. Joanna had been told by the hotel manager that such a box was waiting for her in the refrigerator, but she had elected not to check it out. And now she was glad she hadn't.

Judging from the way Steve kept referring to the food and asking endless questions about it, it was clear that he hadn't received anything and perhaps even resented the omission. Joanna saw this as her opportunity. In her mind, the old-fashioned advice still rang true: the way to man's heart was indeed through his stomach. She had something Steve wanted: samples of exquisite food. That would be her bargaining chip.

Soon enough, the topic of conversation changed again and Steve remained silent. Joanna didn't even have to look at him to guess what would be going on in his head. Without having to do anything, her plan was already in motion, and she knew it was foolproof. A moment later, she wasn't surprised to see him slump in the armchair next to hers.

'I'm hungry,' he said in a sombre voice.

'Are you really?' Joanna replied casually as she pointed towards the snacks on the table. 'Help yourself.'

Steve winced and shook his head disdainfully, but after a moment he reached out and grabbed a handful

163

of crispy chick peas. He tasted a couple, winced again and put the rest back into the bowl.

Joanna was a bit annoyed by such rude behaviour, but she wasn't going to let that stop her. 'I feel like I've been force-fed lately,' she said. 'I'm afraid it will take weeks before I remember what hunger feels like!' She was trying very hard to find something clever to say, but every time Steve was near her it seemed the effect he had on her reduced her intelligence to that of a sea slug. Yet as long as she could get a conversation going, she knew she could soon turn it to her advantage.

'Well, for the past twenty minutes I've been talking to these guys about food,' Steve replied without looking at her. 'Now that's all I have on my mind!'

'And here's me thinking men only ever had sex on their minds!' Joanna laughed.

'One is not all that different than the other, sometimes,' Steve stated in a low voice, as if talking to himself.

Joanna remained silent for a moment. Last time she had tried to steer the conversation towards sex, it hadn't been greeted by any outstanding demonstration of enthusiasm. If the man wanted to talk about food, she would gladly humour him.

'I'm at the point where I've been offered so much food,' she said, 'I'd have a hard time deciding for myself if I had to choose from a menu.'

'No problem for me,' Steve said as he stared blankly in front of him. 'I'd go for seafood or fruit. The only two things I never get tired of.'

'I see,' Joanna said casually. 'Then I suppose you must have been very pleased by the seafood packages from the Suzusha distributor?'

'Apparently I wasn't on their list,' Steve replied with a long sigh. He vaguely pointed to the men behind him. 'Those guys were. Some people have all the luck.'

'Lucky indeed, I agree.' Joanna said. 'Seems like they picked a few people at random from the list of delegates. I have no idea why I was on their list.'

Steve straightened up and looked at her, now suddenly interested. 'You received a package? You were lucky indeed. How was it?'

Now that she had managed to grab his attention, Joanna decided to make the most of it and dodged the question with laughter.

'My! You are indeed keen on this stuff. What is it about seafood that gets you this excited?'

For the man's behaviour had drastically changed: from wistful and listless, he was now giddy as a schoolboy, his eyes bright and his lips growing to dark crimson.

'I don't know,' he said excitedly. 'I've always had a fondness for marine life, especially of the edible variety. So, how was it?'

But Joanna wasn't ready to reply. 'But what about other food?' she asked. 'Don't you like juicy tender steaks? How about crisp vegetables with a hint of butter?'

'Yeah, give me food, any type of food, and I'll gladly eat it. But make it seafood and you've got a friend for life. Now, are you going to tell me what you had in your package or are you going to tease me like this forever?'

'Tease you? I wouldn't even dream of it! I just want to know what makes you tick, that's all. In our line of business, you know . . .'

Steve interrupted her impatiently. 'Will you just tell me, damn it!' Despite his abrupt tone, Joanna detected a hint of amusement in his voice. In his eyes, the bright sparkle told her he had perhaps had a bit too much to drink. A moment later, he was laughing frankly.

Now she knew she had him hooked. He was a bit tipsy, and that wouldn't hurt if she was to get him to lower his defences. And if just talking about the package and its probable contents had this effect on him, she couldn't wait to see how he would react to the bomb she was about to drop next.

'I can't tell you how it was,' she said quietly. 'I told

you I wasn't hungry. The package is still waiting for me in the refrigerator of the hotel's kitchen.'

Steve's eyes opened wide and Joanna watched as he swallowed nervously. 'You haven't touched it?' he asked in a trembling voice.

'No,' she said as she looked away. She was dying to ask him whether he wanted to join her for an impromptu feast, but she held back, waiting for him to suggest it instead.

'Do you plan to sample it anytime soon?' he asked cautiously.

'I don't know,' she lied. 'Do you think it would still be good?'

'I'm sure it'll be delicious!'

'No,' she laughed again. 'I meant: don't you think it will have spoilt by now?'

He took a moment before replying, probably trying hard to find a way to invite himself. 'There's only one way to find out,' he said finally.

Joanna played dumb. 'What do you mean?'

He chose his words carefully, but his tone was shaky as he blurted out his suggestion. 'Well, perhaps we could go retrieve your package and see what's in there, see if it's still good.'

'But once the box is open, we'll stand an even bigger chance of spoiling it!'

'Then we'll just have to eat it!' he stated triumphantly. 'How about it?'

Joanna counted to ten in her head. Now, all she had to do was take him to the kitchen, which would probably be crowded at this hour, so they would have to find somewhere else to do their tasting. Like in his room, for instance. This was too good to be true, she thought. Exactly as she had planned. The Suzusha company, whatever it was, would never know how appreciated their effort was. Joanna made a mental note to check them out later. Maybe her company could do business with them. That was the least she could do for them.

* * *

166

Steve stood with his back to the wall, silent and motionless but not missing any of the movements of the stewards as they unpacked the box.

Within minutes, a table had been set up in a small function room near the kitchen. Now it was loaded with cooked prawns, oysters in their opened shells on a bed of ice, and smoked mussels artistically displayed on shredded lettuce.

Joanna tried to look casual as she struggled to open a bottle of Californian chardonnay. A fine wine, the perfect match for the food they were about to taste. Not to mention that she needed to steady her nerves and get Steve to relax a bit more.

So far, she was very pleased with how easy it had been to lure him out of the bar. As soon as the food had arrived, she had immediately noticed his jeans bulging at the front. She was amazed by this sudden and unexpected reaction. The best aphrodisiac was the one that didn't even need to be consumed, obviously, for they had yet to take a single bite. After that, getting him into bed was just the next step. Tonight, it would be easy.

As Joanna looked around, she realised she wouldn't even need a bed. The function room was lavishly furnished and right next to the table there were a couple of small divans which looked very comfortable and which perfectly suited her purpose.

As soon as the stewards left, Steve locked the door behind them, took off his tie by pulling it over his head and tossed it on one of the divans. Rushing to the table, he quickly surveyed the goods on display, then closed his eyes and took a deep breath. By now, he seemed to have totally forgotten about Joanna.

She didn't mind, however. She would let him eat for a while, then get the second part of her plan in motion. Already she could hear him moaning as he slowly chewed a couple of mussels, the expression of bliss on his face dangerously reminiscent of that of sexual ecstasy.

His big fingers delicately seized a prawn by the tail and lightly dipped it in a pale orange sauce. Letting his head fall backwards, he stuck out his tongue and softly caught the juicy morsel which he kept in his mouth for a moment before chewing it.

It took him a little while to realise that Joanna wasn't eating. Standing next to him, she watched silently, content to refill both his glass and hers whenever needed. He stopped suddenly and looked at her as if he had just noticed her presence.

'Aren't you eating?'

'I prefer to watch,' she said as she refilled his glass for the third time. 'I've always been a bit of a voyeur.'

He didn't reply and kept on eating. This time, however, he made more of an effort to get her to join him.

'These are so nice,' he said as he grabbed a mussel with his chopsticks and brought it to her lips. Joanna couldn't care less about the food. It was nothing unusual, anyway. And it lacked the Japanese touch, as if the company wanted to show that it could adapt to the Western market by producing its own line of products similar to what had been in European shops for years.

But she ate the piece anyway, if only to humour him. Next came a prawn, which he fed her with his fingers. She grabbed his wrist to guide him, letting her fingertips slide sensuously along his forearm before pulling away.

If that didn't seem to move him whatsoever, the effect on her was like a bolt of lightning. The mere contact with his warm skin sent goose bumps down her chest which translated into a violent erection of her nipples.

Suddenly, she craved sex. She was ready for him and knew that holding back would be difficult. It took a tremendous effort to stay calm. She breathed deeply, increased her grip on her wine glass and forced herself to remain focused. It worked for a while, but then he came back towards her.

This time he was holding a half shell containing an oyster. He squeezed a few drops of lemon juice over it, cracked a little bit of pepper and held it level with her mouth.

'Rather run of the mill, isn't it? It lacks the Japanese flavour.'

'I was just thinking the same thing,' Joanna replied.

'But I'm sure it's delicious all the same.'

'I don't like oysters,' Joanna admitted. 'Can't swallow the viscous consistency.'

'I'm sure you've swallowed worse things,' Steve said matter of factly.

For a moment, Joanna thought the conversation would head for something more suggestive but, just like last time, Steve wasn't interested in talking about sex.

'Nothing worse than overcooked liver, in my opinion,' he explained. 'I'm sure you'll agree and, if your mother was anything like mine, you've probably had more than your share. Come on, now. Try this. They're great.'

His hand gently cupped Joanna's nape and he coaxed her into tilting her head back as she swallowed. Naturally, all she tasted was lemon and pepper, which didn't get exceptionally rave reviews from her taste-buds. However, the touch of his hand holding on to her head whilst his forearm circled her shoulders was enough to make her feel faint. His cologne was spicy and enticing. Curiously, she found the smell of alcohol on his breath was also very sexy. This was the closest she had ever found herself to being in his arms, and immediately she knew it was something she wouldn't readily relinquish.

But already he had pulled away, going back to the table to help himself to more food. Joanna watched from afar, now impressed by the vast array of clams, scallops, squid and other delicacies. After a moment, she made a connection in her mind as she remembered the many euphemisms the Japanese often used when talking about anatomy: shells, clams in particular, were a polite word for female body parts. Since she knew Steve had probably heard it before as well, there was the perfect way for her to steer the conversation to more lewd topics.

'Do you know what most Japanese men would think if you told them you've spent the best part of the evening sucking on clams?' she asked casually as she stepped closer to the table.

Steve grabbed a ball of sticky rice with his bare fingers and swallowed it in a large gulp, then took a sip of wine before replying.

'Yeah, I've heard that before,' he said as he sampled yet more mussels. 'These people sure have a way with words, don't they?'

'I wonder why they picked such words,' Joanna said. 'Is it simply because of the similarities in taste, or do they consider seafood an aphrodisiac?'

'Heaven only knows,' he said with his mouth full. 'From what I've heard, Japanese aphrodisiacs are made mostly from herbs and long things like your average rhinoceros horn.'

'Anything shaped like a dick, you mean?'

'Yeah. Sort of.'

As she talked, Joanna edged closer to the table. Discreetly, she glanced down towards Steve's crotch, sorry to see his erection had subsided. Obviously, she was on the wrong track. Words had no effect on him.

She grabbed the bottle of wine and refilled his glass, hoping more alcohol would help make him randy. He nodded his thanks, but didn't touch the glass. He seemed to be interested solely in food right now. Very well, Joanna thought. She could wait a little longer still. Soon enough, he would stop being hungry. Or he would finish off everything on the table. Whichever came first, it was only a matter of minutes.

She strolled away and went to sit on one of the small divans. The cushions were thick but soft and she found herself sinking in comfortably. Steve continued eating, not paying her any attention. Her hand cupped the rounded edge of the armrest and she absent-mindedly caressed it as she began fantasising.

Already she could imagine the two of them, sprawled over the divan, she with her breasts pulled out of her

170

cleavage and her dress hiked up above her hips, he with his trousers undone and pulled down to his knees. She would make sure he was comfortably seated, and then kneel between his parted leg to give him the best head he had ever had. After that, it would be his turn to kneel and pleasure her with his mouth. Finally, she would get up and kneel on the cushions, entice him to come behind her, then bend over the arm rest and have him take her from behind.

As her mind feverishly relayed these images, Joanna couldn't help but moan. Her clitoris was hard and swollen already; her flesh soaked so thoroughly she feared the moisture would follow the crevice between her buttocks and collect on her dress.

She got up and helped herself to more wine. She knew it was dangerous, she couldn't think straight if she were drunk, but she needed to feel the cool liquid flowing down the back of her throat in the vain hope that it would tame the fire now burning inside her loins.

Just as she had anticipated, Steven only stopped when there was practically no food left. He took his napkin, wiped his mouth daintily and gave a loud smack of satisfaction.

'That was great,' he said. 'Too bad you weren't hungry.'

'I'm glad you enjoyed it,' Joanna replied as she emptied what was left of the wine into his glass. 'Have you had enough?'

He patted his stomach. 'I'm full. I need to sit down.'

Without waiting for her to reply, he made his way to the divan where she had been sitting. Joanna waited a moment before following him, wanting to make sure she didn't look too eager.

She sat over her bent leg, turning her shoulders sideways to face him. Steve was slouching, his legs apart, and his head tilted back.

'I think I ate too much,' he grunted as he put his glass on the side table next to him. 'But it was well worth it, believe me.'

Joanna didn't reply. Some time earlier he had undone the first few of the buttons from his shirt. Now she could see the top of his chest, lightly covered in fine blond hair. She writhed involuntarily, impatient to rub her face against this soft carpet, eager to feel it over her own bare breasts.

She reached out and lightly patted his stomach. 'Are you satisfied, then?' she asked in a husky voice.

Steve closed his eyes and grunted again. Joanna pulled away slightly. What she really wanted to do was put her plan in motion. She longed to huddle next to him, to guide his hands exactly where she wanted them and to rub her body against his. But first she needed a sign, any sort of sign, that he wouldn't refuse her.

She came closer again, so close her nose practically touched his cheek. 'What else would you like right now?' she asked in a suggestive whisper.

Steve stirred lightly and opened one eye. 'Huh?'

One look was enough to convince Joanna she would have to work harder. Content and quite drunk, Steve was about to fall asleep. Slowly, she slipped her hand inside the opening of his shirt and caressed his chest.

Just as she had thought, it was incredibly warm and soft. The heat of his skin travelled up her arm and sent a tingle to her nipples. Twisting her shoulders, she brushed her breasts against his hard biceps. His elbow was rather pointy and was the perfect thing with which to tease her nipples. Her mouth fastened on his neck and she nuzzled him for a while.

Steve didn't seem to react, but didn't protest either. Daringly, Joanna let her hand glide down his abdomen, lightly fingering his belly button before venturing further. When she noticed he had undone his belt and the button of his trousers, she couldn't believe her luck. Naturally, he had just eaten like a pig and probably needed to undo his belt to feel better, but for Joanna it was more than she could have expected.

Her fingertips slowly glided under the waistband of his trousers, losing themselves in the forest of his pubis.

Her other hand had cupped his head and guided it towards her hungry mouth.

As she writhed on the divan, her dress rode up her thighs and now the fine curls of her mound, drenched and glistening with her dew, were in plain view. All he had to do was reach out and touch her. Yet he seemed unwilling to do so. Joanna nibbled on his earlobe as her hand reached his flaccid prick and she gently tickled the base of his shaft with her fingertips.

Only then did he react. At first Joanna thought she heard him grunt. But as a series of similar sounds followed, all evenly spaced and constantly growing louder, she realised with horror that Steve was in fact snoring.

She pulled away suddenly, unable to believe that he could have fallen asleep as she was touching him so intimately. Even when her arm slipped out of his shirt and popped open another button in the process, he didn't even stir.

Silently, she examined him for a moment. His face was serene and still. He was as peaceful as she was excited. She was so taken aback it took her a moment to decide what to do. His breath now stank of alcohol, and Joanna cursed herself for having made him drink so much. She should have let him ask her if he wanted wine. He had never really asked for it, and he had already drunk quite a bit at the bar. She knew she didn't want him under these conditions; she would have him on her terms, and sober. As her hand casually fell on her bare thigh and lovingly rubbed it, she felt angry at herself and frustrated beyond belief.

Yet her arousal hadn't subsided. If anything, her anger only served to fuel it. Her flesh clenched repeatedly, now impatiently demanding its reward. In Joanna's mind, a wicked thought rose. Sitting with one leg on the floor, she brought the other up on the divan. As she bent her knees and parted her legs, her skirt rode up and immediately her sex was in plain view. Her vulva gaped and seeped its excitement. Its musky fragrance quickly rose and reached her flaring nostrils. With both hands, Joanna lovingly rubbed the inside of her thighs, teasing herself by constantly bringing them closer to her mound.

Her eyes were fixed on Steve. In a way, she was doing this for his benefit, like a stripper enticing a punter. But the touch of her own hands made her moan with delight and she couldn't stop at that. Reclining against the armrest, she reached inside her cleavage with both hands and pulled her breasts out. She lightly fondled the underside, amazed at how soft and fluid her skin felt. Her nipples had been so hard since she had arrived in the room that she was surprised Steve hadn't noticed them pushing against the fabric of her dress.

Even now, they were like small pebbles and so sensitive after having been kept prisoner all evening that the mere flick of her fingertips over them made her squeal with glee. Should Steve wake up, he would be treated to an incredible sight. But Joanna doubted he would. In any case, she no longer cared. She continued caressing her breasts with one hand as the other slowly glided down between her legs.

The folds of her flesh quivered as her hand settled on them and gently stroked up and down. She was incredibly wet, perhaps more so that she had ever been in her life. Her skin was fluid and hot under her fingertips, her bud hard and swollen. Her whole body craved quick release, and she didn't waste any time getting herself to the point of orgasm. She couldn't hold back any more.

She tried to withhold her cries of pleasure, undecided as to whether she wanted Steve to wake up or not. But soon pressure gathered round her pelvis and the fire of her forthcoming climax grew so strong that she couldn't stop herself moaning loudly. Having him so close, yet totally unaware of what she was doing, was extraordinarily stimulating. Now she wished he would wake up. He would definitely be enthralled by the sight of her quivering flesh, her fingers repeatedly delving inside her, her thumb forever circling her throbbing bud.

She came with a loud scream, a cry only echoed by

Steve's snores. Joanna remained still for while, now imagining what it would be like to have him wake up at that very moment. There was no doubt in her mind that he would be unable to resist her. Her climax subsided in a few aftershocks, but Joanna soon wanted more. This wasn't at all what she had expected from this evening. She was still wanton and filled with unsated desire for the man sleeping next to her.

She wanted to take her dress off, to rub her naked body against his and tease him until he woke up. Yet he seemed to be a sound sleeper. As she continued fantasising, she mindlessly fingered her slit, her whole hand now slick with her own juices. She was hot for him and he had absolutely no idea. It would be easy to slowly undress him and caress his chest with both hands as she had been wanting to. And it would be just as easy to get the gorgeous prick she longed to feel inside her out of his pants. For there was no doubt in Joanna's mind that Steve's member was nothing short of magnificent.

He was deeply asleep, but even then Joanna knew she would find a way to tease and coax him into suitable hardness. She was good with both her hands and her mouth. Besides, she had done it before. Her fingers itched to glide inside the opening of his jeans. Reaching towards him, she set her moist hand on his leg and lasciviously let it ride up. Her fingertips touched the zipper of his jeans and she tugged on it a couple of times.

But at the last minute, Torima's instructions came back to haunt her. The man had been very clear: she had to seduce Steve without using any tricks. And taking him as he slept was exactly that. So, no matter what she managed to get out of the Texan, it wouldn't get her any closer to joining Torima's group.

She pondered the dilemma for a while. Part of her wanted to send Torima and his sidekicks to hell. This evening, she'd be happy just to have Steve. She'd be vindicated, knowing that she had finally managed to have him. End of story. But as she took another look at him, she realised she didn't want him like that. She wanted him to take her as well. He had to come to her willingly, mad with lust and unable to resist her.

For a moment, Steve stirred languidly in his sleep. Joanna held her breath, her heart pounding with anticipation. Was he waking up? But when he turned around, curled up in a ball on the divan, and started snoring even louder, Joanna knew there was no hope of getting anything from him tonight. Even if he did wake up, he would be so groggy that it wouldn't even be enjoyable.

Totally discouraged, she got up, straightened her dress and looked at her watch. It was already past midnight. Without even one last look at Steve, she grabbed her handbag and left. So much for the perfect plan.

Chapter Sixteen

Somehow it didn't seem worth the effort any more. As she kept staring at her itinerary, Joanna felt dejected. Defeat was hard to swallow. In just a couple of days, she would be leaving Japan. Since she had failed to seduce Steve, the people from Jasmine Blossoms would not be in touch.

At least she had slept soundly and was ready to tackle this last day of the boring conference. A hot shower had cleared her mind but despite this calmness there was no mistaking the feeling of frustration from the fiasco of the previous evening.

Normally, this lack of fulfilment would have spurred her on, increased her determination to seduce the man who had remained so insensitive to her charms. There was still time, of course. There was always tonight. But her chances of getting anywhere with Steve were slimmer than ever. By now, he was probably back in his own bed, nursing a formidable hangover. Even if he came out of there eventually, there was no way of knowing what his mood would be.

Joanna got up and started throwing a few items of clothing in her suitcase. A moment later, she was interrupted by a knock on the door. Automatically she checked her appearance in the mirror. She hadn't had time to get dressed and was still wearing the pink and green kimono she had thrown on upon getting out of bed that morning.

At the time, she hadn't even thought about it, but now she was glad she had made such a choice. The combination of colours enhanced her skin tone and nicely complemented her blond hair which flowed freely on her shoulders. Her visitor would be greeted by a lovely vision.

The surprise was Joanna's, however, as she opened the door and found Greta waiting in the corridor. The woman had lost her flamboyance and stood with her head bowed, her face all red and drenched with tears.

'I'm so sorry,' she sobbed as she barged into the room. 'I haven't slept all night. I don't know who to turn to.'

Vaguely puzzled, Joanna hesitated before closing the door behind her. Greta had come in without even being invited, and immediately Joanna feared she would have a hard time getting rid of her. Yet this blatant sorrow was so out of character for Greta, whom Joanna had only ever seen cheerful and effervescent, that she couldn't help being curious as to the cause. Then she also remembered how it was practically impossible to shut her up, and how annoying the New Yorker could get after a while. Thankfully, she still had to pack, there was work to be done, and she wouldn't be lying if she used that as an excuse to get Greta to leave.

She watched as Greta strutted across the room. Again today the woman wore incredibly high spiky heels which made her hips wriggle with every step she took. Her red skirt, long and frilly, looked vaguely Spanish. Her blouse was some kind of cheap, slightly worn, crushed velvet in a shade of apple green which simply didn't match. Making herself at home, Greta collapsed on the bed and pulled out a couple of tissues from a box on the bedside table.

'It's Steve,' she sobbed as she wiped her eyes. 'I think it's over between us.'

Joanna sat on the other side of the bed and listened

without replying. Greta seemed truly heartbroken, and Joanna realised that obviously there was more going on between these two than just sex, at least on Greta's side.

'I thought he liked me,' Greta continued. 'At first, he was always all over me. When we met in Tokyo, we connected right away and it felt so right that I even resigned from my job because of him. I knew he wasn't due to head back to the States for a while, so I thought I could travel with him and help him with his work. He didn't seem to mind. But the more we travelled about, the more he lost interest. Then he started asking for separate rooms. I suspected perhaps there was somebody else, but who? We've been on the road constantly.'

She grabbed another tissue and loudly blew her nose. Joanna listened intently. Suddenly, she had once again become interested in Steve. From the moment she had met him she had been quite unable to read him, figure out what made him tick, and she was interested to hear what else Greta had to say. After all, the New Yorker had succeeded where Joanna had failed.

'I wanted him to love me as much as I loved him,' Greta continued. 'But we had so little in common. I had a feeling it was going to come to this. Recently, he has been avoiding me. I left messages for him all over the hotel but he never replied. So, last night, I managed to get a key to his room and I waited there to confront him. But he didn't even come back! He was with another woman, I'm sure of it!'

Joanna bit her lip. If only Greta knew what had really happened to Steve the previous night, she wouldn't be so hurt right now. But Joanna couldn't tell her. Not even if she omitted the reason why she had lured Steve into the small function room.

Suddenly, Greta's revelations stirred Joanna's competitive spirit. In a way, things were very much as they had been in Tokyo. Obviously, if Greta thought she still had a chance, she would go after Steve once again. For Joanna, that was just enough to make her decide to stay in the race. Both women were after the same man, only this time Joanna was ahead of Greta as far as getting Steve was concerned.

There was still hope for her. There was this last day. The least Joanna could do was to give it her best shot. She would find a way to keep Greta as far away as possible. But for now she wanted to see what else the New Yorker had to say. After that, she'd find a way to turn this information to her advantage.

'I guess he's like all the other men,' Greta said. 'He was only interested in one thing.' For a moment, she stared blankly into space and a sad little smile played on her lips. 'I have to admit that he was very good in bed,' she whispered to Joanna. 'At least until . . .'

Her voice broke and she started crying again. Joanna crawled over the bed and came to sit next to her. This was going exactly where she wanted it to. Moreover, she now saw something else in Greta, something quite attractive in her vulnerability. Reaching for a tissue, she handed it to Greta and put her arm round her shoulders.

'Until what?' Joanna asked.

'Well,' Greta said hesitantly. 'He started asking me to do these things, you see . . .'

'What sort of things? What do you mean?'

'At first, he was all over me when we were in bed. Then, he started suggesting that I do things to him, but I didn't want to.'

Joanna felt her patience quickly vanish. Her excitement was growing as she felt Greta's body warm against her. She wanted to know every detail, but Greta didn't seem eager to volunteer the information. 'What things?' Joanna repeated. 'You can tell me, you know. I won't tell anybody.'

Greta stared at the bunch of crumpled tissues in her hands. 'He wanted me to tie him up,' she whispered as she began to tremble. 'He showed up one night with this horrible leather outfit that he wanted me to wear. At first, I thought it was just for fun, but then he wanted me to order him around, to make him crawl on the floor and even to slap his butt with his belt.'

180

Joanna felt herself melt. Greta's Brooklyn accent seemed more pronounced the more upset she became. For Joanna, this was undeniably charming and arousing. In addition, what Greta had said sounded almost too good to be true.

'Did you do it?' Joanna asked in a husky voice. She was thrilled by the notion that Steve might be into submissive games. At the same time, Greta's words translated into images in her mind and she quickly established a parallel between that and the evening she had spent at Torima's banquet. The memories made her blood rush and her heart pound with excitement. Once again she was a voyeur, and she couldn't wait for Greta to tell her more.

'I couldn't,' Greta admitted. 'I'm not like that. Besides, why would he want me to be so cruel when I was just lying there, willing for him to do what he wanted with me? I was happy just to let him have his way and take me. But that's not what he wanted. If I had agreed, God only knows what he would have asked next!'

Joanna took a deep breath and fought very hard to hide her smile. So, it seemed Steve was into submission. Unfortunately for him, Greta was probably more the passive type. Already, another plan was taking shape in her mind. Now she knew why she hadn't gained any ground with the Texan: he wasn't receptive to subtle cues. He needed to be ordered around, in no uncertain terms. And Joanna knew she was good at doing just that.

Greta finally turned her tear-strained face towards her and smiled gratefully.

'I'm so glad you were here,' she said as she laid her hand on Joanna's knee. Joanna's kimono had spread opened to reveal her shapely legs. Greta probably thought nothing of touching bare skin, but the effect on Joanna was immediate. As soon as the heat of Greta's palm penetrated her, her thoughts took another direction and her plans for Steve were put on hold. All of a sudden, she stopped seeing Greta as some annoying bimbo. Perhaps there was something else she could get out of her.

'I needed to talk to someone,' Greta continued. 'And I knew you would understand. I just don't know what to do next.'

'There are several options,' Joanna suggested vaguely. Earlier, she would have told Greta just to pack up and leave, but now she wanted her to wait a while. Her frustration had swelled and she saw a way to get the release she so desperately needed.

'I know,' Greta said. 'Early this morning, when I came back to my room, I was so upset that I packed my things. I know there's a flight I can take this afternoon and in just a few hours I'd be far away from here. But I don't know whether I should still talk to him, see if there's a chance for us after all.'

'Are you willing to let him see you like this?' Joanna countered. Her mind was feverish, juggling both her plans for Steve and her unexpected, more immediate intentions towards Greta. Here was an opportunity to clear the way for herself. 'I mean, if you go to him now, you'd look as though you're begging for him to take you back. And what would he say if he knew that you waited in his room last night?'

'I know,' Greta admitted. 'He's still not back. I'm sure he's with a woman. Did you see him last night?'

Joanna hesitated, wanting to formulate her reply to discourage Greta, but without implicating herself or saying anything Steve could subsequently deny. 'I saw him in the bar,' she said as she also set her hand on Greta's leg. 'He was talking with three women, but I don't know which one he was interested in. We had a snack later on, but I left him around midnight to come back here. I have no idea where he went after that.'

She stopped there, knowing this was as much as she could tell Greta. Technically, she hadn't lied, but she hadn't exactly told Greta everything either. And she really didn't know what had happened to Steve after she had left. Judging from his state at the time, Joanna

182

knew he could very well still be asleep in the function room, and would remain there until the cleaning staff came in. And as he awoke, the memory of the previous evening would probably be sketchy at best. But that was the kind of information she couldn't give Greta. If the New Yorker were to find him before she left, would she believe that he had fallen asleep? That would sound like the lamest of excuses. But since Greta seemed so desperate to hang on to him, she would perhaps disregard his excuses.

Looking down, Joanna saw Greta's hand paused on her thigh. The long fingernails painted in bright crimson reminded her of her first female lover, Anita. That was years ago already and, except for the fingernails, Anita didn't look at all like Greta. But the effect on Joanna was the same.

She was hot, unexpectedly so, and she yearned for contact with Greta's naked body. She needed once again to feel warm soft female skin against hers. Under normal circumstances, she would never have even dreamt of it. But this morning she was beyond trying to make sense of anything. Her instincts urged her to take action. Gently, she increased her hold on Greta's shoulders and pulled her closer.

'I think you should leave with your head held high,' she whispered in Greta's ear. 'Forget about Steve. You deserve much better than that.'

'I know, Joanna. But I think I'm really hooked on him. It's very physical, you see. I need to have someone near me, I need the contact.'

Her words only enhanced Joanna's wantonness. 'I know,' she whispered. 'So do I. But does it really have to be him? Does it have to be a man?' As she spoke, she softly stroked Greta's arm with the palm of her hand, letting her fingertips lightly brush the side of the woman's breast. Now she couldn't hold back.

Greta looked down and stared at Joanna's hand now fondling her breasts. She didn't try to pull away, which made her only the more appealing in Joanna's eyes. 'Are you suggesting what I think you're suggesting?' she asked in a little voice.

In reply, Joanna lay Greta on the bed. They held each other's gaze for a while, then Greta closed her eyes. She shivered slightly in Joanna's arms, then yielded immediately and went limp as a rag doll. Joanna recognised just how passive Greta could be, and this submissive stance gave rise to sudden and violent desire.

'It's my first time with a woman,' Greta said dreamily. Yet the tight embrace in which she hugged Joanna betrayed her willingness. Their mouths met and Greta's kiss was anything but demure. Her lips moved languidly, revealing her appetite and earnestness. The woman was indeed keen on sex. It was obvious even in her kisses. Perhaps that was what Steve had first seen in her.

But there was no doubt as to her lack of initiative. She just lay on the bed and soon released her hold on Joanna as if waiting for something to happen. Her only reaction was to moan gently when Joanna slipped her hand under her skirt and quickly pulled down her knickers. A moment later, her legs instinctively parted.

Joanna let her hand run up and down the New Yorker's thighs as she continued raising her skirt. Sitting up, she admired them for a moment. They were firm but not muscular, pale to the point of milkiness and very smooth. Undeniably gorgeous, those legs no doubt would stand out if only Greta had more sense than to stick to ample frilly long dresses and exchanged them for something tight and short.

Joanna bent down and softly kissed the white skin, directing her mouth towards the inside where she knew it would be warmer and even smoother. Greta held her legs parted further while she remained lying on the bed with her eyes closed.

Joanna continued her leisurely strokes for a moment. She hadn't touched female skin since the night she had been in the dressing room with Keiko and Atsuko. As images of that evening returned to her mind, she knew that this scenario would soon repeat itself. Only now she would be the one to provide pleasure, show the New Yorker that women could also be great lovers.

Greta would probably remain passive for a while. Joanna's suspicions were confirmed when she lay on the bed and Greta still didn't move. That would likely change once she got her excited enough. The thought made her impatient.

With a swift movement of her wrist, Joanna undid the buttons on Greta's blouse. She had always found it odd to undress a woman because of the way the buttons on a woman's blouse were placed differently from a man's shirt. It felt naughty, forbidden, and increased her excitement.

Pushing aside the fabric, she stared at Greta's chest. Her bra was rather matronly, thick, completely covering her breasts and fastened at the front by a row of strong hooks. The ceramic beads of Greta's necklace, still resting underneath her throat, created the strangest of contrasts. Her heaving chest begged to be freed. Joanna was happily surprised by her own dexterity as she quickly undid the hooks. Greta's breasts popped out of the cups, large and perfectly round. The skin was just as milky white and inviting as the woman's thighs. Joanna slowly caressed them, watching the rosy nipples pucker under her touch.

Bending down, Joanna let her tongue trail all over Greta's chest before lightly flicking over the hard peaks. Her whole face pressed against them, her nose digging into the fluid skin. She used it to brush the hard nipples as she moved her head sideways to caress Greta with her cheeks as well. Pulling away, she stared at the inviting bosom before gathering it into her hand to direct it towards her mouth. Her hand slowly followed the curve of each breast as she drew a nipple in her mouth and suckled it gently.

Although her caress was smooth, Greta shook in a spasm underneath her and let out a loud moan. This reaction suddenly excited Joanna and she grew into a sort of sensuous frenzy, which in turn made Greta moan even louder.

Unable to hold back, Joanna sank over Greta's idle half-naked body and covered her completely. The sash of her kimono came loose and undid itself. Gradually, Joanna's chest and abdomen were uncovered as she continued writhing over Greta. Her hips gyrated lewdly over Greta's pelvis. Joanna slipped her hands under Greta's limp hot body and held her tight. Excitement grew for both women.

Greta's excitement was obvious in her strangled moans and breathing, and in the way she returned Joanna's kisses. Yet it seemed that was all Greta had to offer. Joanna had to take her hands and guide them over her own body to get Greta to finish undressing her.

Somehow, having to show Greta what to do was incredibly arousing. Once again she was the mistress, and she had to direct her pupil. Soon enough, she thought, Greta would show some initiative.

Setting her hands on either side of Greta's shoulders, she slightly lifted herself up. She increased the hold of her lips around her lover's mouth as she twisted her shoulders to rub her chest against Greta's. Her own nipples were as hard as Greta's and both women moaned in unison as the heat and the softness of their skin mutually teased them. Joanna recalled the tall blond girl at Torima's banquet, the way she had used her slave's mouth. Climbing further along Greta's body, Joanna directed her own nipples over the New Yorker's mouth. Greta's lips gaped languidly, but her tongue remained lazy

Joanna couldn't stop writhing voluptuously, caressing herself using the half-naked body lying underneath hers. Her legs straddled Greta's abdomen and her hips thrust forcefully. Her wet flesh glided up and down along Greta's smooth belly and Joanna increased the pressure to heighten her arousal.

Yet this still wasn't enough for Joanna. Suddenly sitting up, she took hold of Greta's hands and placed them on her own breasts. She wanted to see the red fingernails caress her, to feel them gently scratch her nipples until it became unbearable. Greta obeyed readily but didn't take the initiative and do anything more. Greta's lack of fervour began to make Joanna impatient. Not only was Greta inexperienced, but it seemed she was also incredibly lazy and preferred simply to lie still and be caressed. No wonder Steve had soon grown tired of her! Yet Joanna's desire for the body writhing on the bed didn't subside. It didn't matter if Greta remained still for now. Joanna wasn't done with her.

In fact, this lack of enthusiasm at times bordered on submission, and it only encouraged Joanna to be more passionate. She slid off Greta's body and went to kneel between the woman's parted legs. Raising her skirt a little higher, she then delved towards the dark glistening mound, and attacked it ferociously.

It had been such a long time since she had tasted female flesh that she wondered how she could have done without it. Against her lips, the warm soft sex was exquisitely enticing, fragrant and sweet. Joanna teased it with long hungry licks, covering the whole slit with her tongue and grabbing the folds in her mouth.

On the bed, Greta moaned loudly. Soon after, she sat up and looked down at Joanna.

'You're so good at this, darling,' she panted. 'Better than any man I've ever been with. And some of them were very good.' Her last words strangled into a cry of pleasure. She moaned again as she reached out and gently caressed Joanna's soft hair.

Joanna pulled away, looked up and smiled. 'And the best is yet to come,' she announced before resuming her caresses on the wet flesh. This time, she inserted her tongue deep inside Greta's vagina and used the tip of her nose to tease her swollen clitoris. Greta squealed with delight and lay back again.

At that moment, Joanna went for the kill. Seizing the stiff bud between her lips, she sucked it earnestly. Her fingers danced over Greta's throbbing sex and plunged repeatedly into her tunnel. It clenched sporadically, at an increasing pace, which told Joanna that Greta was climaxing. But even as her lover tensed violently and then relaxed as pleasure swept her, Joanna didn't let up. She couldn't get enough. She wanted to keep going for as long as she could, or at least until Greta begged for mercy.

To her disappointment, Greta soon grabbed her head and pushed it away. 'Enough,' the New Yorker panted. 'I can't take any more.'

Joanna smiled and rose to her feet. She stood between Greta's parted thighs, feeling them brush her own soft skin. Looking down, she stared at the quivering woman who bore little resemblance to the Greta she had seen so often before. Her hair was the same, only as it was spread around her head, it looked softer, tamer than usual. Since Greta wasn't wearing any make-up either, little remained of the woman one of the delegates had nicknamed 'the Valkyrie'. Her large breasts, with the nipples still fully erect, wobbled violently as her chest continued to heave. Her face, flushed and occasionally twitching with small spasms of ecstasy, was now more at peace than when she had shown up at Joanna's door earlier.

Sitting next to her, Joanna once again seized Greta's hand, put it on her own belly and bent down towards her lover.

'Touch me,' she whispered in Greta's ear as she softly kissed her cheek.

Greta's hand ran lazily over Joanna's chest, unsure and hesitant. Joanna lay down and closed her eyes, expecting Greta to sit up and caress her whole body. She wanted to see those red fingernails on her rosy skin again. But the New Yorker seemed to be falling asleep instead. Turning her head, Joanna stared at Greta and was surprised to find her wide awake.

'Thank you,' Greta said in a little voice. 'That was very nice.'

'And it's not over,' Joanna replied with a smile.

'No? You want to do it again?' Greta appeared to come out of her torpor for a moment. Her eyes shone and she writhed voluptuously before parting her legs. 'I can't say no to an offer like that,' she admitted. 'But not just yet. Let me recover first then you can do it again.'

Joanna laughed frankly. 'Actually,' she said, 'I thought you'd be more eager to return the favour!'

Greta bit her lip. 'I told you,' she said in a small voice. 'I've never been with a woman.'

Joanna turned on her side and moved away from her slightly. Greta's admission once again afforded Joanna the opportunity to play the teacher.

'Just look at me,' she said as slowly she ran her hand along the side of her ribcage and her hips. 'Don't you find me attractive?'

Greta looked at Joanna's bare body for a moment and smiled again. 'You are very beautiful, that's true.'

Joanna closed her eyes again and whispered suggestively. 'Touch me. Feel how hot and soft my skin is. See how smooth my breasts are, and how my nipples react if you tease them.'

Greta rolled on to her side to face Joanna and silently obeyed. Under her gentle touch, Joanna's skin broke into goose bumps and a delicious shiver ran down her spine. Joanna bit her lip and sighed.

'That's it,' she sighed. 'You're doing well.' Rolling on to her back, she parted her legs and invited Greta to touch them. 'Now for my thighs,' she purred. 'Tease them with your nails. I like to be scratched on the inside.'

Greta continued, but not before showing some hesitation. Her hand trembled as it glided over Joanna's belly but totally skipped her hairy mound. She did stroke the inside of Joanna's thighs, but remained quite far from her sex.

Joanna opened her eyes. 'I don't want to wait any longer,' she said. 'I want you to make me come now.'

Greta pulled away. 'I don't know,' she said. 'That's too much for me. I don't think I can do it.'

Joanna sat up and parted her legs. 'Look,' she said as she lovingly stroked her slit with her fingers. 'I'm all hot and wet for you. Touch me.'

Greta reached forward but pulled away just before touching Joanna's expectant flesh.

'Maybe some other time, OK? I'm really not ready for that.'

'Aren't you curious to see what another woman feels like?' Joanna leant forward and kissed Greta on the neck. Her lover's sigh made her believe it wouldn't take long to convince her. 'Aren't you curious to taste me?' she whispered as she softly blew into Greta's ear.

But Greta pulled away again. 'I'm sorry,' she said. 'I'm too tired. I haven't slept all night and after what you've put me through I really don't feel like doing anything any more. I just want to lie down and go to sleep.'

Joanna was suddenly incensed by Greta's lack of response. Too tired! If that was her way of enjoying sex, by lying still and just passively taking pleasure while refusing to return the favour, it was no wonder that a man like Steve would soon have enough of her.

Greta quickly got up and refastened her blouse. Sprawled on the bed, Joanna continued caressing herself, pretending that Greta wasn't even there. She really didn't care any more. She needed release and if the New Yorker didn't want to cooperate, she'd take care of it herself.

Greta watched from the corner of her eye but didn't seem at all impressed or interested. 'Thanks again, Joanna. You really made me feel better. You're right: why should I bother with Steve? Now that you and I are friends I'm sure you can give me all the affection I need.' She shivered and smiled wickedly. 'I can't wait to do it again. You really are good. And maybe next time I'll be less shy, who knows?'

Her suggestion only made Joanna angrier. 'What do you mean: next time?' she asked sarcastically. 'You're heading back to the States this afternoon, aren't you?'

Greta gave her a puzzled look. 'But that was before,' she stammered. 'Now that we're together, I don't really have to go, right?'

'Sorry,' Joanna said coldly. 'I'm leaving for Vietnam first thing tomorrow morning.' That wasn't exactly true, but close enough to crush Greta's expectations.

Greta turned to stone and stared incredulously at Joanna as her face turned livid. A sad smile played on her lips and she slumped on the bed. 'I'd really like to go with you,' she sobbed loudly. 'But I don't have any money left. Steve was very good and provided for me after I left my job, but I don't suppose you could . . .'

Joanna laughed and interrupted her. 'Even if I wanted to,' she said, 'my company has already made all the arrangements and there's no provision for taking anyone with me.'

Greta stood again. 'I see,' she said as she made her way slowly towards the door. Suddenly her face lit up and she turned to Joanna. 'What if I gave you my address in New York?' she suggested giddily. 'You could come and visit me! And perhaps I could come visit you in London!'

Joanna didn't reply. Although she hadn't planned for this turn of events, it was satisfying to be able to exact some sort of revenge on Greta. How conceited of the woman to think she could just impose herself in that fashion and assume that Joanna would invite her to tag along. In addition, if it hadn't been for this fool, Steve would be with Joanna right now, and she'd be on her way back to the mysterious inn.

'Yeah,' Joanna said vaguely after a while. By now she was voluptuously rolling around on the bed, wrapping herself in her kimono and enjoying the soft warmth of the silk on her sensitive skin.

'Good!' Greta said. 'I'll go pack, then I'll come back so we can exchange addresses!'

'Why don't you do that?' Joanna suggested. What she really wanted was to tell her to go to hell but it hardly seemed worth the effort. Besides, if Greta was stupid enough to expect her to come to New York just to give her orgasms, that didn't make any difference to Joanna, who had already decided she didn't ever want to see the woman again.

Greta's shrieking voice made Joanna's blood boil. Just when she thought it was finally safe to come out of her room, it seemed the New Yorker still wasn't out of her life. As she turned round, she saw Greta barge across the foyer of the hotel, dragging an enormous shoulder bag while the porter followed behind with the rest of her luggage.

For a moment, Joanna couldn't believe she had been intimate with that woman. Greta was back to her old self, wearing a shiny, shocking pink jumpsuit that must have been very fashionable when it was made in the seventies, but which totally clashed with the wooden African jewellery hanging round her neck; not to mention the burgundy-coloured lipstick and matching eyeshadow.

'There you are!' she clamoured as she rushed towards Joanna. 'I was afraid I'd miss you!' Fishing a piece of crumpled paper out of her pocket, she slipped it forcefully into Joanna's hand.

'My address and telephone number,' she explained. 'When can you come? Didn't you say at some point that you'd be back home by the end of May? I'm sure your boss will give you some time off after such a long trip. Why don't you come then? Or maybe I could come over instead? I don't mind being on my own all day, you know, as long as we're together in the evening!' She finished her sentence with a wink, which only made Joanna more anxious to drop her next bomb.

As Greta kept talking, Joanna ushered her out of the door and gently coaxed her into a taxi. Greta looked at her watch. 'Just in time,' she said. 'I barely have enough money to pay for my ticket home. I can't miss that plane.'

'No, you can't,' Joanna said with a devious smile. 'By

the way, did you see Steve before leaving? Have you said goodbye?'

Greta's happy mood turned sour for a moment. 'I decided he wasn't worth the effort,' she said. 'I don't know where he is and I don't ever want to see him again. He doesn't have my address in New York and I tore his up. For all I care, he's probably still with the same woman he was last night.'

'I sincerely doubt that,' Joanna said as she stepped away from the taxi. 'You see, I'm the one he was with last night.' She waited a few seconds, feeling vindicated by the sight of Greta's surprise and sudden anger. Contemptuously, she took the piece of paper Greta had given her, rolled in into a ball and tossed it on to the New Yorker's lap. Without giving her a chance to say anything, Joanna knocked on the driver's window and gestured for him to drive off.

Now that the Valkyrie was finally on her way back to the States, Joanna could get on with her task of seducing the man Greta would never see again.

Chapter Seventeen

*T*here was still time, Joanna reasoned. She could still do it. Her encounter with Greta had empowered her. She felt a bit of remorse for having treated the New Yorker so poorly as she had got into her taxi, but she quickly brushed that aside. With her out of the way, Joanna could now use her renewed enthusiasm and concentrate on Steve.

In less than a couple of hours, she had arranged her trap. All she needed now was to get him to fall into it. She casually strolled into the exhibit hall some time towards the end of the day's demonstrations. Having read Steve's itinerary, she knew he was scheduled to attend this one. In fact, she was counting on it. She was pleased but not too surprised to see his blond head towering above those of the other delegates. Quietly, she made her way to where he was standing, immediately noticing he looked cool and rested. Either his hangover wasn't as bad as she would have thought and he had quickly recovered, or he was suffering beyond belief but managed to hide it well. As soon as the demonstration finished, he turned to Joanna and smiled.

'What happened to you last night?' he asked immediately. 'I woke up this morning and you were gone. There wasn't much food left, but by then the stench was pretty awful. What happened? Why did you leave me in there?'

Joanna laughed as she walked out of the room. 'Don't you remember?'

'I remember eating and drinking a lot. After that, I must have passed out on the sofa because it's all a blank. At what point did you leave?'

'It was about midnight. You fell asleep and I got bored. I tried to wake you up but you didn't even react.'

'I'll have to take your word for it,' Steve admitted. 'My last memory is of you and me sitting on the couch. You said something, I think, but I can't remember what it was. Then I woke up feeling awful, my mouth dry and my stomach completely upside down.' He stroked his abdomen as he spoke. 'I'm still reeling from it. It was good, that much I remember, but believe me, it's going to be a while before I do anything of the sort again!'

Joanna pouted to show her disappointment. 'That's a shame,' she said. 'I received something this morning that I thought you would enjoy.'

Steve raised his hand and Joanna felt he was about to refuse her invitation, but then she saw him hesitate.

'What exactly did you have in mind?' he asked cautiously. 'Does it involve vast amounts of food and alcohol?'

Joanna laughed again. 'You just said you wouldn't go through anything similar again, and already you're changing your mind?'

'There are invitations that are too good to pass on,' he stated. 'Tell me more!'

'This morning I received a very elaborate basket of fruit. There's this company with which I just signed an important contract and they sent me the basket with their sincere thanks. It's too good to waste, but I'm leaving tomorrow and I can't take it with me. Since you mentioned you liked fruit, I thought you'd be interested in taking part in a modest but tasty feast.'

It was all a lie, but Joanna wasn't going let that stop her. She had herself ordered the fruit, remembering what Steve had told her, and she was banking on this weakness to lure him to her room.

In a fraction of a second, Steve's hesitation vanished. 'Fruit? That's always a possibility. How hard can it be on my stomach? Besides, I think fruit is a good cure for a hangover, no?'

He seemed eager as he waited for her to reply, and Joanna knew she could have taken him to her room right then and there. That was too soon, however. Looking at her watch, she pretended to hesitate, when in fact she had it all figured out.

'I have something I need to deal with at the moment,' she lied. 'Why don't you come up around eight? I'm in room 1104.'

'Eight o'clock?' Steve looked at his watch incredulously. Since it was barely six, he would have to simmer for a while. At least, that's the way Joanna wanted it.

'Eight,' Joanna repeated. 'I should be back by then.'

Without waiting for him to confirm, she gave him a friendly pat on the shoulder and turned around. She knew he had nothing planned for the next couple of hours, and the delay would only make him more eager.

From the moment she heard him knock on her door, Joanna knew there was no looking back. From the bathroom, she yelled for him to come in, having left the door unlocked on purpose.

'Help yourself,' she told him from behind the closed door. 'I'll be out in a second.'

She waited a little longer, wanting him to find the fruit, which she had cleverly laid on the table, and start eating. The preparation had taken her the best part of the afternoon, but it was well worth the effort. Coming out of her hiding place, she rushed towards him, satisfied to see he hadn't wasted any time. Already he had grabbed a large chunk of fresh pineapple and was happily chomping on it.

'Sorry,' Joanna said as she casually picked a small bunch of grapes. 'I wasn't quite ready.'

Immediately, he noticed her dress. 'Isn't that what you were wearing last night?'

Joanna pretended to be embarrassed. 'It is,' she admitted sheepishly. 'I'm afraid everything else is already packed.' That was yet another lie. The truth was that she had failed to find anything that would better suit her plan for the evening. And, if Steve had remembered the dress, it could only mean that he had noticed it the previous night.

'I know it's not very becoming for a lady to wear the same thing twice,' she continued.

'That's quite all right,' Steve interrupted her. 'It looks good on you.'

Joanna pretended to blush and twirled to let him look at her again. He kept his eyes on her and smiled.

'It really does look good,' he repeated. 'It's very sexy.'

That was something Joanna didn't need to be told. She had increased the setting on the air-conditioning system to make sure her nipples would remain erect and obvious. In addition, she had lovingly scratched them with her fingernails before coming out of the bathroom just to make sure Steve would notice. And, just like the previous evening, she wasn't wearing anything underneath.

As Steve returned to the table, she directed her gaze towards his crotch. Just as she had hoped, he was already hard. Was it because of the food or from the sight of her? She couldn't be sure. Maybe both. In any case, she intended to work on that as the evening progressed. In the meantime, she tried to set her plan in motion.

'Sexy, you said?' she asked in a suggestive tone. 'I'm not embarrassing you, I hope?'

Steve swallowed a large apricot and looked at her again before replying. 'Not quite,' he said with a smile. 'At least not as long as there's food to keep my mind occupied.'

'And how long will it take before your stomach is sated and you start noticing more of me?' She came closer as she spoke. Her high heels made her taller than usual and she arched her back in a subtle move to get him to notice her swollen breasts.

'What makes you think I haven't already noticed?' he replied as his eyes glanced at her chest.

Joanna's eyes followed him and she burst out laughing. 'Oh my,' she said. 'I can see why you would say that. I hope I'm not too obvious.'

'Just rightly so, I would say.'

'Hmm. I see.' She grabbed a lychee and slowly peeled it. Its rounded shape had always reminded her of a glans and she seductively looked at Steve as she lasciviously slid it into her mouth. She closed her eyes, sucked it gently, then looked at him again. He hadn't missed any of that, but he didn't seem very impressed.

His lack of enthusiasm suddenly impelled Joanna to get on with her plan. She had waited long enough already. He was here, right where she wanted him, and there was no point in continuing this charade any longer. Casually, she reached forward and picked up the large mango she had left at the top of the display. Steve had seen it, too, and he silently stared at her as she took a small knife and began to peel it.

'Is this the only one?' he asked as he pointed towards the fruit.

'It is,' Joanna replied without looking at him.

'It looks good.'

'It's very juicy,' she explained as drops of juice trickled down her wrist. She stopped peeling the fruit, brought her hands towards her mouth and stuck out her tongue to playfully lap up what had dribbled. Once she had finished peeling it, she led Steve to one of the armchairs she had placed next to the table, made him sit down and handed him the mango.

'There,' she said. 'You're the guest. You can have it.'

He didn't hesitate and avidly took a large bite of the flesh. Just as Joanna had hoped for, juice immediately trickled down his chin. That didn't seem to bother him and certainly didn't stop him from taking another, greedy bite which only caused more juice to pool in the dimple on his chin. That was exactly what Joanna wanted. Moving towards him, she set her hands on the armrests, leant forward, pushed her chest towards his and insinuated her face between his and the fruit. Before he could understand what she was doing, she once again stuck out her tongue and slowly licked the juice off his chin.

She closed her eyes in ecstasy, moaned loudly, smacked her lips, then moved back and waited for him to take another bite. Against her knees, she felt his legs parting. Seizing the opportunity, she straddled his left thigh and sat on it. Her flesh was already wet with excitement and she unwittingly ground it against his hard muscle as she slowly writhed.

Opening her eyes, she looked at Steve. He hadn't uttered a word, but the look on his face was exactly what Joanna had been wanting to see ever since she had met him. In his eyes, she read both amusement and desire. He didn't do anything in return, but she didn't let that worry her. Her message couldn't have been clearer, and the fact that he hadn't protested spurred her on.

After he took another bite, Steve purposefully pulled his hand away as he expected her to lick his chin once again. But Joanna was already one step ahead of him. Her heart pounding with excitement, anticipation, and even fear, she grabbed the mango from his hand, and moved away.

Steve protested. 'Hey! I was enjoying that! You said I could have it, didn't you?' His tone was playful, and Joanna knew the time had come for her to go for her last strike. Slumping into her armchair in front of him, she forcefully crushed the mango in one hand as she raised her dress above her hips with the other.

Parting her legs, she exposed her dark, pink and glistening flesh, and voluptuously spread the pulp from the mango all over it. All the while, she defiantly stared at Steve, who didn't miss anything. For a few seconds, they held each other's gaze. That was when Joanna knew she had finally won.

'You still want it?' she said in a husky voice. 'Then come and get it.'

Steve slowly stood up and took two steps towards her. His hand reached down but she stopped it before it touched her flesh.

'No,' she said. 'Not like that. Get on your knees and use your mouth.'

As he obeyed silently, Joanna was thankful for what Greta had told her. And the New Yorker had also been right when she had told Joanna that Steve was a great lover. From the moment his tongue delved at Joanna's swollen folds in search of the pulp she had smeared, she went into a wickedly excited frenzy.

There he was, kneeling in front of her and caressing her with his mouth. It had all been so easy, in the end. Yet Joanna wasn't sorry it had taken so long. It was well worth the wait. All along, she could have had him anytime if only she had thought of this earlier. But never would she have thought that he would be the type simply to submit. And she would test his yearning to be dominated to the extreme.

Underneath the cushion of the armchair, she had taken the precaution of hiding a small cat o'nine tails, which she had bought earlier that day. As he continued licking the juicy pulp off her flesh, she retrieved the small whip and waited for the appropriate time. Already he had swallowed what was left of the mango and licked Joanna clean, but that didn't stop him. Now Joanna was vindicated. Triumph enhanced her arousal yet she wasn't ready to leave it at that.

'Lick me harder,' she ordered as she lightly hit him on the back with her whip. He set his hands on the floor to brace himself and pushed his face closer to her sex.

Joanna writhed and rubbed her thighs against his arms before slowly lifting her legs to bring them over his shoulders. Squeezing her knees together, she held his head in a tight grip, unwilling to let him go until she had climaxed.

Steve's mouth relished her more thoroughly than if she had been the most delicious piece of food. His lips quickly surveyed the whole of her slit, grabbing her sensitive labia and pinching them lightly for a while before letting them go again. But although his caresses were very methodical, he stayed clear of her stiff bud, which had grown bigger as a result of his tactics.

He pulled back a few inches, then once again went for her with his tongue. Joanna squealed as she felt it cover her completely, hot and wet and pressing against her sex as he wiggled it forcefully.

'Enough,' she said as she panted. 'Make me come now. Suck my clit and make me come.' As a precaution, she lightly hit his back again, if only to emphasise the fact that she was the one in control.

Steve obeyed once again, attacking her without waiting any longer. His lips took hold of her bud and he lovingly drew it in his mouth. The tip of his tongue toyed with it as he increased the suction.

Joanna's climax surged suddenly and rampaged violently through her. She bucked on the armchair, dropping the whip on the floor and digging her fingernails into the thick fabric of the armrests. A powerful orgasm rose from deep within her, gathered, swirled and burnt the whole of her pelvis. Joanna couldn't help screaming, each of her breaths louder than the previous one, and didn't stop until her throat hurt.

'Keep going!' she yelled as pleasure shook her time and again. She afforded herself the luxury of several orgasms, taking as much as she could whilst the man was still at her feet. It was just too good to pass over.

After a while, however, out of breath and totally exhausted, she had no choice but to ask him to stop. She pushed him away, picked up the whip, rose to her feet and looked down at him.

'Good boy,' she said contemptuously. 'Now get up and undress me.'

Steve didn't even look at her as he seized the bottom of her dress and slowly pulled it up, peeling the dress off her as if it had been a second skin. The image that formed in Joanna's mind was too good to resist. Reaching towards the table, she grabbed a banana, quickly peeled it and handed it to Steve.

'You know what to do,' she said as she set her hands on his shoulders and bid him to kneel at her feet again. This time she remained standing, placing her hands on his head for support.

Her exposed skin throbbed with heat and from the pleasure that had just shaken her. At her feet, her lover was still fully clothed, and Joanna decided it would remain like this for a while.

With great dexterity, he pushed the banana deep inside her and pulled it out several times. Joanna took more satisfaction out of this wicked motion than from the actual feel of the fruit inside her. It wasn't big enough to stretch her and trigger anything pleasurable. Yet it had long been a fantasy of hers to do something so naughty, and that alone was enough to delight her. Her satisfaction was short-lived however. Soon the fruit grew limp and was reduced to a shapeless pulp. But Joanna wasn't done with it.

'Take it out with your mouth,' Joanna ordered as it became clear that nothing else was practical at this point. Sucking loudly, Steve drew the banana into his mouth inch by inch, swallowing it in large gulps. Once he was done, he sat back on his heels and looked up at Joanna.

His face betrayed all the pleasure he had experienced whilst obeying his mistress. But there was another gleam in his eyes, something Joanna caught but couldn't quite identify. His jeans strained at the crotch, and Joanna fought hard to resist the urge to order him to undress. She was eager to see him naked, finally to discover his body and his manhood, which had now undoubtedly attained a full erection.

She stood naked in front of him, and she allowed him

to observe her for a while, basking in the knowledge and the satisfaction that he found her beautiful. The admiration in his eyes was unmistakable. By now, Joanna knew he wanted her. But she had herself waited so long for this moment: she would make him wait as well.

'You may touch me,' she said in an authoritative tone. 'But only with your hands.'

Steve straightened up and rose on his knees. His hands, the hands Joanna had so often fantasised about, came up and softly paused on her flat stomach. They were hot and only slightly moist, and his touch was so intense that she felt the heat spread through her.

They glided around her hips and surveyed the contours of her buttocks. Joanna sighed and tilted her head back. He was going to tease her, she just knew it. She wanted him to come back up and grab hold of her breasts, but for now he was content to caress her behind and her legs, letting his hands slowly run down the back of her thighs to her calves and her ankles.

His fingertips tickled the back of her knees and their caress sent a shiver of excitement which vibrated upwards and echoed in the midst of her sex. The palms of his hands then settled on her calves in a perfect fit and he gently massaged them.

Instinctively, Joanna parted her legs. Steve didn't look up at her but he understood what she wanted. His hands slid up along the inside of her thighs and headed inexorably up towards her flesh. She could feel every inch of their progression and waited impatiently for the time when they would reach the junction. But at the last moment she decided it was too soon for that. She pressed her knees together to stop him from going any further.

Steve pulled back, and once again set his hands on her hips. This time he guided them upwards, seizing her waist tightly and letting his fingers walk up until they touched the underside of her breasts. His thumbs lightly brushed her globes, following their smooth curves and not missing a single inch of their roundness, but he completely avoided her nipples which now peaked fully and eagerly awaited his caresses.

But his hands changed direction and slid towards Joanna's back. There, he slowly felt each tiny bump of her spine, up and down, coming back down to rest in the small of her back for a while.

His method was driving Joanna mad. Yet she controlled herself and didn't let it show. If only she had let him touch her sex, he would have seen how wet she was, how swollen and ready her flesh had become under his caresses.

Her impatience grew as he started to stroke her arms. Setting his hands on her shoulders, he merely let them fall, letting his thumbs and his fingers envelop her biceps on the way down. His wrists brushed the sides of her breasts in the process and this time Joanna couldn't help moaning. If Steve heard her, he didn't let it show. Finally his hands seized hers in a way she recognised as a silent request for further instructions. She took his fingers and placed them directly on her hard nipples.

As if he had read her mind, he knew exactly how to touch her. At first, he barely brushed her, letting his fingertips glide over the hard peaks. Joanna moaned again. His caresses were maddeningly light, but incredibly arousing. Despite herself, she couldn't help twisting her shoulders, guiding her own breasts under his fingers. She came very close to collapsing and begging him to give her even more, but she managed to grab hold of herself at the last minute.

'Enough,' she said as she pushed his hands away. 'No more touching. Put your hands behind your back and suck my nipples.'

Steve obeyed immediately. His lips gently took hold of Joanna's left breast and slowly drew its peak into his mouth. He suckled gently at first, but soon grew rather enthusiastic and started licking both her breasts with long strokes of his tongue.

His breath grew shallow and Joanna knew he was getting even more excited. Now she was glad not to have let go of her whip and she prepared herself in case he needed to be disciplined.

He grabbed her ribcage and pulled her closer to him. That was exactly what Joanna didn't want.

'I said: don't touch me,' she grunted as she raised her arm and prepared to strike.

But he surprised her by rising to his feet and seizing her wrist before she could hit him. 'No more stupid games,' he said as he took the whip out of her hand. 'It's grown rather tiresome.'

Joanna was taken aback by his reaction and desperately searched for something to say, a way to regain control. However, before she could figure out what to do, he quickly went to the bedside table, turned off the light, and come back to kneel in front of Joanna again.

Although he resumed his caresses on her body, this time it was clear he was the one in control. Joanna quickly surrendered. She knew there would be no going back, so the whole domination session was no longer necessary. She now much preferred to let him lead the way.

His arm snaked around her waist and he held her tight as his mouth fastened on her nipple again. His other hand immediately glided between her legs and his fingers didn't waste any time discovering her wanton flesh. Joanna grunted with delight as his thumb settled on her hard clitoris and rubbed it so skilfully that she reached another orgasm in a matter of seconds.

She shook violently in his embrace as pleasure stormed through her. He continued stroking her slit, never letting her climax completely subside. Rising to his feet, he seized her mouth in a passionate kiss that only made her want more. His tongue searched hers and caressed it softly. Against her cheek, she could feel his warm breath and she knew her victory was complete.

'That was what you wanted, wasn't it?' he whispered in her ear before he started kissing her neck.

'Yes,' Joanna replied dreamily. 'I want you so much. I've been wanting you for so long.'

'Well, now you can have me.'

Joanna immediately went from a state of blissful oblivion to renewed erotic frenzy. Grabbing the opening of his shirt with both hands, she pulled forcefully to make the buttons yield. There was no time to undo them one by one. She could barely see his chest in the darkness but she could already feel its heat. Crushing her breasts against his torso, she writhed endlessly as her arms glided under his shirt and her hands caressed his back.

It was just as she had imagined, perhaps even better. Steve stood immobile, letting her quickly undress him. She practically tore his shirt off his shoulders and immediately started kissing his neck and his chest. His skin was soon covered with her saliva as she let her tongue cover every inch. She sucked his nipples just as passionately as he had sucked hers, pinching them with her lips and tweaking them with the tip of her tongue. She grunted with hunger, unwilling to relinquish this hard, muscular body against which she now pressed and rubbed herself.

Lower down, she could feel his hard dick held prisoner against her pelvis. Her hips swayed voluptuously, pushing it and grinding on it. She was amazed at how exciting it felt for her. She caressed, licked and sucked the whole of his neck, his shoulders and his chest, using her mouth, her hands and her whole body.

Her fingernails lightly dug into his skin and it was his turn to grunt with delight. She let her tongue trail up and down his biceps as if in a desperate rage, wanting more of him, always more. Drunk with desire, she finally dropped to her knees and undid the front of his jeans.

She didn't need to see his prick to know how beautiful it was. Holding it in her mouth and in her hands, she caressed him as best she knew, panting with want, her breath so fast and shallow she soon felt dizzy.

Steve moaned loudly as she drew his erect prick into her mouth and sucked him hard. His reaction only fuelled her arousal and she turned into both vulture and vampire. Writhing at his feet, she grabbed his buttocks with both hands to draw him closer still. His shaft throbbed in her mouth and the evidence of his forthcoming orgasm was just enough to jolt her out of this lustful oblivion. It had gone too far. She didn't want him to come just yet.

She pulled away and grabbed his shaft with one hand. With a quick movement of the wrist, she stroked him up and down to make sure he would remain at the same level of excitement but without ever quite reaching the point of no return.

Without releasing her grip, she rose to her feet and kissed him on the mouth. His hand snaked between her legs and he began to tease her again. They stood immobile for a moment, facing one another, the movement of their hands on each other's body their only form of communication.

Steve spoke first. 'If I had known you were going to be like this, I would have come to you much sooner,' he said as he softly kissed her lips.

'I suppose I wasn't obvious enough,' Joanna replied.

'What a waste of time.'

'I know. You shouldn't have bothered with Greta.'

In surprise, Steve stopped his ministrations on Joanna's slit for a second. She increased her hold on his prick and intimated to him to keep going.

'How do you know about that?'

'She was here this morning,' Joanna explained. 'She told me everything.'

'I see. I guess we just weren't suitable.'

'She's too passive, too lazy,' Joanna stated. 'She just likes to lie there and let you do all the work.'

Steve laughed softly. 'How would you know? Did she tell you that as well?'

'No,' Joanna said in a suggestive whisper. 'I had her.'

Steve turned to stone and stepped back. 'You? And her?'

Joanna took his hand, brought it to her mouth, and slowly licked each of his fingers. 'Exactly,' she sighed. 'Does that shock you?'

Steve came closer and embraced her. 'Shock me? Not exactly.'

'Then what?' Joanna asked as she toyed with his nipples. 'What's your first reaction as you imagine her and me together?'

Steve backed away once again and his move made Joanna worry suddenly. Now she wished she hadn't let him turn off the lights. She would have liked to see the expression on his face, to know what he thought at that moment. She heard him fumble with his clothes for a moment and she supposed he was getting dressed. Panic seized her and she became so desperate not to lose him that she thought she was going to cry. She had come so close to her goal, she couldn't let it slip away now!

But as Steve came back to her and took her in his arms, she felt his bare thighs brushing hers and she realised he had in fact finished undressing.

'I have a very hard time imagining you with her,' he said as he lay her on the bed and reclined next to her. 'Why don't you describe it to me?'

Joanna's next sigh was one of both relief and pleasure. Her worries quickly vanished and she realised that perhaps Steve was sensitive to words, so long as she knew what to talk about.

'She put her hand on my thigh,' Joanna began. 'I saw her long red nails and it reminded me of the first woman I had ever been with.'

'Did it excite you?' Steve asked as he covered her chest with light kisses.

'Tremendously. I raised her skirt and pulled down her knickers. She didn't protest.'

'She's easily excitable. But just too lazy for my taste.'

Joanna threw her leg over his hips and lifted herself

208

up. In a flash, she had straddled him and seized his prick, ready to insert it inside her.

'I take it you prefer women who are more assertive?'

Steve let out a moan and grabbed Joanna's breasts in his hands. 'I do,' he said as he thrust upward to penetrate her.

Joanna squealed as his phallus filled her and rekindled her arousal. Finally, after having waited and hoped for so long, she had achieved her goal. It had been worth the wait. She swayed slightly, feeling him twitch inside her. Contracting her thighs, she rose and fell repeatedly, moaning loudly every time she fell back upon him. After a moment she stopped, bent forward and kissed him again.

'I've never been to Texas,' she said in a whisper. 'If I come to visit you, will you teach me how to ride?'

'I don't think you need to be taught,' he said as he thrust faintly. 'You seem to be a natural.'

Setting her hands on his hips, Joanna held him down to stop him from thrusting. Right now she wanted to control the pace and the intensity. Seeking only her own pleasure, she pulled away until his dick almost popped out of her, then let herself fall back again, forever enjoying the feeling of penetration.

Steve was happy to let her take the lead. Lying on his back, he gently toyed with her breasts as she continued to arouse herself. In a way, she was sorry she couldn't see him. She thought about turning on the light, but the lamp was too far for her to reach and she couldn't bear the idea of parting from him, albeit for a brief moment.

She continued to glide up and down his length, riding him at first by simply rocking back and forth, then increasing the movement of her hips as she felt him growing bigger inside her, her arousal now mounting quickly. She panted in joy and in pain as the muscles of her thighs soon tied in a burning knot, yet she continued to move rapidly up and down upon his shaft, her knees locking under the strain.

Her vulva was quickly melting on to his member,

quivering with delight, as Joanna willed herself to continue her assault despite the pain in her exhausted legs. The swollen head stroked her inside, up and down the smooth walls of her tunnel, triggering that sensation which would soon take her to the point of no return. Her stiff clitoris rubbed itself on the hard shaft as well, only enhancing the pleasure she could already feel was about to explode.

She was breathless, highly aware of the pressure building up within her, yet her climax almost took her by surprise. The head of his member nudged repeatedly at her entrance and triggered the explosion. Joanna still quickened the pace, dismissing the burn in her thighs as she bounced violently at an ever-increasing speed, unwilling to stop until she reached another orgasm. Her head jerked back and forth a few times as successive sobs escaped from her mouth.

Pleasure swept her just as powerfully as the first time. She heard Steve moan as her flesh contracted forcefully around his shaft. He thrust a couple of times, so hard she lifted off the bed. But by now Joanna was so exhausted that she could only collapse on top of him, lifeless and unable to do anything to enhance his enjoyment. This one was to be all hers.

She slid off him and remained idle, catching her breath and waiting for her heart to return to a normal pace. Despite her weariness, she was still keenly aware that it wasn't over yet. She had been waiting so long to find herself finally with Steve, she wasn't going to let it stop now.

Without a word, she coaxed him into turning on to his stomach and she languidly climbed on top of him again. His back was just as hard as she had imagined, muscular and well defined. She writhed on his hot skin, feeling the heat penetrate her. She wanted to relive her dream, to make it real. Slowly, she traced a wet path across his back with her tongue, stroking his shoulder blades as she reached them. Her hands hugged his ribcage on either side, her fingers neatly fitting between each ripple of his muscles. Reaching far underneath, she found his nipples and toyed with them as she gently dug her thumbs into his back.

He moaned several times and his hips pushed deeper into the bed. Joanna shifted her weight accordingly, knowing his hard dick was probably crushed underneath him, rubbing against the roughness of the embroidered bedspread.

As they writhed together, it became clear that Steve couldn't hold back much longer. Fire built up between their bodies, the heat of Joanna's belly reflecting off his back. She moaned again as her arousal increased anew. To know he was so close to climax was strangely stimulating and enhanced her own passion.

Her nipples were erect and extremely sensitive. Twisting her shoulders, she brushed them against his back a few times, then let herself give under her own weight to crush them mercilessly. Her hips heaved against his buttocks; her loins growing warm and her moist flesh throbbing. Her tongue settled on his neck, probing behind his ears, then continuing forward to circle the bump at the base of his jaw. She quickly left a wet kiss at the corner of his lips, then came back to tickle his earlobes as she breathed huskily.

Although Steve had been rather passive, he suddenly stirred and threw her off with a powerful thrust of the hips. Joanna let herself fall on her back, satisfied that he couldn't hold back any longer and eager to have him take the lead.

Seizing her ankles, he brought them on to his shoulders as he knelt between her parted legs. Forcefully grabbing her hips, he pulled her towards him and penetrated her in one swift jab.

Joanna screamed in joy and surprise. He took her completely, pushing in as far as he could and stretching her with his girth. He thrust slowly but powerfully, withdrawing almost entirely before delving back in again. Joanna threw her arms above her head and let him do what he wanted. The back of her thighs rested against his abdomen and his silky hair tickled her deliciously. His warm hands, wrapped around her legs just above the knees, soon glided down and his fingertips gently caressed the soft skin on the inside.

He held her solidly and soon increased his tempo. On the bed, Joanna's body slid up and down under the force of his thrusts, and her breasts wobbled voluptuously. Each move brought her closer to climax, the swollen head of his dick probing deeper and deeper inside her and increasing her pleasure.

Her wet sex responded to the caress of Steve's phallus by giving the delightful, squishy noise Joanna found so enthralling. She was also unusually receptive to the sound and the feel of his thighs slapping against her buttocks with such violence. Steve grunted with each jab and Joanna couldn't help whining loudly with each breath. The sounds all mixed together and resonated in Joanna's head, making her dizzy with want.

Against her back, the bedspread rubbed in a way she usually would have found annoying and scratchy, but tonight it seemed to generate erotic torture of a new kind. She could hardly see her man in the darkness. She hadn't pulled the curtains but there was barely any light coming in through the window. At most, she could make out his broad shoulders, topped with her feet, and his bent elbows as he held on tightly to her legs. Now and again, the aroma of the fruit still left on the table floated towards her and increased her sensitivity.

All at once, the sounds, sights, smells and sensations blended into one and combined with the stimulation imposed by Steve's thrusts to result in an overwhelming orgasm which lasted a long time. It swept, transported her and took her on such a high she didn't want to come back down again.

But soon after, Steve started moving faster, his thrusts growing shallow, and Joanna could feel her whole body vibrating as a result. Sweat collected and trickled between his belly and her thighs. Suddenly, he stopped, tensed, and gave a strong final thrust. His hands clasped around her thighs and Joanna thought he would never let go. His head dropped back and he let out a loud scream. He panted repeatedly as his pelvis contracted and Joanna felt his member twitching powerfully inside her. A moment later, he collapsed next to her on the bed.

In a matter of seconds, the atmosphere in the room changed drastically, going from overloaded with lust and passion to absolutely still and sedate. They lay silently side by side as they both recovered from the storm that had just devastated their bodies.

Throwing her arm over his chest, Joanna let her fingers gently run up and down along Steve's ribcage. Under her hand, the pounding beat of his heart took forever to subside. His skin seemed even softer than before and she nestled against him as he slid his arm under her head. The bedroom was filled with the scent of their bodies, their coupling and the persistent aroma of freshly cut fruits, but not a sound could be heard except for their breathing and their occasional moans as waves of pleasure surged faintly and slowly vanished.

Chapter Eighteen

*T*he sound of the door opening woke her up. Joanna blinked a couple of times, then stared at the blushing cleaning lady. The woman stopped in her tracks, quickly muttered her apologies and left the room.

Joanna yawned as she stretched her arms and shifted her shoulders. Rolling around a few times, she luxuriated in the softness of the bedsheets. The sun was already up in the sky and she was amazed that its brightness hadn't woken her earlier. The smirk still hanging at the corner of her lips turned into a broad smile as she gradually recalled the events of the previous night.

By the time Steve had left, the horizon was already bathed in the pink light of the rising sun. Initially, Joanna had wanted to sleep in his arms but she hadn't dared ask him to stay. She was anxious to see him leave, fearing that eventually he would say or do something to break the spell, destroy the magic of their wonderful evening.

Later today, he was due to leave for the Philippines. That was going to be the end of it for the two of them. Their brief affair would remain just that. Joanna couldn't even imagine having a relationship with him. They were worlds apart, in more ways than one. Besides, she still preferred to preserve the lovely memory of their night together, rather than chance being disappointed if things didn't work out between the two of them. As she mindlessly caressed her pillow, she pondered the possibilities. It just wasn't practical. One of them would have to move so that they could be together. Besides, would he want to have anything to do with her after last night? Was it a habit of his to have sex with women he met whilst on business trips?

Joanna knew that he wouldn't easily grow tired of her, like he had with Greta. In fact, she was the one more likely to get tired first, judging from past experiences. Last night she had taken what she wanted, and she would go home with wonderful memories.

The notion of heading back suddenly made her think of Harry. It had been a while since she had been in touch with him, but she wasn't sorry. After what she had been through over the past few days, she had absolutely no interest in him whatsoever. And after having been with a man like Steve, it would perhaps take a while to find someone who could make her feel that way: generate such lust within her and take her to heights she hardly ever reached.

But, curiously, she didn't want Steve again. After such a perfect encounter, she was likely to be disappointed if the next time wasn't at least as good. And how could it be, now that getting him into bed would be so much easier? Her only regret was that she never got to see his body. She had felt the warmth of his skin, tasted his sweet maleness, heard the pounding beat of his heart, but she had missed out on the chance to admire his gorgeous manhood.

Too bad, she thought. The only way she would go with him again was if there was an added bonus, like the opportunity to see him bound and gagged and left entirely at her mercy, like the *salary-man* at Torima's secret place.

She shook herself and suddenly sat up in bed as she remembered Torima. The bedsheet glided down across her chest and tickled her nipples which immediately peaked. Like a flash, their agreement surged in her mind. Now that she had managed to seduce Steve, it was up to the people of the Jasmine Blossoms inn to keep up their end of the deal. There would be an endless series of banquets, more opportunities to show how wicked she could be. Night after night, men would willingly submit, and she knew there would be no end, no limit to the amount of satisfaction she would get out of torturing them.

She lay back again and rolled on to her stomach. Instinctively, her dew pooled between her legs and her hips heaved against the mattress. Just thinking about the possibilities made her hot again. That, she couldn't pass on. Her night with Steve had been passionate beyond belief, but at best that was all he had to offer. Pretty soon, she knew, she'd get bored with him even if he agreed to submit to her wishes of domination. After a while he would know her too well and the magic would be lost.

Torima had much more to offer: sessions just as satisfying but outstanding in their originality, their intensity, and the wicked notion of total domination. Just thinking about it made her excited again. What a shame she hadn't asked Steve to stay.

Now Joanna knew how Greta must have felt the previous morning when she was looking for her. Only in this instance, Joanna's eagerness to find Steve was based on something totally different. She hadn't written down her address on a piece of paper with the intention of giving it to him. All she wanted was to know whether anyone had contacted him to ask about her.

Torima had said he would know if she had been successful in seducing the Texan. But the only way of ascertaining that fact was to ask Steve himself. And since Steve was due to leave any minute, they would have had to have contacted him first thing that morning. Joanna cursed herself for not having asked him his room number. For some strange reason, it wasn't listed on his itinerary. Obviously, Torima's spies weren't as well informed as they could have been.

As a result, Joanna now found herself impatiently waiting in a queue by the front desk, dreading to find out that she had just missed him. When her turn finally came, she was utterly panic stricken and talking so fast that the clerk had to make her repeat her question twice.

Her blood turned cold when she heard he had already checked out of his room. She froze on the spot, but had the presence of mind to ask whether they knew if he had left the hotel. She was informed that he had put his luggage in the hotel's storage room, but no one was able to tell her when he would come to retrieve it.

So she found herself a comfortable seat near the porter's desk and waited, desperate to see him one last time.

Joanna clicked the padlock shut so forcefully that she feared she had broken it. As she finished packing and looked round the room one last time, her anger made her scream with exasperation. Seized with a sudden fit of madness, she grabbed the wrinkled bedsheets with both hands, ripped them off the mattress and quickly tore them to shreds.

For the past few days she had waited so impatiently, yet to no avail, that her frustration overflowed and needed to be vented. Despite standing guard in the foyer for hours on end, she hadn't seen Steve. His luggage was still in the storage room, but the porter had suggested that perhaps it was only part of his belongings and that he had taken the rest with him for his tour of the Philippines. No one could tell her whether he was due back or if his cases would be shipped directly to the States.

But that was only a small contributing factor to her resentment. More than two days after having succeeded in luring Steve into her clutches, she hadn't heard anything from Torima. He hadn't been true to his word.

To Joanna, that was the ultimate insult. Motivated by childish vengeance, she had crumpled the beautiful kimono they had sent her and thrown it in a corner of the room.

She slammed the door shut behind her as she made her way down the corridor, now eager to leave Japan. Although she had spent wonderful and unusual hours, she wanted to move on, to put all this behind her once and for all.

In the lift, the porter tried to start a conversation but Joanna didn't listen. She had chatted with him often over the past couple of days, but now that she had nothing to learn from him she just couldn't care less about what he had to say.

Her attitude towards the clerk at the counter was just as dry. She handed in her key and was about to turn round without even saying goodbye, when suddenly she heard the man say the magic word: 'message'. She stopped and looked at him again, incredulous. With trembling fingers, she grabbed the small piece of paper he was handing her and set her bag on the floor before unfolding it. Tears welled up in her eyes as she recognised the thin sprig of jasmine running along the edge of the sheet.

CONGRATULATIONS. THE TIME HAS NOW COME FOR YOU TO CONFIRM THAT YOU ARE WILLING TO JOIN US. PLEASE LEAVE YOUR LUGGAGE WITH THE PORTER AND ASK HIM TO TAKE YOU TO THE TOP FLOOR.

THERE, THE FINAL DECISION WILL BE UP TO YOU. WE TRUST YOU WILL MAKE THE WISEST CHOICE.

Relieved but puzzled, Joanna followed the instructions. The porter led the way to a lift at the back of the hotel. Once the doors slid behind them, he took out a small card with a magnetic strip and swiped it through a slot. The lift quickly took them up to the top floor. Once there, the porter used his card again to open the door and Joanna understood this floor was only accessible by special authorisation.

The long corridor had doors only on one side; five

identical evenly spaced doors made of heavy oak. As Joanna stepped out of the lift, the porter gave her another folded piece of paper and an entry card.

THIS CARD WILL LET YOU INTO ANY OF THESE ROOMS, EXCEPT FOR THE LAST ONE WHICH IS ONLY STORAGE SPACE. THE CARD WILL ONLY WORK ONCE, HOWEVER. IT IS UP TO YOU TO DECIDE WHICH ROOM YOU WANT TO GO INTO AND USE THE CARD TO GET IN. ONCE YOU HAVE USED THE CARD, IT WILL NO LONGER WORK ELSEWHERE AND YOU CAN ONLY GO BACK DOWNSTAIRS USING THE LIFT.

Joanna stared down the long corridor. She turned to look at the porter who simply bowed and smiled at her before the door of the lift closed on him, leaving Joanna alone with her decision.

One out of four, but which? As she walked towards the first door, she immediately noticed a large peephole. Something told her it wasn't meant for the occupants of the room to see who was at the door, but the other way around.

She placed her trembling hands on the warm oak, leant forward and looked through the curved lens. Just as she had suspected, she could see perfectly inside the room. As her eyes took in the details, her heart jumped and she let out a small cry of surprise.

The room was almost an exact replica of the geishas' dressing room at the inn, from the jars on the counter to the jasmine shrub in the far corner. In the middle, two young women were sitting on low stools and chatting casually. Both wore pink and green kimonos, like the one Joanna had received but left behind in her room in a fit of anger. Now she wished she had kept it. The vision had radically changed her mood. Her anger had vanished some time ago, and now remnants of surprise quickly turned into seething desire as she recognised her friends Atsuko and Keiko.

Her first impulse was to swipe the card to open the door and join them. But as she fumbled to place the magnetic strip the right way up, she suddenly stopped and moved away from the door. Slowly turning her head, she glanced at the next door and paused.

There were other rooms to see. The words from the message she had picked up at the front desk came back to her mind. 'We trust you will make the wisest choice.' Obviously, Torima had other things in mind, other possibilities for her to explore.

Mechanically, she walked to the next door, her mind totally detached from her body, moving as if in a dream. If the sight in the first room had surprised her, what awaited in the next one shocked her even more. The room was decorated like any of the bedrooms in the hotel. Sprawled on the bed was Steve, surrounded by pieces of paper scattered all around him, pen in hand and seemingly absorbed in his work.

Joanna closed her eyes and swallowed nervously. He hadn't left. That's why his luggage was still in the storage room downstairs. Judging by his casual stance, he wasn't being held against his will. But Joanna distinctly remembered he should have been in the Philippines by now. On the other hand, she knew better than to discount the power Torima and his people held. They could easily have offered him money to stay another few days.

She had to force herself to walk away. Again, she wanted to go and join him. But having seen Steve – not to mention Keiko and Atsuko – she now shuddered to think what could be awaiting her in the next room.

She almost ran to the door and braced herself for what she would see through the peephole. This time, what she found made her smile. Dressed in the same ridiculous, mock cowboy outfit, Yukio, the young waiter from the 'roadside diner', was pacing nervously. Joanna remembered the message she had received after he had been in her room a few weeks ago. Torima knew she had more or less initiated the inexperienced waiter to the pleasures of submission. It must have been child's play for Torima's people to track him down and bring him here. She laughed softly and moved away, now impatient to see what else Torima had to offer.

Behind the fourth door, the spectacle awaiting her was nothing short of a grand finale. Lying on his back on the bare hardwood floor, the shivering figure of a naked man was solidly fastened and securely shackled with sturdy clamps bolted to the floor. His body, rather frail but trim, was unremarkable. But the one thing Joanna did notice was his dick, which stood proudly erect, and incredibly long. Although it wasn't very thick, its length nevertheless made the purplish head look smaller than average. Joanna smiled to herself, trying to imagine what could be going through the man's mind at that moment. She didn't recognise his face, but already she had guessed that he was another *salary-man*, probably waiting for his fantasy to become reality.

A strange suspicion entered her mind and she checked the last door, just for the sake of it. But the message hadn't lied: it was indeed a storage room which contained several chairs piled up in one corner, stacks of bedsheets and blankets on a trolley, a large round table propped up against a wall, and several cleaning items. Joanna walked away and stopped in the middle of the corridor.

Her head spun from what she knew awaited her. Was this meant as a test or a reward? Probably the former, judging from what the message said. The choice was up to her, and she had to be wise about it.

She couldn't help smiling when she thought of how wicked Torima's plan was. He was giving her the possibility of reliving any encounter, but only one. During the past few weeks, she had never been issued such a challenge.

At first glance, any of these people could give her the pleasure they had provided in the past. If she had to pick the best, she would have gone for Steve. But perhaps that was exactly what she shouldn't do. However tempting it appeared, Joanna sensed she was on the wrong track.

221

Obviously, Torima knew she had succeeded in seducing Steve, or else she wouldn't be here. Ultimately, he had kept up his end of the bargain, even with this added twist. Joanna's decision would have to reinforce the certainty that she was worthy of joining their group. That meant proving to them that what she valued above all else was the pleasure stemming from domination. She smiled as she remembered what she had been asked during her first visit to the Jasmine Blossoms inn, the night of the seemingly innocent banquet. What was the ultimate pleasure? Now she had her answer, or at least the answer Torima would like to hear.

Decisively, she walked to the fourth door and swiped the key card through the slot. The doorknob gave a click and she grabbed it. It turned without resistance. Joanna's heart pounded as she forcefully pushed the heavy oak door open.

Chapter Nineteen

*F*rom the moment she entered the room, Joanna
realised it was much bigger than she had previously
thought. There were many details the peephole hadn't
allowed her to see. The light was faint and diffused,
coming from a dozen small light bulbs in the low ceiling.
The walls were soundproof and muffled even the sound
of her breathing.

She was only mildly surprised by the presence of two
young men, attendants, sitting on a bench in the corner.
They stood and bowed to her. Joanna bowed back. One
of the men gestured towards a trolley next to him, which
was covered by a white sheet. Curious, Joanna pulled
the sheet off. Underneath, she recognised the same
panoply of instruments which had been put at her
disposition on the night of the banquet. Only this time
they didn't lie in a heap. Each item was carefully placed,
like surgical instruments in an operating theatre. This
strange set-up didn't do much for Joanna. Somehow it
wasn't nearly as exciting as the first time.

As the other attendant invited her to turn round,
Joanna noticed a small table set with fresh fruit, sushi
and an open bottle of wine, presumably for her. She
couldn't help laughing at how typical this was of
Torima: sex and food went hand in hand.

Finally, she turned to the man on the floor. She had sensed his eyes on her from the moment she had appeared, but she had purposefully avoided looking at him. He could wait, she had decided. In fact, the longer he waited, the better. He smiled sheepishly as Joanna walked around him a couple of times. Whereas at first she had read apprehension and fear in his eyes, soon she detected a glimmer of amusement, even contempt. Puzzled by this sudden smugness despite his precarious position, she realised that he had been peeking underneath her skirt as she walked round. That was enough to stir her domineering instincts. Swiftly stepping back, she decided that from now on, he wouldn't be allowed to see anything at all.

She turned to the attendants. 'Turn him over,' she said in English. 'On his stomach, and make sure he can't move.'

The attendants bowed in reply and obeyed her orders. Judging from the *salary-man*'s cries of protest, this wasn't an element of his fantasy. 'That is not what I asked for!' he yelled repeatedly, in Japanese, as the attendants solidly refastened the shackles once they had turned him over. Yet Joanna noticed his protest was only verbal. He made no effort to stop the attendants from carrying out her instructions. His prick remained erect, another sign that perhaps he wasn't entirely against Joanna's decision. In fact, he was probably even more excited by the prospect of having her dominate him totally.

He lay spreadeagled on the floor, his face slightly turned to the right. Joanna stood at his hips, straddling them. That way, no matter how he tried to move his neck, he couldn't see anything but her legs. After taking off her jumper, she nonchalantly let it fall to the floor, right in front of her slave's nose.

With a deliberately slow movement, she then pulled down the zip of her skirt. It gave with a grating, metallic sound. Joanna saw the skin on the man's back break into goose bumps, and the sight of it enhanced her feeling of superiority.

She let the skirt glide down along her legs, making sure it brushed the man's bum as it reached her ankles. She stepped out of it, picked it up and dropped it to the left of the man's face. He turned to look at it, then closed his eyes and breathed deeply. For a moment he seemed mesmerised by it, as if her perfume still lingering on the fabric brought him to a state of ecstasy.

Writhing on the floor as much as his restraints would let him, the man desperately tried to look at Joanna. She moved away even further, stood near his parted legs and finished undressing.

Her minuscule cotton bra quickly joined the rest of her clothes. Having tossed it with amazing precision, it landed only inches from the man's nose. At first he seemed rather excited by this sight, but soon she felt him growing impatient for what was to come next.

Keeping her back to him at all times, she sidled across the room so that he wouldn't be able to see her bare chest. Turning her head to see his face, she was satisfied that he never took his eyes off her. By coincidence, that morning she had chosen to wear simple white cotton knickers. Now she was glad she had chosen them, knowing that in this country many men still held a fixation for pristine juvenile-looking underwear. The contrast with her black high-heeled shoes was only the more pronounced, and Joanna knew the sight would excite him even more.

But Joanna didn't allow her slave the pleasure of admiring her pert cotton-clad bottom for very long. Without a word, she grabbed the blindfold that lay on top of the trolley and handed it to one of the attendants. Once again the *salary-man* protested loudly as the attendants tied the white piece of fabric round his head. But Joanna didn't care. She was in charge, and if she chose not to let him see anything, there was nothing he could say that would make her change her mind.

Again, she could detect falseness in his cries. From

what Torima had told her, the men who came to him sought to fulfil their fantasies of submission. Only, he hadn't explained to what extent these enactments were dictated by the men themselves. It would have been too simple, predictable, to follow their instructions to the letter though. The real thrill lay in the unknown.

Having seized a riding crop, Joanna returned to straddle the man's legs. His back pearled with fine drops of sweat, and she could see veins bulging in his forearms as he pulled on his restraints. He was still protesting, but now his cries sounded more like whining, dull and annoying. Joanna made him shut up with a couple of well-placed blows on his buttocks. He cringed and twisted in vain, but finally ceased complaining.

Setting the tip of the crop at the base of his neck, she lightly tickled him, moving from one ear to the other, and in large circles over the bump at the top of his spine. The man shivered under the rough caress. Joanna watched, mesmerised, as goose bumps surged all over his body. The fine hair on his back and on his buttocks stood on end as she directed the crop down along his ribcage, lightly brushing his armpits and trailing across his back in a zigzag motion.

Now and again she slapped him a little, dispensing stinging blows on his parted cheeks until they grew red and slightly swollen with marks. Each time his muscles contracted, playing under his skin and making his buttocks look like two perfectly kneaded balls of dough. Their sight made Joanna hot.

Without letting go of the riding crop, she took off her knickers and crouched over the man's bum. Setting one hand on the small of his back for balance, she pressed her flesh against his raised skin and swayed back and forth. Her blows had turned his bum into a hot rough-textured rock, and Joanna enjoyed rubbing herself against it.

He bucked underneath her, lifting his hips as if wanting to feel more of her wet flesh against his own skin. But Joanna wouldn't tolerate that. She was in charge, and she wasn't afraid of reminding him with a quick blow of the crop right between the shoulder blades.

His skin was incredibly hot and raised, and the effect on her moist flesh was unusual and pleasant. Soon her clitoris reared and demanded more stimulation. Her thighs ached, and the high heels of her shoes didn't afford her good balance. She needed something more drastic and immediate to enhance her enjoyment. Fortunately, the solution was right in her hand.

Placing the handle of the riding crop between his bum and her sex, she used it to caress herself, enjoying the rough touch of the braided leather on her stiff bud. The pain in her thighs was soon forgotten as her arousal grew. Joanna wanted to abandon herself, enjoy the release of this first orgasm. But a better idea rose in her mind: she would have her slave pleasure her instead. Panting with want, she quickly stood and went to sit in front of him on the floor, legs apart. Her glistening slit was just inches from the man's head. She saw him fidget as she got closer. He had probably heard her but was unable to guess what she was doing.

Grabbing him by the hair, she lifted his head and slid her bum closer, bringing her flesh into contact with his mouth. His tongue came out lazily and he took a taste of her fragrant dew before closing his mouth again. Incensed by his lack of interest, Joanna decided simply to take what she wanted. She held on tighter, writhing against his mouth to pleasure herself. She liked the way his tight lips felt against her swollen sex.

The man breathed in deeply. Her dew smeared across the bottom half of his face seemed to arouse him. Once again he licked her hesitantly, but soon he grew more eager. His behaviour prompted Joanna to think that perhaps he had never kissed female flesh before. She also took strange pleasure in the notion that he couldn't see her. His hesitation was only short lived as she seized the crop and hit him on the back again.

The effect was immediate. From reluctant and lazy, her slave rapidly became insatiable, as if contact with her sex was an acquired taste. Before long he relished her thoroughly, incessantly delving inside her and coming back out to discover the whole of her slit. His breath grew shallow and fast, as his nose dug deeply within her toffee-coloured bush and his lips pressed against her swollen bud.

Holding his head with both hands, Joanna continued her writhing, directing his mouth where she wanted it. His saliva mixed with her dew and she felt it trickle down the crevice of her bum to pool between her warm skin and the wooden floor. She pressed his head harder against her flesh, practically choking him, but so close to climax she didn't want to let go.

He grunted as he increased the strength and the speed of his caresses. Joanna came with a loud cry, and immediately pulled away. As pleasure rioted through her, she was fascinated by the sight of his tongue still searching for her, moving blindly across his lips in a vain attempt to reach her. But already she was up and walking away from him. She wobbled slightly, feeling the aftershocks of her orgasm, as she pondered her next move. Her climax had been intense, but soon she knew she would want more.

For a few seconds, she was at a loss, not knowing what she should do next. Suddenly remembering the impressive sight of his long dick, she ordered the attendants to roll the man on to his back. A moment later his erection reappeared in the soft light of the room, looking longer and stiffer than before. The man thrust in vain, his hips instinctively pushing towards the ceiling. He was ready. But Joanna decided he could wait.

She walked leisurely to the table and contemplated the food on offer, surprised to realise that she was hungry. Obviously, Torima had known she would be and she was grateful for his generosity. She quickly prepared a helping of sushi for herself, picking a large chunk of raw tuna fish and smothering it with a heavy dollop of green *wasabe* paste before rolling it up in a handful of sticky rice. She bit off almost half of it and slowly chewed, letting the flavours mix in her mouth and the vapours of the fiery *wasabe* drift up the back of her throat. This was better by far than simple horse-radish, hot and spicy, and just what Joanna needed to rekindle her arousal.

The attendants both watched her with blank expressions, as if unimpressed by what they had just witnessed. Joanna couldn't care less. She had no need for them except to handle her slave if need be.

A bottle of white wine awaited in an ice bucket. Joanna poured herself a glass and took a large gulp to wash down what food was left in her mouth. The spices and the alcohol gently warmed her stomach and she gave a sigh of satisfaction. Suddenly, she was hot again and ready to return to her slave.

Orange segments cut up and artistically placed in a shallow bowl gave her an idea. She grabbed a handful and turned to the man writhing on the floor. Standing tall near his torso, she squeezed the orange flesh and let its juice dribble all over his chest. Its fragrance rose and made her hungry again; not only for the fruit, but for the man as well. Yet she still wanted to take her time. Quietly kneeling down, she watched the man's nipples contract and peak as the juice trickled down the side of his ribcage. She held her breath, not wanting him to know where she was nor what she was going to do. She wanted to proceed slowly and attack him by surprise.

She bent down towards him as silently as she could. Using only her tongue, she swiftly lapped up each drop of juice, all the while making sure this was their only point of contact. The man's body contorted from the first touch and twisted even more violently as Joanna drew his nipple into her mouth and sucked it hard. Glancing sideways, she saw his stiff prick rear and a fine drop appear in the tiny slit.

Suddenly, she longed to feel him inside her. Never had she seen anything so long, and from the moment she had first seen it she had wondered what it would be like to feel it inside her. In the past, proportions had never really mattered to her. But now it was unusually enticing. Her flesh was hungry for it; she had kept it waiting too long.

On the other hand, she knew she couldn't give her slave the pleasure of penetrating her just yet. Instead, she crouched over him once again and let her clenching flesh lightly brush against the swollen, purplish head. The shaft twitched and lifted, as if animated, with a mind of its own. It hit her directly on the clitoris, and Joanna squealed with surprise and pleasure.

Forcefully grabbing the hard rod in one hand, she directed the head over her slit, caressing herself until she came close to another orgasm. The swollen glans was the perfect instrument with which to stimulate her arousal.

The man tried to thrust a couple of times but Joanna managed to avoid him. Yet his moans made it clear that he wanted to penetrate her. He was hard and stiff in her hand, pulsating dangerously as if he were on the verge of reaching his peak. So Joanna decided to cool him down.

Seizing the base of his shaft, she held it tightly until his erection subsided. Even in a semi-flaccid state, it was impressive to behold. But then Joanna changed her mind and decided she preferred it in its full glory. Lightly tickling his shaft and his balls with her fingertips, she quickly roused him back into full erection. She let go of him and went back to the table to see what else she could use. Her eyes paused for a moment on the *yoroi-gata*, the latticed penile sheath she had been handed at Torima's banquet. Only this time the surprise factor was lacking and she didn't fancy using it.

Without a word, the attendants stood and went to open a door at the far end of the room. Puzzled, Joanna watched as they entered the adjoining storage room, the same room she had glanced at from the corridor some time earlier.

230

Together they rolled out a large round table. As they brought it to Joanna, they laid it on the floor and she saw that it was only about a foot high. The base was solid but a revolving panel had been affixed on top. Joanna had seen such double-panelled tables before. They were quite common in Asia, especially for large communal meals where food was laid on the table and everyone helped themselves by revolving the panel. It looked very ordinary, although its rich mahogany colour made it quite appealing. As she came closer to examine it, Joanna noticed its special feature and couldn't help smiling.

Right in the middle, a hole about four inches in diameter had been carved through. Joanna immediately knew what purpose it served and gestured for the attendants to bring it closer. Obediently, they lifted it and set it over the man. One of the attendants bent down, reached underneath and guided the man's long dick through the hole.

Obviously, Torima's employees were well trained. She hadn't asked for the table; she hadn't even known it was there. It was as if they had read her mind, seen that she was indecisive about her next move and simply wanted to show her another option. It had been the same night of Torima's banquet, when someone had handed her the latticed penile sheath which perfectly suited her purposes then.

Once set on the floor, the table was impressive to behold. Despite the thickness of the two wooden panels, the man's erect prick still protruded from the top by about four inches. The man had no idea what was happening, but he sensed something was wrong. Only his head and his feet were visible; the rest was shielded by the table. Peeking underneath, Joanna saw that the bottom of the table barely cleared his body. His chest heaved with each breath and his nipples mercilessly brushed against the rough wood.

Yet Joanna didn't let that bother her. Climbing on the table, she knelt over his dick, setting her bottom directly over his member. She sat back and let it penetrate her. The stretching sensation enhanced her arousal. It wasn't all that unusual, but what really excited her was the notion that her slave couldn't feel much else. She waited a while, basking in this satisfaction. He couldn't see anything, so he wouldn't know about the table. Therefore, he couldn't even imagine what was going on. If he was bewildered now, in a moment he would go right out of his mind.

With a brief nod of the head, she instructed the attendants to push the panel slowly in a clockwise direction. Inside Joanna, the gliding sensation defied description. A couple of rotations was enough to make her crazy with lust, and it didn't stop there. She remembered how Atsuko had so skilfully twirled the large ivory dildo inside her. She also recalled how the tall blond girl at the banquet had inserted the long metal chain inside her vagina and made it twirl as well. The feeling was new, intense and immensely pleasurable. She closed her eyes as the room revolved around her, wanting to avoid any distraction to concentrate better on the feeling inside her pelvis.

Under the table the *salary-man* thrust in vain, the movement of his hips at times so strong that Joanna felt him hit the table violently and practically lift it up even with her on top.

It soon became clear that the attendants were highly skilled in this manoeuvre. The speed they imparted on the revolving panel was timed so that Joanna could enjoy the maximum of stimulation without feeling dizzy or nauseous. Arching her back, she let her head fall backwards. Her soft folds rotated endlessly over the man's erect prick, its swollen end caressing her without pausing so much as a fraction of a second, and in a fashion so unusual that the mere notion of what was happening was enough to make Joanna mad with pleasure. Her hips heaved by instinct, enhancing the sensation even further.

Bending forward again, she curled up into a ball,

pressing her stiff and throbbing bud against the man's hard shaft. She wiggled her hips incessantly, wanting to experience more stimulation from this weird contraption. Her flesh clenched repeatedly, gripping the man's phallus and reluctantly letting it go as her folds spun over it. Her orgasm built up slowly, softly. It was born at the entrance of her tunnel, right where the contact with the man's long dick was at its maximum. As it rose, she moaned loudly. Soon it scattered inside her, branching out through her abdomen and she could feel it even in her breasts. The sensation lasted longer than anything she had ever experienced and made her pant with pleasure. It crept up and lifted her, a blissful delight that was amazing in its delicacy.

The intensity of her climax was only matched by the speed at which it subsided. Soon after, Joanna stopped feeling anything. The member twitching inside her was just as stiff, but Joanna's flesh barely felt it. Her whole body had become numb and she was exhausted, out of breath after having screamed her joy at the top of her lungs. It had all been too much. Weakened by the constant stimulation and the power of the wave that had just swept her, she made the attendants stop, crawled down from the table and on to the floor as she caught her breath.

Disregarding the man who now violently protested under the table, the attendants came to Joanna and helped her to her feet. One of them supported her as the other opened the door to what Joanna had thought was a closet, but which in fact led to the adjoining room, the same room where she had seen Yukio before. Only now the young man was nowhere in sight. The attendant helped her lie on the futon whilst the other brought in her clothes. Reclining, still naked, on the soft cotton cover, Joanna soon fell asleep, without so much as another thought for the man she had just left writhing under the table.

Chapter Twenty

*J*oanna awoke to the feel of a hand stroking her weak thighs. Before she even opened her eyes, the scent of jasmine reached her nostrils and she smiled to herself. There would be no end to this; now she knew.

As she lifted and turned her head, she was pleasantly surprised to find her friend Yukio had returned. Even more surprising was that he was accompanied by another young man who could easily have passed for his brother. Both men were of identical height and build. Even their hairstyles and facial features were similar. Thankfully, neither of them wore silly mock-cowboy outfits. All they had on was some sort of leather thong, which tightly encased their swollen genitals whilst allowing Joanna to admire their perfectly sculpted bottoms.

In fact, their bodies were no less than perfectly shaped, looking even better than Joanna remembered. Even Yukio's face seemed different. He looked more mature, more serene, and his eyes had lost the puppy-like enthusiasm and innocence that Joanna had initially found so attractive in him. Yet she couldn't help thinking that this change in him was a result of how she had treated him. It was plain to see that after having been her pupil, he had become a real man.

Together the young men slowly massaged Joanna's thighs as she repositioned herself on the futon. She lay on her stomach, legs parted and arms folded under her head, with the men on either side of her. The muscles in her legs were indeed sore after all the squatting she had done in the other room. In fact, even her arms needed to be stroked. She writhed slightly and stretched. Yukio left his companion to do her thighs and proceeded to minister to her shoulders and arms instead.

Soon Joanna found herself totally relaxed but wide awake. She glanced at the other young man, wondering how he knew Yukio and how the two of them had found their way here.

'What's your name?' she asked in a groggy voice.

'Tsunemi,' he said simply. He didn't even look at her as he replied, but Joanna couldn't care less. She didn't need to know his life story, really. All that mattered was the way his hands moved smoothly over her thighs, gliding with just enough pressure to soothe their soreness.

Her skin glistened softly, covered with oil, and she couldn't resist the temptation to rub her smooth thighs together. Tsunemi's fingers were momentarily caught in between, but the layer of oil on her skin allowed him to escape her grip. Yet the move had aroused Joanna, and now she wanted the men to touch more than just her arms and legs. Turning on her back, she sprawled on the futon, issuing them a silent invitation to caress more of her.

But neither of them seemed to receive the message. Yukio stood, moved to the wall and slid open a panel. Glancing in his direction, Joanna caught a glimpse of the bathroom. Soon after, Tsunemi helped her up and ushered her in there.

In the middle of the room, an elevated round white porcelain bathtub was filled to overflowing with fragrant water. Without waiting any further, Joanna climbed the few wooden steps and stepped into the bath. The water enveloped her, filling her with warmth and relieving the lingering ache in her muscles. The oil on her skin dispersed but there remained a soft slippery sensation all over her body when she let her elbows caress her flanks and her legs rub together as she sat down.

The water had a relaxing effect on her. She had no idea how long she had slept, but she knew it couldn't have been more than an hour. Despite that, she felt tremendously rejuvenated and was ravenous.

She had expected her young suitors to follow her into the bath, but they didn't. Yukio came forward carrying a large sponge, whereas Tsunemi brought her a tray loaded with food. Joanna sat back and let out a long sigh. They knelt near the edge of the bath, which unfortunately shielded the magnificent view of their hips and buttocks. All Joanna could see was their bare chests.

On the tray presented by Tsunemi, a selection of prawns, chunks of crab meat and smoked mussels lay on a bed of fruit. The sight reminded her of Steve and how he had confessed this was his favourite food. For a moment, Joanna let her imagination wander as she seized a prawn and delicately slipped it into her mouth.

Where could he be now, she wondered? Probably on his way to the Philippines. She firmly believed that Torima's people had found a way to delay him, to put him in the room just to taunt Joanna. But once she had chosen otherwise, they would have no need for him and had probably let him go.

Joanna also realised she had completely forgotten about the plane she was supposed to take to Vietnam. In fact, she should have been on board quite a while ago. Yet it didn't matter any more; she wasn't returning to work for International Emporium. From now on, she would concentrate solely on obeying Torima's instructions. Judging from the treatment she was now receiving, there was no doubt in her mind that she had indeed made the wisest choice. It was obvious even as she watched the way her two companions took care of her.

Yukio knelt by the side of the bath tub and plunged his naked arms under the water whilst Tsunemi stood by, keeping the tray within Joanna's reach.

This time the massage Joanna received was more energising, and much more arousing as well. The young waiter's hands travelled over her ribcage and he softly caressed her breasts, which the water had rendered weightless. Joanna moaned as he expertly fingered her nipples. The way he worried them into hardness was astounding, and Joanna could hardly believe this was the same young man whom she had had to tell what to do not all that long ago.

Suddenly, she no longer wanted to be in that bath. She wanted to go back to the futon, take both men with her and entice them into showing her what else they were capable of. After all, if Yukio had already been with her, it was only fair that Tsunemi should get his chance as well.

She fantasised about having them both, together. What started out as a vague image in her mind quickly grew into an overwhelming impulse and gave Joanna the energy to step out of the tub. Her new friends wrapped her in a large towel and preceded her into the bedroom.

Once there, she flung the towel across the room and threw herself on the futon. Staring at them daringly, she let her hands glide across her flesh to the junction of her legs. They both stared in reply but didn't make any move towards her. Joanna was puzzled by their lack of response. It was clear from the big bulges in their thongs that the sight of her had a definite effect on them, yet they didn't act on it. Sitting up, she held out her hands towards Yukio. She expected him to pounce on her, like he had done the other night in her room. But he remained unmoved.

As she reached forward to caress his hard body, he stepped back. Joanna turned to Tsunemi. He, too, didn't seem to want to come near her. Joanna was speechless, unable to think of anything to say to encourage them.

But she wasn't about to give up on them so easily. If words failed her, she would resort to body language.

With a devilish smile, she lay back, parted her legs to expose her wet flesh and naughtily stroked her slit with her fingertips. Her flesh was already moist with her dew, slightly gaping with expectancy. Her swollen folds quivered as she touched them and she sighed with delight. Against her palm, her throbbing bud was already erect, and she just knew that the two young men by her side couldn't miss it. They both watched religiously and after a while she even caught a glimmer of admiration in their eyes. Yet that wasn't enough to move them.

When they turned round and left the room altogether, Joanna sat up abruptly and cursed aloud. Where were they going? Quickly retrieving the towel, she wrapped herself in it and stepped out of the room. But by then it was too late. She barely had time to see the doors to the lift closing behind them.

Coming back to her room, she slumped on the bed, lay back and stared at the ceiling. Her body once again craved physical release and the men's sudden departure only enhanced her need, leaving her frustrated, angry and confused. What on earth was going on? Was this another part of Torima's wicked plan? Did he want to test her still, to find out how much frustration she could endure? She couldn't understand why he would do that at this point. She had managed to seduce Steve, as ordered. By choosing to go into the last room in the corridor, she was convinced she had done the right thing. And finding these two young men to cater to her when she awoke had convinced her that everything was fine. Obviously, she would have to wait for further directives.

She fetched her clothes and quickly got dressed. She had no idea what she was supposed to do next, having been through too many ups and downs. She had to trust that Torima would find a way to get further instructions to her. In fact, there was probably another message waiting for her at the reception desk at that moment. As she was about to leave the room, she stopped, turned round and stared at the panel hiding the door to the adjoining room.

She had to go back there, one more time, just for the kick of once again seeing that formidable table. Carefully, she opened the door and peeped in. The *salaryman* and the attendants were gone, and the food had been cleared. The round table was propped up against the wall, suddenly looking totally innocuous. With great difficulty, Joanna set it back on its feet and reached forward to make the top panel spin. The wood felt warm in her hand and she let it slide softly against her skin for a while. She couldn't help laughing as she forcefully grabbed the panel and made it spin faster and faster. As she watched it revolve, she tried to imagine how it would feel to find herself once again mounting the man, but rotating at this increased speed.

A voice suddenly coming from behind her dragged her out of her contemplation.

'I've often heard the phrase "sit on it and spin" but I always thought it was meant as a polite way of telling someone to get lost. I never imagined it was actually feasible.'

Joanna straightened up as a sudden rush of warmth invaded her. Steve's cynical tone was unmistakable. Her heart pounded and excitement flowed to her loins. A second later, she felt her flesh melt. She turned round slowly, wondering whether her imagination was playing some nasty trick on her, or if indeed Steve had come back and was standing right behind her.

'I guess I was wrong,' he continued as he came closer. 'We should never underestimate the inventiveness of the Japanese.'

Joanna stared at him incredulously. It was really him, in the same clothes he had been wearing when she had seen him through the peephole earlier that evening. Only now, there was no door separating them. She didn't move as he came closer and examined the table.

Joanna was frozen with delight and surprise. She wanted to reach forward and touch him, to ensure that it wasn't just an illusion. He was right there with her, in the same room! It couldn't possibly be.

Images flashed through her mind and immediately Joanna knew she wanted him again. She couldn't wait to have him slip underneath the table and give him the same treatment which she had administered to the *salary-man* earlier.

Steve reached down and made the top panel spin. 'Very ingenious,' he conceded.

Joanna leant against him and seized his hand to pull it away from the table. 'Would you like to try it?' she asked in a husky voice. 'It's like nothing you've ever experienced before, I'm sure.'

Steve winced and then smirked. 'I'll take your word for it,' he said. 'Not really my game.'

Joanna's excitement was quelled by sudden irritation. Now what? How dare he refuse her? Would she have to put together another silly scenario to get him to want her again? His lack of enthusiasm and his sarcastic tone were suddenly downright annoying. As much as she wanted him, she wasn't about to go back to square one and come up with another scheme to get him into bed.

'Then what is your game?' she asked coldly.

He looked at her, smiled smugly and gently grabbed her hand. 'Since you're asking . . .' He didn't finish his sentence but dragged her out of the room. To Joanna's amazement, he led her quickly through the adjoining room where he walked past the futon without paying it any attention. Instead, he pushed yet another sliding panel and a moment later Joanna found herself in the room where she had seen him earlier.

Obviously, these rooms all communicated, and Joanna realised that Steve knew more than she did about the set-up of this place. But how did he know? She didn't have time to ask him. They entered his bedroom and he quickly closed the door behind them. As they had progressed from room to room, her mood had changed again. Her irritation vanished and she began to suspect Steve did have lewd plans for her.

It was now early evening and the room was almost completely dark. The only source of light came from the window. Joanna walked towards it, remembering the mesmerising sight which had greeted her upon her arrival in Tokyo. Only then did she realise that the other rooms didn't have any windows and this was a welcome change. Although she wasn't in Tokyo any more, and the street several floors below wasn't as busy, the coloured neon lights shone just as brightly and everything else seemed strangely familiar.

It was happening all over again. Would things take a different turn tonight? Would she go to bed alone? Behind her, Steve crept up slowly. His hands followed the curve of her waist and paused on her belly as his lips delicately pinched the smooth skin of her neck. Joanna shivered as she abandoned herself in his embrace, pleased to see how wrong she had been about him, and how all was not lost in the end. Relief filled her and left her feeling somewhat lethargic. Suddenly, she was too tired to make him crawl like she had done before. What would be the point? Already his kisses had grown bolder and Joanna was more than willing to be taken on his terms.

His fingers crawled underneath her jumper and lifted it up. Joanna was content to raise her arms to help him take it off, but nothing more than that. She preferred to remain idle, not knowing what to expect but certain that he wouldn't disappoint her.

As soon as her hot skin was exposed, he released his embrace. He quickly undid the zip at the back of her skirt, which fell to the floor, and held her hand as she stepped out of it. But that was their only contact. Joanna shivered as his fingertips undid the hook of her bra. He wasn't close enough to touch her, but she could definitely feel his warm breath on her shoulders. Now she stood almost naked in front of him, but with her back turned, waiting expectantly for him to make the next move.

His arms returned to circle her waist and he kissed her neck again, this time more passionately. She felt herself growing limp and faint in his arms. His hands massaged her hips in large circles, his fingertips slipping ever so slightly under the waistband of her knickers, teasing the hair at the top of her mound. They then glided upwards to tease each of her breasts in turn, using only one hand whilst the other held her close to him. Her nipples responded stiffly to the caress of his fingertips and she sighed with delight.

Now Joanna had lost the notion of where she was. The street down below was lost in the cloud of mist her breath had left on the glass pane. Steve's mouth quickly grew eager. As his hands surveyed her chest, he used his lips and his tongue to work her back. His hot large hands kneaded her breasts in a soft but determined motion, all the while tweaking her nipples with his fingertips. He was growing excited as well, his breath becoming shallow and fast, warm and hard against her sensitive skin.

His thumbs slipped decisively underneath the elastic band of her knickers and he knelt as he pulled them down. Setting her hand on his head for support, Joanna lifted one foot after the other and let him slip the small cotton undies from around her ankles. Finally she was naked, still facing the window, with the man who had triggered in her such intense pleasure kneeling behind her.

She whined as he bent down and covered her calves with hot kisses. He paused briefly as his mouth reached the back of her knees. A moment later, his tongue began to lazily bathe her smooth skin. Instinctively, Joanna parted her legs. Just as she had hoped, his fingertips crept up the inside of her thighs and lightly caressed her moist folds. His thumb slid inside her, slowly caressing and stretching the smooth walls of her tunnel, giving her a taste of what was yet to come.

His knuckles strummed her hard bud. Joanna squealed as each pointy bone teased her swollen shaft, flickering over it lightly but with such intensity she felt faint. Her knees trembled under the effect of such an unusual tactic. Her arousal was at its peak, but his touch was perfectly calculated to keep her precisely near the point of no return without actually pushing her past it.

Now she wanted him to use his mouth as well, but she didn't dare ask him. The atmosphere was strangely calm and devoid of the harsh notion of domination she had now grown accustomed to. There was incredible tenderness in his touch, and Joanna didn't want to talk for fear of breaking the spell.

Soon his whole face pressed against her bare thighs and she relished the smoothness of his cheeks. He grew even more eager, his breath becoming shallow as his mouth endlessly covered her hot skin. Seconds later, as if in a frenzy, he quickly made her turn round.

Joanna leant against the window as she parted her legs. The glass felt refreshingly cool against her back, but it wasn't sufficient to quell the fire now burning within her. For Steve's rising passion was contagious. If, only a moment earlier, Joanna had basked in a soft warmth and a mellow atmosphere, now she was just as hot and keenly excited as he was. The smell of her own dew, coupled with that of his cologne and his male aroma, had rendered her senses acute. Her brain had enhanced the sensation and transformed it to increase her arousal.

She let out a cry as his mouth reached her sex. His tongue danced rapidly over her flesh, the tip lightly but expertly worrying her bud. Joanna moaned loudly as she felt her first climax approaching. Again she was amazed by how quickly he could make her come. The mere notion that he wanted her was in itself enough to bring her to a state of high arousal. He could make her cross the threshold with a mere flick of his fingers or his tongue.

She moaned again as pleasure filled her, warm and

ethereal. It was strong but not violent, yet immensely satisfying as it softly billowed inside her. It subsided soon after, leaving her feeling sluggish but fulfilled. As she quietened down, Steve rose to his feet and held her in a passionate embrace.

'What would you like now?' he whispered breathlessly in her ear.

'I want to see you naked,' she sighed. 'Turn on the lights and undress for me.'

'Not yet,' he said as he laughed softly. 'Let me take you first.'

'As you wish,' she purred.

He made her face the window again, rapidly coaxed her to bend forward slightly and part her legs. Although she could no longer see him, she could sense he had grown into a sudden frenzy. Behind her, she heard him grunt with impatience as he quickly undid his trousers. Only a moment later she felt the head of his hard prick nudging at her entrance.

In a matter of seconds his excitement and impatience had reached their peak. He entered her in one swift move. Joanna's flesh contracted around his hard prick as if it recognised its shape. The rough fabric of his jeans grazed the soft skin of her bottom; the metal buckle of his belt dug into her tender skin, enhancing the heat that enveloped the whole of her pelvis. She moaned as she set her hands flat on the window, feeling his member piercing her repeatedly, her body crushed against the glass pane. He pushed her up laboriously, heavily panting under the effort, groaning with every jerk.

Joanna felt her vulva stretched every time she slid up and down his thick shaft. Her pleasure returned, growing more intense with each of his jabs. He took her powerfully, crushing her against the window and practically lifting her off her feet, forcing her to stand on the tip of her toes. Repeatedly, he thrust with all his might. Joanna opened her eyes and stared at the street below, knowing no one could see her but feeling overwhelmingly aroused by this strange situation.

Steve's hands clasped her hips and he held her tight as he rammed into her. He grunted loudly, practically lifting her off her feet with each thrust. Joanna's hard nipples slid up and down against the window pane. At first the cool dry glass pulled mercilessly on her skin, but soon her own sweat eased the motion.

Her cries echoed his as she climaxed again. After a while, his hands glided up to recapture her breasts and she squealed her delight. His attack lasted a long time, as if he had been waiting forever and now had to completely exorcise his desire in an unending invasion. She felt him tense and he pressed his chest against her back. Inside her, his phallus twitched powerfully as he climaxed. He gave an ultimate jab, shaking under the force of his orgasm. His last moan resounded in her ear, and made her skin break into goose bumps.

For a moment, neither of them moved. Joanna was still looking down at the street below, but she didn't really see it any more. Her mind and her body were overwhelmed with an intense satisfaction that had been eluding her for so long and that she had feared only the thrill of total domination could give her. Now she knew that wasn't the case, not as long as Steve was around.

Pleasure still shook her from time to time. She was grateful that Steve was standing behind her, otherwise she knew she would have collapsed by now. He pulled away slightly and lifted her in his arms. Demurely, she slipped her arms around his shoulders and nestled her head in the groove of his neck. She liked the feeling of finding herself totally naked in his arms, especially since he was still almost fully clothed.

He lay her on the bed and quickly undressed before joining her between the sheets. In the dim light coming from the window, she saw the vague contour of his naked body but she was too exhausted to reach to the bedside table and switch on the lamp.

Rather, she elected to use her hands to discover him. As he lay next to her and gently caressed her soft mound with the palm of his hand, Joanna quickly regained her strength. She rolled on to him and pressed her naked body against his. Her hands searched him from head to toe as she blindly discovered him, her mouth following closely behind. She wanted to remember each hair of his chest, each ripple of his flat stomach, and each sinew of his strong thighs. She wanted to taste every inch of his skin and ensure the memory of it would forever remain embedded in her mind.

This slow procession was electrifying in its intensity and rekindled Joanna's arousal. However, the rest of her body just couldn't take any more. Once she was satisfied that she would recognise him amongst hundreds of naked bodies, she lay back and relaxed.

For a long time he remained still, his hands gently resting on her back. Delicately, he lifted her off him and made her lie on her back next to him. Drained of her strength following such extreme exercise, Joanna was numb and on the verge of falling asleep.

Yet as he got up and turned on the lamp on the bedside table, curiosity got the better of her and she blinked. From the armoire at the foot of the bed, he took out a robe and put it on. Noticing that Joanna was staring at him, he smiled and came to sit next to her.

As he approached, Joanna's strength suddenly returned. She had recognised the familiar pattern of the kimono he was wearing: the pink jasmine sprigs on the pale green background. With trembling fingers, she reached forward and hesitantly touched the fabric. As hard as it was to believe, she had now connected the final pieces of the puzzle in her head.

Without any hesitation, she grabbed the edge of Steve's kimono and pulled it aside to reveal his naked body. He didn't try to stop her and simply smiled as she stared incredulously at the motif tattooed on his pubis, which was a perfect match to that on the silk kimono.

'You . . . You are one of them,' she stammered.

'As you are,' he said as he leant forward to gently kiss her temple. 'You deserve it, believe me.'

Chapter Twenty-One

*L*ovingly, Joanna ran her fingertips along the thin, pink and green design now adorning her groin. Her skin was still a bit red, raised and somewhat sensitive, but the tattoo artist had assured her the swelling would subside in a few days. So much the better, Joanna thought. In less than a week, she was to attend another of Torima's banquets, and she was hoping it would have healed by then.

She took another plum from the basket next to her and bit into its hard skin. Underneath, the pulp was sweet and juicy, and she sucked rather than chewed it. Sitting naked on her bed, her small computer on her lap, she was trying very hard to finish writing her letter of resignation.

Only a couple of days ago her head office had advised her that they had found a replacement for her. The new buyer was heading straight to Vietnam to continue the tour Joanna had started, and Joanna could now return to London. That made it even more difficult for her to announce she no longer wanted to work for them. There was no way she would return to London, at least not just yet.

She glanced round the small flat, and once again tried to find something wrong with it. Just like before, she failed to see anything that wasn't to her liking. The place was comfortable, cosy, nicely decorated and looked better than it would if she had done it up herself.

Torima was more than generous. The location was convenient, the rent was paid for, she had a chauffeur and a maid. Every day wonderful food arrived for her, packages of fine delicacies that she knew she would never grow tired of. Free from the constraints of a full-time job, she was able to come and go as she pleased, doing whatever she liked, secure that money was no object as Torima provided for her every need and fancy. It was just too good to be true, and now Joanna understood why Stacey had sought to become part of his organisation.

She remembered Stacey as a woman unhappy with having to work, who nurtured vain fantasies of caviar and champagne parties, who was desperate to find a way out of the rat race and to enjoy the high life. But in return she would have had to attend Torima's gatherings and obey his instructions. Having discussed this with both Steve and Torima, Joanna had concluded this was probably the factor that had prompted Stacey's decision to give it up at the last minute.

But it wasn't a problem for Joanna. In fact, she couldn't wait to go back to the Jasmine Blossoms inn, eager for yet another series of steamy sexy performances. Her only regret was that Steve wouldn't be in attendance.

His role in Torima's organisation was to recruit foreign women. He did work for an American company, although he was based permanently in Japan. More importantly, he worked for Torima as well. Whilst attending international food fairs and similar functions, he kept an eye out for women with a taste for fine foods, hot sex and the other small pleasures of life, and who would fit in with Torima's plan.

He had admitted to Joanna that concentrating on Greta had been a waste of time. Initially, he had thought her brash ways and enthusiasm would make her a good candidate. Yet in the end he had been utterly wrong: the New Yorker just didn't have that talent. But whereas Steve spoke of his mistake with a tinge of irritation, Joanna was grateful for it. If he had paid attention to her instead, he would soon have spotted the mistake and worked out that Joanna wasn't Stacey. Eventually the situation would have been rectified and Joanna would never have received further messages.

At first, when Steve and Torima had finally told Joanna the whole story, she had been somewhat miffed. All this time, she had thought she was working on seducing Steve. In reality, he had been advised well in advance that she would be coming on to him, and his resistance was merely a ploy to get her to work harder, to test her ingenuity in seduction. It had paid off in the end.

There was always a reward, Torima had explained. That was why Yukio, the young waiter, had acted so detached with Joanna when she had found him on the top floor of the hotel. Although he had been totally besotted and unable to resist her on their first encounter, he had been instructed to hold back the second time round. In exchange, he was entitled to a reward. Only he and Torima knew what he stood to gain from obedience; that was their secret. Yet Joanna knew it had to be good. Why else would he refuse a woman like her?

As overwhelming as it all seemed, Joanna also knew that what she had seen so far was only a small part of it. Torima had contacts everywhere: in every city, every hotel, restaurant and bar. It was almost ironic that she had been mistaken for Stacey. Only seldom did Torima make a mistake, and that was one. And Joanna couldn't have been happier about it. Now she was officially part of the organisation as well.

All that was left to do was to leave her job. As she resumed typing her letter, she paused and wondered what excuse she could use. Whatever the reason she provided, everyone would suspect she had been offered a job with another company, a competitor. So it didn't matter if her reason sounded lame. In fact, that could even be funny. Now was the time to be creative and Joanna decided that the more outrageous, the better.

A wicked smile played on her face as she punched a few keys. 'I am terribly sorry for all the inconvenience this will cause', her message concluded, 'but the sad news of Richard's passing has hit me harder than I would have thought and I just can't see myself going back to work if he is no longer there. It just wouldn't be the same.'

She sat back and smiled to herself once again, satisfied that, in the end, it was indeed all Richard's fault.